Taming me

By

Alexandrea Weis

This is a work of fiction. Names, characters, places, and incidents are products of the author's imagination or are used fictitiously and are not to be construed as real. Any resemblance to actual events, locations, organizations, or person, living or dead, is entirely coincidental.

Copyright © Alexandrea Weis 2015

Licensing Notes

All rights reserved. No part of this book may be used or reproduced in any manner whatsoever without written permission, except in the case of brief quotations embodied in articles and reviews.

Cover: BookFabulous Designs
Editor: Maxine Bringenberg
Editor: Karen Hrdlicka

Day 1

Sitting in my agent's office on that cool spring day, I half-listened to the man's nasally voice lecture me about how I was getting barn sour as a writer—something I thought only horses did when left in the stall for too long. According to Al Berger, my agent, writers could be the same way. He was insisting I get out in the world and do a little research to find a new idea for a book. How could I do that? Venture into the world of living, breathing people and have to interact with them? That was death to any writer. We hated interacting with anyone...except for our characters.

"You need to face facts, Lexie. Your book sales have tanked, and I can't get another publisher interested in you. You need something new to put out there," Al insisted, leaning his pudgy arms on his crappy little wooden desk. He was too cheap to invest the money in a bigger one.

What I needed was a new idea for a story, a marketable idea for a book that would sell. The grinding feeling in my stomach made me painfully aware of the harsh reality of being a writer; you had to sell books to be able to write more books.

"You've written four tame romances about hot doctors falling in love with different kinds of women. It's getting stale," Al droned on. "Your readers are bored. Hell, I'm bored reading your books." He mopped his hand over his red, sweaty face.

Al's face was always red and sweaty. For the five years I had known him, I had never seen the short, dumpy Jewish guy without a red, sweaty face. I know cliché, but that was Al; a myriad of clichés. If you looked up unsuccessful literary agent, with a heart of gold, in the dictionary, you wouldn't find Al; he would be listed in the asshole section.

"What do you want me to do?" I stood from the flimsy Ikea chair in front of his desk and began to pace the floor of his cramped corner office. "I can't think of anything else to write."

Al slapped his chubby hand down on my latest failure of a manuscript, which was sitting on top of his desk. "This shit doesn't sell anymore. Sweet romances are fine for little girls, but every woman over the age of twelve, nowadays, wants to be tied up in leather and fucked until the cows come home."

Al always had such a way with words. I was amazed that he had never taken pen to paper.

Glaring at him with my brown eyes, I tossed my deep brown hair about my shoulders, attempting to look angry, but I was pretty sure I failed miserably.

"Hey." He pointed his stubby finger at me. "Don't give me that look. Get your ass out there, hit the pavement, and find something sexy to write." He stood from behind his desk, giving me an unwanted view of his protruding belly. "You know this *Fifty Shades of Grey* is killing you and every other romance writer out there. So get me something like that. Tie the woman up in your next book and have her banged the hell out of by a Dorian Gray type."

"You mean Christian Grey."

"Who gives a shit what you call him? For Christ's sake, just do it and then I can sell the hell out of it."

"Tie them up?" I snickered with all the contempt I had in my sinful little soul. "I can't just tie women up without a story, Al. And I don't know the first thing about bondage."

"Google it!" he shouted. "Like everybody else."

Folding my arms, I huffed for a moment, languishing in my self-pity. I should have gone to nursing school like my mother had suggested. I could have married a doctor and taken up tennis like every other woman dreams of doing. No, I had to become a writer, to express my creativity and give myself a goddamned ulcer.

"Whatever I write will sound like everyone else's Googled crap, Al." I shook my head, knowing I needed something different, something real. "If bondage sells, then I have to find a way to make a real story out of it. To do that, I have to make it real to me."

Al appeared stunned for a moment. His beady brown eyes were all over me. "Real? What you gonna do? Go out there and actually hang out with those sick fucks that tie each other up and other weirdo shit?"

The idea was intriguing. "Maybe that's what I need to do."

The laugh he gave me was not only offensive; it spurred on my sudden desire to prove him wrong. Arrogant little shit.

"Sure. Why not?" I threw my hands up. "Maybe I need to go to a few of those seedy clubs in the Quarter and hang out with that crowd."

Al's face paled—well, got even paler than it already was. "Are you out of your mind, Lexie? This is New Orleans. Every sick pervert hangs out in the Quarter."

"I know that, Al. I was raised in the Quarter, remember?"

"Yeah, but that was twenty years ago, when it was nice and just filled with drunk tourists and hookers. If you're not careful, you'll end up in a ditch somewhere with your throat cut." He waved his hands about looking like a fat, flightless bird. "I can't allow you to do that."

"Allow?" I hiked by eyebrows, incensed. No one allowed me to do anything. Even the lunatic I was married to knew better than to say anything like that to me.

Al sighed. "I just meant, I don't think it's a good idea. Don't get your independent female panties in a twist. I wasn't telling you what to do." He rolled his little eyes. "God forbid, anyone tells Alexandra Palmer how to live her life."

How to live my life? I'd always had too many people telling me how to live my life. The only problem was they didn't seem to be doing any better with their lives, so why bother taking advice from someone who was as clueless as me?

I picked up my leather five-gallon purse from the chair in front of Al's desk. It would seem I had said about all I could to my agent. He wasn't going to be much help.

"Thanks for the advice, Al."

He gawked at me like a bullfrog dazed by the beam from a flashlight. "What are you going to do?"

"Research." I tugged my heavy purse over my shoulder, making a mental note to clean the damn thing out before I gave myself a hernia.

"Oh, I don't like the sound of that." He shook his head. "You're going to do something stupid, I just know it."

"If you don't hear from me in a week, call the police and file a missing person's report."

"Aww, for shit's sake, Lexie, don't say crap like that to me." He plopped down in his squeaky desk chair, sounding like he was sitting on a family of mice. "Now I'm going to worry about what crazy ass horseshit you're pulling out there."

"Who cares what I do, Al?" I smacked my hand down on the assortment of papers that always seemed to be cluttering his desk. "If I can get a great book out of it, make us both some money, it will be worth it, right?"

That shut the greedy little bastard up. Mention money to an agent, and he would stuff his grandmother in bandages, then try to pass her off as an Egyptian mummy to a bunch of archeological students.

As his eyes looked up and down my five-foot-four-inch frame, I could tell he wasn't going to argue with me. He never argued with me; he just ranted, and then told me to do what I thought best.

"You do what you think best," he whined.

Did I know the man or what?

He raised a pencil in his hand and pointed it at me. "But if you get into any kind of trouble, don't call me to bail you out."

"Thank you, Al. That's exactly what I would expect my agent to say."

He sighed and sat back in his chair, making it squeak louder than before. "You know I love you, Lexie. I would love to see you back on top, but don't do nothin' stupid, all right? No book is worth ruining your life for."

The man called himself a literary agent? I was a writer; the only thing worth ruining my life for was a book. Men, family, pets, even the fear of death never mattered. As long as I was writing my next book, all was right in the world, and everyone could go to hell.

"Sure, Al." Why bother enlightening the man? "Thanks for caring."

He raised his black eyebrows up on his bald head. "Who said I cared?"

I turned from his desk, chuckling to myself. Agents...got to love them. Lucifer probably started out as an agent. Who else could piss off God, but a guy wanting ten percent of everything he had created.

Walking out of Al's five-story square office building on Baronne Street, I stopped and took in the hum of the city around me. For a moment, I was distracted by the sights and smells of New Orleans. God, I loved this city. Hedonistic, eccentric, wild, provocative, and alive with the ever-changing human condition, no matter where I went in this town, it always thrilled me with some new discovery. Not a lot of places could do that—especially to a writer—but New Orleans could. It's probably why so many creative people came from this place; it always stirred the imaginings of the soul.

Heading down the sidewalk to the car park, I mulled over my meeting with Al. The only problem with any new project was where to start. Like putting down the first words on an imposing white page, finding a starting point for a story was always difficult for me. Hell, it was difficult for any writer. I had heard a professor in college once say, "There are two points when a writer feels at their best in a book: when they type the first word, and when they type the end." Then again, the asshole who'd taught that class never wrote a New York Times Bestseller. I had, and there was a hell of a lot more angst with the first word than the last.

After retrieving my beat up Honda Accord from the garage and making that absurd drive down all those levels—cursing the schmuck who designed parking garages for a living—I veered out into the traffic in the city's Central Business District and decided to head to the river.

I always headed to the Mississippi River to think. Ever since I had been a kid, I would escape to the banks of the river by the French Quarter. I'd get lost in the flowing dirty water and colossal trade ships maneuvering the dangerous bend. It grounded me, making the torrents of my life appear miniscule next to the tide of that immense river. Being raised by a single mother who was always working had made for an interesting childhood, albeit a lonely one.

At eight, I was given a key on a chain around my neck and told by my mother that I was old enough to stay home after school by myself. I was too young to know the impact of such a decision, only that it scared me. Thank God for the good neighbors that lived around our little cottage on Burgundy Street. Without them, I would have been completely alone.

I never voiced my fears to my mother. Telling Lily Palmer what to do was about as bad as telling me. Every lesson on independence I had taken from my mother. An operating room nurse who thrived on work and a series of unsuccessful relationships, she had tried to be there for me, but never was. Probably the reason we rarely spoke...she had her life, and I had mine.

Leaving my car in the lot in front of Woldenberg Park at the edge of the French Quarter, I crossed the streetcar tracks that carried the Red Lady line of trolleys up and down the riverfront. A hot tourist destination, the park offered majestic views of the river and assorted sculptures. During the festival season, it was the place to take in some of the best music the city had to offer.

On this chilly spring Tuesday, the park was relatively empty except for the smattering of tourists. There were always tourists in the Quarter. I had grown up dodging them on the sidewalks outside of our cottage, giving them directions when they were lost, and always telling them to be careful. After all, this was New Orleans.

Finding a metal bench painted a morose shade of blue, I had a seat and breathed in the humid air from the river. I already felt better. Eventually, my mind wandered back to the task at hand. What in the hell was I going to write about?

In the distance, the sound of a lonely saxophone drifted over the dingy yellow floodwall along the edge of the park. Meant to protect the French Quarter from the overflow of the river when it was built, no one in the city had much faith in such eyesores anymore. We had all learned our lesson after Katrina.

Katrina was a name that made every New Orleanian quake with ungodly memories. It was bad enough we had to survive it, but doing so on a world stage only made the pain more...pathetic. I had been one of the lucky ones. My apartment, at the time, had been on the fourth floor of a building not far from the college where I had been finishing my journalism degree. I had been spared from the destruction of the black water, but not from the looting. Shuddering at the image of my apartment when I had returned home from my two-month exile, I wondered how I had rebuilt my life. Still, Katrina had made me stronger. A few years later, when my brief marriage had ended, I was better equipped to handle the rebuilding process. After Katrina, anything was possible.

Putting all the ugly thoughts from the past out of my head, I concentrated on discovering a story. To me, a story came like a desired lover in the night…softly, with adept hands that caught hold of my insides and never let go.

The simile made me shake my head. That was exactly the kind of shit I needed to avoid for this next book. Bondage, hot sex, men in leather…those were the kinds of things I had to put in my story. Considering the only leather I was familiar with either came in shoe, handbag, or coat form, I had a strange feeling I was in for a very difficult journey.

"Excuse me." The deep voice next to me instantly hooked me.

Peering up, I could not see the tall owner of the intriguing voice for the glare of the morning sun behind him.

"Do you have the time?" he asked, making my insides quiver.

The time? I almost laughed out loud. Before the advent of cellphones, that would have been a plausible excuse to talk to a woman, but now it sounded like a cheap pick-up line. Figuring this was some bum—or worse, a serial killer in search of his next victim—I stood from the bench, ready for a quick getaway.

"I'm not sure. My cell phone's dead." Oh, I was very proud of myself for that one. Quick thinking, Lexie.

It was then he moved out from the sun, and I was better able to see his face. Stunning was the first word that came to mind. With angular features, jutting cheekbones, a round chin covered in dark stubble, and a high, square forehead, he was almost too good-looking. Then I saw his eyes. That was where the attraction ended for me. They were very cold, almost evil in their design. It was not so much how they appeared, but how they made me feel that was the most disturbing. Such eyes did not belong to normal people.

"I'm sorry." He dipped his head slightly, and the gracious gesture lowered his eyes from my view. "I was waiting to meet a friend and my cell phone died, as well." The slight smile that curled the edges of his thin red lips was as hypnotic as the rest of him.

Taking a step back, I was able to evaluate his body. Toned and towering over me, he wore a black pressed suit, without a tie, and very nice black leather loafers. His hands were the next thing that caught my eye. Fine, pale, almost delicate, they were the hands of a priest, or some other kind of spiritual man.

I smiled nervously. With those looks, he was probably a real successful serial killer.

"I hope I didn't startle you." He had not the slightest hint of a New Orleans accent, making me all the more paranoid about mine.

"No, not at all." I pronounced, sounding a little too formal.

"I saw you sitting here and I…." His perfect smile grew a little wider, taking away from the unsettling stare of his eyes. "I couldn't help but notice that you seemed lost in your thoughts."

Lost in my thoughts? Yeah, he was a serial killer.

"No, I ah...." Gazing about, I searched for some friendly witnesses to my abduction. "I was just thinking."

His calculated smile spread. "Do you always come here to think?"

I know I should have made a beeline out of there, but despite the warning signals going off in my head to ditch this guy, I could not make my feet move. I was not an idiot. Of course I was leery about him. Yet, there was just something...soothing about his voice, the way he leaned ever so slightly toward me, and he was exceptionally handsome, so I had to see where this went.

"Sometimes...well, a lot of times." Running my fingers through my hair, I hoped I came across mysterious and not ditzy. "I grew up around here, so this place is...comfortable."

"You're from New Orleans?"

I nodded. "Born and raised."

"What a fascinating city to call home. I just moved here from Dallas." He held out his hand to me. "I'm Garrett, by the way."

I took his hand, and the instant our fingers touched there was a spark. It was what I used to write about happening between two strangers, alluding to their destiny. For the first time in my life, it had happened to me. It was not as all-consuming as I had written about, but more unnerving. The problem with running into the "touch of fate," as I called it in my books, was that you didn't know if this was going to be a good kind of fate or a bad one.

"I'm Lexie." I pulled my hand away as a feeling of dread began to rise in me. Suddenly, I felt like prey.

"Lexie?" His eyes narrowed on mine. "Is that short for anything?"

"Alexandra, but I never use it."

He stood back slightly. "Why not? It's a beautiful name."

"It's a little too formal for me." I shrugged. "I'm just a Lexie."

Those deep brown eyes flashed with an alluring intensity, as if my words had set off a crescendo of ideas. Now, I was drawn to his eyes; hell, I was seduced by them. Never had I met a man who could sweep me away with a look. Christ, I needed a cold shower.

"Garrett!" a voice called from down the path next to us.

Turning in unison, a man in a casual gray suit was coming our way. He was tall—with the same chiseled features as Garrett—walked with a cocky arrogance as his light brown hair flapped in the breeze, and was carrying a black iPhone in his hand.

"There you are," the stranger remarked, coming closer. "I tried your phone."

"My phone's dead, Colin."

I looked from Colin to Garrett. Damn, there were two of them. I could have died a happy woman, right there and then.

Garrett's eyes veered back to me. "Looks like my friend is here."

The pained expression in his eyes was breathtaking. Was he really that upset to see his friend?

"Hey," Colin said breathlessly, standing next to us. His piercing blue eyes darted from me to Garrett.

"Oh, forgive me." Garrett appeared to emerge from his trance. "Colin, this is Lexie. We just met. She's from New Orleans."

Colin held out his strong hand. "Lexie, nice to meet you." His blue eyes had none of Garrett's coldness or allure. They were nice guy eyes…the kind you admired when you were walking out his bedroom door after spending the night naked, beneath him.

"Pleasure, Colin." We shook hands, but I didn't get the same belly-shock from him that I had gotten from Garrett.

"Sorry, I got held up." Colin shifted his eyes to his friend, as if to ask if there was anything going on between us.

"Are you from Dallas, too?" I figured they were business buddies.

"No, I'm from here," Colin replied. "Garrett and I went to college together."

"And what do you guys do?"

Both men looked thunderstruck, and then Garrett casually waved one of those seductive hands in the air.

"We're architects. I was sent here by my firm in Dallas, a few months back, to set up a new office."

Architects? That sounded intriguing. Perhaps I should do a story about some kind of architect love tryst. Starring Garrett, the wonder-hunk.

"What do you do, Lexie?" Garrett's voice had just a twinge of huskiness about it, making my stomach do flips.

"I'm a writer."

Both men nodded, seeming impressed. For the life of me I didn't know why.

"What do you write?" It was Garrett, being flirty.

I smiled and tucked a loose tendril of brown hair behind my right ear, flirting back. "Fiction, romantic fiction."

The stunned look I got was completely expected. I always got that reaction from men when I told them what I did. It was like asking their opinion on dishwashing liquid. They never used it, had no idea there were different kinds, and believed it was something only women used because it smelled nice.

"I'm sure it's probably something your wives might have read," I explained, still confronted by their blank stares.

"We're not married," Colin offered.

If jumping up and down were an Olympic sport, I might have won the gold medal about then. Instead of showing my exuberance, I merely grinned.

"Well, marriage isn't for everyone," I quipped.

"Are you married?" Garrett's voice sounded deeper than before.

"No, divorced, actually."

He frowned at me, but his eyes were far from sad. "I'm sorry."

"I'm over it."

"So, ah, Garrett," Colin cut in. "We should get going. We have that meeting in ten minutes."

Disappointment tunneled through me. For the first time in my life I met two great-looking men at once, and they had to run off to a meeting. It was so unfair.

"Yes, we should go," Garrett asserted, but he kept his eyes on me. "Will you be here tomorrow, thinking again?"

By this point in the conversation, all the reservations I had felt about the man initially had disappeared. I had met his business associate, discovered his job, learned about his relationship status, and knew where he was from. Did serial killers work as architects? I figured I was safe.

"Yes, I could be here tomorrow…thinking again."

"Around noon? I could come by and we could get some coffee. Might help you to think better."

I saw Colin grinning next to him. "I don't know; Colin, should I?" I asked, flashing a sly smile.

Colin motioned to his friend. "He's a very good listener. In fact, you could say he's a master at it."

"A master, eh?" Shaking my head and beaming like a schoolgirl, I knew I was done for. "Fine. Noon, tomorrow."

Garrett's resplendent smile was breathtaking. "I will see you then."

Colin held out his hand to me. "Lexie, I'm sure we will meet again."

I took his hand. "I hope so, Colin."

Colin took a few steps to the side to give us some privacy. Garrett waited until he was out of earshot. "I'll look forward to tomorrow," he softly said to me.

"So will I, Garrett."

With a last sinful look he turned away. Standing by my bench, I watched the two men saunter toward the round glass tower of Aquarium of the Americas. As they strolled along the riverfront, women making their way down the red-bricked path gazed hungrily their way. I hoped I had not been that obvious. Then again, who was I kidding?

Day 2

There were gray clouds in the sky threatening rain when I arrived at the same bench in Woldenberg Park, the next day at noon. I had spent about two hours deciding on my outfit. Why it would take anyone two hours to decide on jeans and a nice blouse was beyond me, but that was what men did to women…made us fashion morons when it came to selecting clothes for that hot date. Everything either made us look fat and frumpy, with butts the size of Cleveland, or reminded us of our mothers.

Rolling over a number of topics to discuss with Garrett, I began to have those invariable doubts about whether he would show. Second-guessing my behavior had started the day before and become my favorite pastime. Had I been too flirty or too forward? Perhaps he was just being polite, and wanted me to walk away feeling good about myself. A cavalcade of "what ifs" surrounded me. Just as I had talked myself into going home, and forgetting the entire affair, a pair of black loafers stood before my bench.

"So you came." His voice was like chocolate liqueur, and I was the ice cream.

My eyes traveled up the neatly ironed crease in his blue jeans to his white button-down shirt. After taking a moment at the top to peek at his exposed chest behind the two strategically undone buttons, I raised my eyes to his round chin, and then to those deceptively ravishing brown eyes. The same dark, disconcerting stare that had greeted me the day before was back, only this time instead of frightening me, it drew me in.

"Hello, Garrett." I stood from the bench and held out my hand.

He took my hand, and gripped it suggestively. His hand was warm, supple, and I could tell there was strength behind his firm handshake. It was the kind of strength that came not from the body, but from the mind.

"I wasn't sure you would come." He let go of my hand.

"Why did you think that?"

He shrugged, placing his hands behind his back. "I'm a stranger, and some women might be wary about being alone with a man they don't know."

"Why, are you a serial killer?"

His laugh was beyond musical, it was enchanting. "No, but if that's what you were suspecting, then I'm glad you took a chance on me."

"Yeah, well, I'm a writer. We like to take chances."

That made him smile. "Do all writers feel the same way…about taking chances, that is?"

Yes, insanity was part of the job description, but I did not need to scare the hell out of him, just yet. "Some do. We'll do anything for the story in our head."

"And what story is in your head, right now?"

The story. I had not been able to think of a story since meeting Garrett. "Actually, I'm in the middle of doing research for my next novel," I lied, thinking I sounded successful.

"I would love to hear about it." He motioned to the bricked walkway next to the bench. "Why don't we head over to Café Maspero for some lunch, and you can tell me about your book."

Great! Not only did I have to come up with a book concept, I had to come up with something to keep Garrett entertained and interested. If this scenario had been a story I was writing, I could have deftly given my heroine a bunch of ideas to impress our romantic lead. Unfortunately, this was real life, and I absolutely sucked at it.

"Actually, I have no clue what I'm going to write about," I blurted out, strolling beside him. "That's what I was thinking about yesterday when you came up to me. My story."

"Ah, that's why you looked so sad."

Stunned, I stopped walking. "I looked sad?"

"When I saw you, you were hunched over, with your head bowed down. You acted lost, like you didn't know what to do next." He waved his long hand down the path, and I fell in step beside him. "Does that happen often?"

"Which one, being sad or lost?"

"Both." He showed me his profile as he took in a group of tourists gathering at the Toulouse Street Station to board the riverboat *Natchez*.

Christ, if I kept this up the guy was going to think I needed Prozac. "Actually, neither." I made an effort to sound upbeat. "I guess I just look like that when I'm thinking."

"Really? I find that interesting." He nodded thoughtfully. "So what's the story you were thinking about?"

"Not a story, more like an idea for a story...well, actually more like something I need to write a story about, or my agent wants me to write about."

"Your agent?" He crinkled his eyebrows, making his eyes appear darker. "Does he usually tell you what to write?"

"He tells me what will sell." I sighed as the historic structure of Jax Brewery loomed ahead. "The problem is that everyone is writing about bondage these days."

"You're joking. Bondage?" His laughter was as deep and as devious as his eyes. I was entranced by the cadence of it, the resonating tone, and how it wound itself inside of my body, sending chills along my skin. That laugh was my undoing.

"Yes, I know, it's ridiculous. But since *Fifty Shades of Grey* everyone in the romance game has been—"

"That book was pure garbage," he emphatically proclaimed.

I turned to him, astonished by his statement. I had not encountered many men who had read the book. The only men I knew who had read it used it as a handbook for picking up women, thinking all of us wanted to be tied to a bed and ravaged.

"You've read it?" I inquired.

"Does that surprise you?"

I stopped at the entrance to Jax Brewery. "Most men steer clear of romance novels like that one, even if it was very popular."

He tucked his hands behind his back, appearing self-assured. "I read it to find out what all the fuss was about...and to test its accuracy."

"I don't understand. What do you mean by 'accuracy'?"

Without hesitation, he said, "The relationship between the submissive and the dominant. I wanted to see how it was handled in the book."

My mind went into overdrive. How in the hell did he know what a submissive or dominant was? Maybe I had been sleeping with my laptop for too long, and men were more in tune than they used to be before I was married, but the comment still took me off guard.

"You know about those things?"

He folded his arms over his stunningly broad chest and gave me a catlike grin. "A bit. What I've read and what I've experienced."

I took a hesitant step toward him, feeling as if I was very close to an interesting story lead. "Care to tell me about your experiences?"

His eyes stayed intently focused on mine, as if trying to determine how I felt about his disclosure. "Does that excite you?" His voice was steady, and hypnotic.

I snickered and turned my head to the side, not wanting to show him that his attempt at seduction was really getting to me. What I needed was a story in my head and not a man in my bed.

"You have no idea how that would excite me. To actually talk to someone who has some insight into that lifestyle. It would give me a great angle to get—"

"I was talking about exciting you, as a woman," he interrupted, sounding frustrated.

My snicker turned into a full-on laugh. "As a woman? You must be kidding. I haven't been one of those since I was married, and even then...forget it." No point in boring him to death with my pitiful past.

The playful frown that stared back at me was tantalizing. Honestly, how did he do that? I had to remind myself to play it cool.

"That's a shame." Those crafty eyes were studying me again. "It's a man's job to remind a woman of her worth."

"Did you get that off a Hallmark card?"

"No, it's a personal philosophy of mine."

I became distracted by a few tourists milling about and taking pictures. "Nice philosophy, but unfortunately your sex is lacking in a consensus of exactly how to do that."

"Are you always this feisty?"

My eyes shot back to him. "Now you sound like my agent."

His laughter made several tourists gathering outside of Jax Brewery turn our way. "You're not like other women I've met. You don't shy away when I talk about what I like to do."

"I told you, I'm not a woman...I'm a writer." I folded my arms over my chest, determined to meet his obvious attempt at shocking me with my bulldogged determination. "So what are you into? Whips, chains, leather accessories?"

His hand cut through the air between us. "Nothing like that...and nothing like what was portrayed in that book." He shook his head. "I think that book has done more damage to our culture than good. Exposing people to an alternative lifestyle, without fully explaining its appeal, just sets the young and naive up for a lot of bad experiences."

"What kind of bad experiences?"

Taking in the people around us, his lips drew tightly together. "I've seen many young women think, after reading that book, that they want such a life. They join bondage websites, and pair up with people they think will be billionaires with hearts of gold, only to find themselves in abusive relationships with men who mistreat them. I think there needs to be an accurate portrayal of what being in such a relationship entails. Something that can educate the masses."

"So why not tell me about it? I can write an accurate story about your lifestyle."

"It's not that simple...." His wistful sigh only teased my curiosity. "You can't just tell someone about this lifestyle. You must live it."

"Then tell me your story. When did you start this...stuff?"

"Stuff?" His amusement was etched all over his face. "It began as an experiment. In college, when I was studying architecture."

What kind of college did he go to? And why didn't I go there?

"Is this an architect thing?" I probed after a brief silence.

His black eyebrows went up. "You're funny."

Thrilled I had ruffled his composed exterior, I quickly asked, "Come on, tell me about your experiences. I really want to know."

His eyes were pensive. "Am I to be research for that story of yours?"

"Think about it, Garrett. With your help, I can write something real, something believable, and protect a lot of young girls from getting hurt in the future." In an instant he had gone from hot guy to badly needed research guy. The funny part was the research side of the man interested me more than the hot guy. I made a mental note to get my hormones checked.

He stared at me for several seconds. I became swept up in the way his long black lashes curled over his eyelids. Damn, even his eyelashes were sexy.

"What's in this for me?"

Now I was the one being floored. I had never expected having to broker a deal to get information. "I guess like you said…the chance to get the story right and tell the truth about your lifestyle. Don't you want the world to know the truth?"

"Truth is overrated," he flatly announced. "What else are you offering?"

I did not like where this was headed. "What do you want, Garrett?"

His eyes once more swept over my figure. I began to suspect I was going to have to give up more than my time for this story. As the seconds ticked by, I contemplated if I had the moxie to do what he was obviously thinking.

"Let's have lunch and discuss what I want." He waved to Café Maspero across the street from us.

"No, let's talk about it now," I insisted. "No point in going any further with this if what you want is…." I shifted uncomfortably on my feet, dreading what I was about to say. "More than professional."

He chuckled and folded his arms over his chest, taking another brief moment. "What I want is this. I tell you my story, and you must give me access to whatever you write, but I have final say so over the content. If I don't like it, it goes. I want this book to be as accurate as possible."

I almost stumbled forward with disbelief. "That's it?"

He cocked an eyebrow. "What were you expecting?"

"I don't know...sex, possibly."

"With you?" He chuckled again, but this time I wasn't entertained by his warm laugh. "That's not what I'm after with you." He unfolded his arms and moved closer to me. "I would never force a woman to be with me as some sort of negotiation. When I take a woman to bed, it's because she wants it more than I do."

In my experiences with men, it was usually the other way around. Intrigued more than alarmed, I decided to agree to his terms. I was willing to allow him approval of my story, if it got me what I wanted. At this point, I was willing to do just about anything.

"All right. You can have final approval of my book. But we discuss any changes you want to make before they are made. This is fiction and does have to be tweaked to be believable."

"I'm sure the information you get from me will make it more than believable." He motioned ahead to Decatur Street. "Shall we?"

We started walking toward the stoplight. "I have one last condition. You can't use my name in your book, Lexie. I have a reputation to protect. A reputation I've spent years cultivating." The tinge of discomfort in his voice fired my curiosity.

"Fine, we can call the main character...Ralph, if you like."

"Ralph?" He scowled at me, making me grin like a malicious child. "We'll have to work on the name."

"Sure, Garrett, anything you want. Just tell me your story."

He placed his hand in the small of my back, escorting me across the busy street. "My story? They're just experiences, Lexie. You're going to need a lot more than that to make your book convincing."

"Like what?"

"We'll discuss it over lunch."

Anyone who has been to New Orleans can tell you about Café Maspero and the food, but for me the allure of the restaurant was the family who owned it. Charlie, the owner, had known me since I was a little girl, when my mother had frequently sent me to the crowded corner restaurant for takeout orders. Charlie Jr., better known as CJ, had taken over the reins from his father a few years back. As we stepped through the heavy wooden doors inlaid with glass, I spotted the dark, curly mop and lanky figure of my childhood friend behind the bar.

"Hey, Lexie," CJ called to me.

"CJ, how are you?" I shouted out.

"A friend?" Garrett asked bedside me.

"Old friend," I assured him.

CJ emerged from behind the bar and came up to me, giving me a big hug. "Damn, girl, where you been? I haven't seen you in months."

"Working, CJ, always working." I gestured to Garrett. "CJ, this is Garrett… ah…." I realized I didn't even know his last name.

Garrett held out his hand to CJ. "Hughes, Garrett Hughes."

"CJ Toupopolis."

The two men exchanged a cordial handshake. I was always intrigued by the way men shook hands. Taught to do so from a very young age, I found it odd that boys were encouraged to shake the hands of strangers and girls were not. Yet, men refrained from touching, almost avoided it, thinking it unmanly. Women did nothing but touch, caress, and revel in that special sense. I pondered what Freud would have made of that one?

"So, you two here for lunch?" CJ guessed, displaying his crooked smile that I had always adored.

"You know it, CJ," I replied.

He gazed about the packed dining room. "Take that one in the corner, Ashley's table." He pointed to a table by the open french doors that overlooked the sidewalk on Toulouse Street. "What can I get you two to drink?"

I glimpsed Garrett and shrugged. "Iced tea?"

Garrett nodded, smiling back at CJ. "Two iced teas, CJ, thanks."

Winding our way through the maze of packed wooden tables that were spread about the cement floor, we finally reached ours. The cool breeze that came through the open doors helped blow away the mix of humidity and the stale smell of fried food that permeated the restaurant. As I went to have a seat, Garrett stepped behind me and pulled out my chair.

Whoa, that was a new one for me. I was lucky if the guys I dated were sober enough to get into their chair, let alone pull one out for me.

"Thank you," I said, taking my seat. "It's been a while since a man did that for me."

"Why do I not find that surprising?" Garrett commented, taking the chair next to me. "It pains me to see how many men have forgotten the simple acts of chivalry."

I had to laugh at that. "Is that part of that Hallmark philosophy of yours about women?"

He lifted his chair closer to mine, then rested his arms on the table. "Can I ask you a question?"

Those were the words every writer hated to hear, because they always led to a question we never wanted to answer, usually about ourselves.

"Why are you so hostile toward men? Does that come from your divorce?"

Hostile? Was I being hostile? I thought I was being female. It was, after all, called the battle of the sexes. Unless there was a recent truce declared that I missed on CNN, I was pretty sure the war continued.

"No, all women feel this way about men, because all women at some point in their lives have been hurt by a guy," I explained.

He inched in closer. "And who hurt you?"

I sat back in my chair, glaring at him. "We came here to talk about you."

"Does that mean I can't ask you any questions?" He squared his shoulders. "How can I get to know you as a writer, if I can't ask questions, Lexie?"

"If you want to get to know me as a writer, you could just read my books." I knew that was a silly thing to say, and tried to regroup my thoughts. "All right, yes, you can ask questions, but let's not talk about who has been hurt more or any of that stuff. We each have enough pain in our lives without brooding over it."

"Fair enough." He was inching closer again. "Then I would like to ask the first question."

I grimaced, searching for an escape route. "Fine."

"You know my last name, but I don't know yours."

I sulked down into my seat. "Sorry, you're right. Palmer, my last name is Palmer. And yours is Hughes."

"How do you know CJ?"

"I grew up down here." I glimpsed out the open doors next to our table. "Not far from this place on Burgundy Street."

"It must have been wonderful to grow up around these historic buildings." He sat back in his chair, and the sudden distance between us made me feel a little sad. I liked him being close to me.

"Yes, it was." I checked my feelings. "I knew many of the people who lived down here. They were friends. It's not the same anymore. Most of the people I knew have moved away, and the quaint homes are now shops and noisy bars. The Quarter isn't the neighborhood it used to be."

"Where do you live now?"

"I have an apartment in a subdivided house on Esplanade Avenue." I figured it was time to ask my questions. "Where do you live?"

"A penthouse in the Warehouse District. Fifteen stories up with a great view of the river."

His eyes brightened a bit when he spoke of his penthouse. "You moved here from Dallas to start an architectural business, right?"

He nodded. "I work for Parr and Associates, based out of Dallas. Hayden Parr, the owner, wanted to branch out. He sent me here to open an office and see what kind of business we could get. With all the rebuilding going on since Katrina, he figured there might be some opportunity."

"Oh, there is plenty of opportunity since the storm. So many homes have yet to be rebuilt."

A skinny waitress, with long brassy blonde hair tied back in a ponytail and wearing a wide beige apron, came to our table. Plopping down the two iced teas, she smiled at Garrett and completely ignored me.

"Hey, I'm Ashley. CJ said to treat ya'll special." I assumed her drawl was all for Garrett. "Any idea what you'll have, or do you need some menus?"

I tilted toward her. "I'll have a special with the works and fries."

Garrett glanced over at me. "What is the special with works?"

"Hamburger with everything including cheese."

He turned to Ashley. "Two specials with works and fries."

She jotted the order on a pad of paper. "Sure thing, darlin'." Then she winked at Garrett.

My stomach turned. Why were some women so obvious?

Watching her shake her butt as she walked away, I returned my focus to the question I was about to ask before Ashley had interrupted. "Are you originally from Dallas?"

"Yes. My family is there." He pulled two sugar packets from the container in the middle of the table. "But I really like New Orleans. It's different here. It appeals to my…eclectic side." He ripped open the packets and dumped them both into his tea.

I reached for one packet of sugar and sucked in an antsy breath, wanting to get to the topic at the forefront of my mind. "How did you first get into BDSM?"

The change in his demeanor cut through the air like a knife. I had probably pushed a little too hard and fast with my interview, but I didn't care. The story was all that mattered.

As he sat back in his chair, those dark eyes weighing me, I could see the apprehension in his face, but it was also tempered by a heady dose of fascination.

"First of all, BDSM is a catch-all phrase used to describe a wide range of activities, different types of interpersonal relationships, and various subcultures. For me, it's about the relationships and the psychological aspect of D & S, or dominance and submission." Stirring his tea, he paused. "You have to understand, my experiences are very limited. I'm not an expert, nor do I claim to be. No one can be an expert in BDSM."

I dumped my packet of sugar in my tea, then crumpled the paper in my hand. "I just want to hear your story, Garrett."

"My story?" He removed his spoon from his glass of tea. "I started in college. I belonged to a fraternity at UT in Arlington. Part of the initiation rite was visiting this club, a sub-Dom club in the city. Several of the guys in the fraternity were into the whole BDSM culture. There, I met Ruth." He took in a deep breath, expanding his chest, and making me painfully aware of his proportions. "She took me under her wing, taught me, and made me her submissive. After a time, I moved on." He drank from his tea.

Oh, this was better than I'd anticipated. "Is that when you started tying women up?" I stirred my sugar into my tea.

His eyebrows went up again. I was beginning to realize that this was not a good sign with this man. "Tying them up?" He put his tea down and leaned toward me. "What exactly do you know about BDSM?"

I dropped my spoon on the table and angled away from him. "Not much, only what I've found on Google. I don't have any experience with it."

"Ah, I see." His eyebrows relaxed and his grin returned. "Have you ever wanted to be dominated by anyone?"

The revulsion that I was sure registered on my face was totally unintended.

He laughed when he saw it. "That is the reaction I usually get from people who are unfamiliar with the art."

I picked up my tea. "I don't get it. What art?"

"This isn't about domination or submission, Lexie. It's about seduction; the need to be seduced by the power of another. The need to give yourself, willingly, to someone else is something that is hardwired in all mammals. Look at dogs, monkeys, lions. In every pack there is a hierarchy, those who are submissive to a dominant male, or even female. In our species, the role of sub or Dom often shifts. This power exchange is constantly evolving in all types of relationships. With what I do, all parameters of control for the sub and the Dom are discussed and agreed to ahead of time. There are rules that are followed. The key mantra in BDSM is 'safe, sane, and consensual.'"

"People aren't monkeys, Garrett. They have ideas and opinions and can't throw all that aside for what…great sex? Society dictates that—"

"Society is an illusion, a pretense that keeps us from reverting back to our true animal nature." His eyes traveled down the front of my blouse, hovering over my small breasts, making me blush. "You're blushing because I was admiring your body. Is that a societal response," he paused and lowered his head closer to mine, "or an animal one?"

I bolted back in my chair. "But the whole dominant-submissive thing is not—"

"Which one do you think you are? Dom or sub?"

"What?" I reached for my tea. Was it getting warm, or was it me?

He put his hand on my tea glass and took it away. Setting it in front of him, he stared at me. "Don't drink that."

"Why not?"

His face was cold, almost cruel. The change in him was compelling. "Because I said so."

"Because you said so?" I reached for my glass.

"Don't drink it, Lexie," he growled, sounding like a pissed off Rottweiler.

"What is wrong with you? One minute you're staring down my shirt, the next you're barking orders at me." I gulped back the tea and slammed the glass on the table.

He clapped his hands and let out a loud, low rumble of laughter. "You're definitely a Dom."

My mouth fell open. "Was that some kind of test?"

He waved his hand over the table. "Of course. I was trying to prove a point. A real Dom can never be happy as a submissive. God knows it was never for me."

"So you're a Dom?"

He slowly nodded his head. "When we first met, I thought you to be a sub. That's why I came up to you. I've been on the lookout for one since I arrived. A woman I could…make mine."

I should have known it was too good to be true. The first attractive guy to come up to me, and he happened to be hunting for a bondage partner. The odds had been stacked against me.

"Why did you think I was a sub?" I pressed.

"Your body language. That is the first thing I look for in a candidate. A sub will be more timid, cringe easily, cower, and appear…lost."

I sat back in my chair with a thud. "That's why you came up to me and invited me to lunch, so you could…what…lure me to your torture chamber?"

He chuckled, reaching for his tea. "I don't have a torture chamber."

"What do you have?"

After sipping from his drink, he plunked his glass on the table with a thud. "You're being nosy."

"No, I'm doing research." I shifted closer, lowering my voice. "Don't you want a chance to set the record straight? Have me write a book that would show the truth about…." I waved my hand at him. "Whatever it is you do."

His lips slammed together, not looking entirely convinced. "Do you really want to learn about this, Lexie? When you find out what it is that we do, you may not like it."

"You're a 'we' now. I thought you had limited experience?"

He wiped his hand over his striking features. I wanted to smile, knowing I was breaking down his defenses, or I guess his Dom armor.

"I know I'm going to regret this," he mumbled.

I touched his arm, and he pulled away from me. I thought his reaction a bit much, but let it go. Maybe being a Dom meant you weren't the touchy-feely type.

"Come on, Garrett. Introduce me to your friends. Take me to some of your clubs. I won't get in the way. I just want to watch."

Uh oh. The eyebrows were up again. "You don't just watch, Lexie." He shook his head. "To get to the core of this lifestyle you have to be a member, you have to participate. For you that would be dangerous."

Dangerous? Now this was getting good. I scooted my chair closer. "Why dangerous?"

He motioned down my figure. "Because you would be something anyone like me would love to possess. A Dom they could switch."

"What do you mean by switch?"

"Switch means to change ideology. It's when you turn from a dominant to a submissive. But only an elite master can do that."

"What is an elite master? Some kind of expert?"

He surveyed the tables next to us, appearing concerned that we would be overheard. "Master is just a general term, often used by subs when referring to their Doms. In some small circles, an elite master is a title given to one who has extensive experience with subs, has trained many of them, and in some ways, yes, is deemed an expert."

"Do you know any?" I asked, with probably a little too much exuberance.

His sigh resonated around us. "Jesus, you're a pain."

"Hey, you brought it up. I want to learn about this stuff, Garrett. Just the things you're telling me now are great. This could be about an elite master, his lovers, how he changes them from—"

"Switches," he interrupted.

"Whatever." I waved my hand in the air. "Just hook me up with some people. I can fake it to be part of the team."

Sitting back in his chair, he slapped his hand on the table. "It's not that simple, Lexie. You can't fake this."

"Sure I can. Just introduce me to your friends, and then your job is done. That's all there is to it."

His eyes became even rounder. "Are you kidding? Without me to protect you, they would eat you alive. No, if I'm going to introduce you to any of the people I know, you're going to have to have me with you at all times. You have no idea what you're getting into. This is a way of life, Lexie, not a weekend barbecue."

I heard the concern in his voice and reminded myself that he was from Dallas, after all. I had been raised on the weird and colorful streets of the French Quarter. Unusual, gothic, cult-like, I had seen it all. Growing up, the man who lived next door to us belonged to a vampire cult. He even took me to one of his meetings. Everybody ate donuts, talked about Anne Rice novels, and drank red-colored coffee. How much weirder could this stuff be?

"Garrett, I can do this." I sat back in my chair, grinning happily. "If it gets to be too much, I'll back out. I'll walk away, I promise."

He sat there for a long time, just staring at me. I could see the wheels spinning in his head. I figured he was planning his angle, some way to sell me to his groupies. As his guarded eyes bore into me, I knew I was winning him over.

"Okay, Lexie. I'll bring you to club I know. A place where Doms and subs meet."

"What club?"

He chuckled, wiping his hand over the five o'clock shadow on his square jaw. "It will give you an idea of what it's like. See if you want more after that. We can go tomorrow night, after we have dinner."

I frowned at him. "Why do we need to have dinner?"

"If I'm going to do this, you have to at least give me some concessions. Dinner tomorrow night with me is one. And I'm picking you up at your place."

"Like a date?"

"No, not a date." He reached for his tea. "This is far from a date. I think there are some things we will need to go over at dinner before we head to the club."

"What kinds of things?"

"Ground rules. Certain ways you're going to have to behave around me, if you're to be credible." He sipped his drink.

I was too pumped up to argue. "Fine. You can pick me up for dinner, and we can talk about your silly ground rules." I reached for my tea, happily fidgeting in my seat. "But I get to pick the restaurant."

Garrett rolled his uncanny brown eyes. "Why am I not surprised?"

Day 3

Dressing for my date with Garrett was much easier the second time around, because I was more excited about the prospect of doing research than actually seeing him. Ever since our lunch, ideas for a new story had been tumbling about in my head. I had even spent a good part of the day at my laptop making notes. I just didn't know enough about the lifestyle to get my arms around the plot.

As I stood before my bathroom vanity mirror and checked my casual black slacks and red silk blouse, I was alarmed at how calm I felt. Fluffing my deep brown hair, I took a moment to scrutinize my reflection. Had I missed something?

My makeup complemented my oval face and creamy complexion. The blush along the hint of my cheekbones was not overstated, despite the tendency of my cheeks to turn pink whenever I was cold, angry, or embarrassed. My lips were full, painted a pale red, and I thought complemented my rather straight features: my small, sharp nose, sort of pointy chin, and curved jaw. My ex, Sid, had called me beautiful when we were first together. After our first six months of marriage, that word disappeared completely from his vocabulary.

Running my hands down the red silk top that showed off my slender figure, I hoped I was presentable as a Dom's date. I made a note to ask him about attire. Maybe there was a dress code.

Exiting the small bathroom with its single shower stall crammed next to the toilet, I walked into the wide bedroom where a row of french windows opened to a balcony that overlooked a modest cemented patio surrounded by gardens. The best features in the gardens were the three majestic oaks with thick, leafy branches that never changed color, no matter the season. I could spend hours on that balcony, and had many times in the past, mostly writing.

That view was the main reason I lived in the subdivided old mansion...that and the great master bedroom, complete with a marble fireplace and twenty foot ceilings. The four other tenants each had what had once been a grand bedroom, with a fireplace and high ceilings. It was just Mrs. Castillo, on the first floor, who also got the paneled library, and Doug Kirsch, in the opposite first floor apartment, who got the intricately plastered living room and grand crystal chandelier.

Outside of my bedroom was a modest living room with plaster-textured walls painted a pale shade of pink, and my collection of antique furniture; a wedding present from my mother. The mahogany and yellow velvet sofa, love seat, and matching coffee table took up most of the room. In the corner, contrasting against the refined antiques, was my shabby, second-hand oak desk. Walking across the living room, I picked up my black purse that was sitting on the breakfast bar that divided the efficiency kitchen from the living room.

The buzzer from the main entrance to the old home rang in my apartment. I went to the speaker situated next to my thick unfinished cypress front door.

"Is that you?"

"Who else are you expecting?" Garrett's voice was bristling with sarcasm through the speaker.

Hearing his gravelly voice made me jumpy, and I prayed I could keep this strictly business between us. Deciding it would be better not to be alone with him in my apartment, I shouted into the speaker, "I'm coming down."

Hurrying out my door, I checked the deadbolt and then rushed along the landing that led to the darkly stained oak staircase. Once the centerpiece of the home, with inlaid white marble steps and a bannister carved to resemble tree branches, the wide stairway always made me feel like a queen whenever I descended it. Only tonight, I was more interested in the man standing on the other side of the arched double doors at the entrance to the house. When I shot back the deadbolt on the massive doors, I drew in a breath.

"Stay cool, girl."

He was waiting on the curved porch, wearing a tailored blue suit without a tie. He was freshly shaven, smelled of musky cologne, and his hair was damp, accentuating the slight wave of his dark brown locks. At first, I was disappointed in his choice of attire. I thought he would have worn something less businesslike.

"What is it?" he asked, eyeing his suit.

"Is that what you wear normally…you know, when you meet with your kind?"

He stepped in the doorway. "My kind? What did you expect me to wear to dinner? Chaps and a bullwhip?"

I shrugged off his wisecrack. "Fine." I walked through the arched doorway and waited until he came out to the porch. After he was standing beside me, he closed the heavy front doors.

"Nice old place," he commented, gazing about the porch lined with four white Corinthian columns.

"It is." I went to the steps that led to a herringbone bricked walkway. "It was built in 1887 by a cotton mill owner. It remained intact as a single family mansion until the early seventies, and then it was divided into apartments." I gazed up at the magnificent piece of New Orleans history I had called home for the past two years.

Admiring the Victorian Gothic design, I could not help but spot the peeling white paint about the long window frames, the rusted porch light suspended from the sloping second floor balcony, and the occasional cracks in the exterior woodwork. The house looked like I felt these days; worn out and in urgent need of rejuvenation.

"Which one is yours?" Garrett asked, coming up to my side on the walkway.

I pointed to my apartment upstairs on the right.

"I want to see your place," he asserted.

"Why?" I challenged.

He cocked his head slightly to the side as he observed me. The effect mixed with a sudden whiff of his cologne was riveting. "When we come back, you will show it to me."

I put my hand on my hip, being obstinate. "No, I will not, and stop issuing orders. I'm not one of your subs or servants or…whatever."

He placed his hands behind his back and nodded apologetically, but I could tell by his eyes he didn't mean it. "I merely meant I would really like to see inside this fine old mansion. I'm an architect, and old homes, such as this one, have a special place in my heart."

"You have a heart?"

Shaking his head, he motioned to the street. "Are you always like this before you're fed?"

I started toward the small black gate at the end of the walkway. "No. When I'm hungry, I'm much worse."

When Garrett stepped around a black BMW 650i, my eyebrows went up. He opened his driver's side door and then gestured to me to open my door.

"Aren't you going to get the door for me?" I pressed.

"Why? This isn't a date." He peered at me over the top of the car.

"What happened to your Hallmark philosophy?"

His eyebrows went up again. "Oh, I'm sorry, were you expecting me to treat you as a woman or as a research partner? Because I'm not sure which one I'm taking out this evening."

"Forget it," I muttered, grabbing at the car door.

Once I had settled into my seat and secured my seatbelt, he turned to me. "Things would be a lot easier, for both of us, if you would stop fighting me."

"Well, how do I know you aren't testing me again? Or worse, trying to turn me into your sex zombie?"

The roar of laughter that came from him was heartwarming, and at the same time infuriating.

"Sex zombie?" He wiped his right eye. "You should use that in your book." After his laughter had abated, he sat back in his seat, his deep brown eyes taking in my outfit. "I'm not out to convert you, Lexie. You're a woman who does not want to be dominated, but to dominate. I'm only interested in someone who can be submissive to me."

"Why do you find that attractive?"

He turned the key in the ignition. "When I take a woman on as a sub, it's not about physical contact or attraction. Sex is not always the final goal."

"There's a shocker." I snorted with disbelief. "So what is the final goal?"

He pulled the car out into the street. "When a sub gives up control to me, it is more out of respect and trust. That transfer of trust we call 'the gift.' It is more of an arrangement, consensual and not coercive. Their trust gives me pleasure, and my control over them allows release. In many ways, the sub has much more control over me than I do of them. I need their permission to be a Dom. To know someone trusts you like that, is ready to hand over their will to you, is very powerful."

"I don't get it."

"Let me put it this way." He maneuvered the car along Esplanade Avenue. "Have you ever wanted someone to take away all of your worries? Lift the burden from your shoulders and allow you to have peace, to not worry about the day-to-day trivialities of life?"

"Sure. Who hasn't? Except what you're talking about is role-playing. My idea of lifting my burdens is paying my taxes, rent, and car note."

He shook his head. "This isn't about fiscal control, although some Doms do that. I don't. I'm not an idiot."

"I'm glad to hear you're at least practical about this."

"Practical? No." Garrett's eyes lifted to his rearview mirror. "What you describe happens every day in your vanilla world. Look at kept women, mistresses, even trophy wives. What I do is no different from those relationships."

"Yeah, but those relationships are all about money. The woman sacrifices control for the money...which, after my last royalty check, sounds like a pretty good idea," I added, acutely aware of my dwindling assets.

"Are you in need of money?" he inquired, his smoldering eyes turning to me.

I squirmed in my seat, not quite sure how to take the question. "I'll survive. I always do."

"What about your ex? Could he help you?"

That made me laugh. "Sid would be the last person I would call." I tucked my purse in my seat, feeling defensive. I hated talking about my ex.

"Was it a bad marriage?"

A bad marriage? The words rolled around in my head like a windswept paper cup in an empty parking lot. How much do you tell a stranger about your life, especially the painful parts? I debated a course of action, and then reasoned that Garrett was giving me insights into his soul, why shouldn't I share my disappointments with him?

"We were...wrong from the start," I slowly began. "Sid was a guitar player who belonged to a few bands in the area. He did pretty well as a musician, and when we started dating, the attraction was intense. Six months later, he asked me to marry him. I, of course, was over the moon. My mother was livid."

"Why wasn't she happy about it? I thought all mothers loved it when their daughters married."

I shook my head and turned to the passenger window. The historical mansions along Esplanade Avenue sped by as we headed toward City Park. "My mother wanted me to wait until I was older to get married. I didn't think twenty-five was too young. She also wanted me to marry someone a lot more successful than a guitar player. She claimed we would end up fighting about money, and she was right. We fought a lot about money, and his screwing around."

"I'm sorry." He actually sounded sincere. "What did your father think of him?"

I shrugged and glanced back at him. "Wouldn't know. He died when I was two of a drug overdose. It was always me and Mom…and whatever boyfriend she had at the time."

"How long were you married?"

"About a year and a half. I've spent the few years since the divorce trying to stand on my own two feet."

"What about your mother? Can she help you?"

"Lily and I don't talk. I haven't spoken to her in over a year."

The impressive homes disappeared as the car came to the edge of Bayou St. John. Made famous by Maria Laveau, the bayou was said to be haunted by those voodoo practitioners of days gone by. Up ahead, the oak-lined entrance to City Park was lit up with spotlights. The park was a refuge from the cramped homes and cement of the city. Filled with trees, lagoons, golf courses, and other attractions, the borders of City Park had always been a welcomed sight to me. Even now, the darkness of the oaks over the land was inviting. I wanted to get lost in that darkness, at least for a little while, desperate to escape from the painful memories of my past.

"Where's this restaurant again?" Garrett's soothing voice brought me back from the abyss.

I pointed to the left of the park entrance. "Tavern on the Park. Just about half a mile down City Park Avenue."

The car came to rest at a stoplight. "Why is it your favorite restaurant?"

I turned to him, smiling weakly. "Because it looks out over the park. Anything that looks out over City Park is my favorite restaurant."

"You like the park?"

I nodded, gazing back to the darkness of the trees next to the car. "When I was little, my mother used to bring me here on Sundays to feed the ducks. Those are some of the best memories I have of my childhood."

Tavern on the Park was a two story converted home built across the street from one of the park entrances. Climbing out of his black BMW, I caught a quick glimpse of oak trees surrounded by tall, lush plants, and the man-made lagoon on the park grounds.

"I went to the New Orleans Museum of Art shortly after I arrived in the city," Garrett disclosed, coming around to my side. "The short drive I took through City Park was quite beautiful. I can see why you like it."

Tavern on the Park Restaurant was lit up with flickering brass gas lanterns about the first floor white-painted stucco entrance. The front doors of dark wood and wide glass were open, and along the side of the oblong building were a row of french windows also done in the same dark wood. Above our heads, a balcony wrapping around the second story offered an unencumbered view of the park. From inside, the din of voices and clinking dishes floated out to the street. As we proceeded toward the entrance, Garrett slipped his hand behind my back. I thought the gesture a little odd, considering he would not let me touch him yesterday. Maybe he was warming up to me.

Fastening his suit jacket, he escorted me up the steps to the restaurant. Just inside the restaurant, we came to a short podium manned by a very petite blonde in a dark blue dress.

"Welcome to Tavern on the Park. Table for two?"

I thought her eyes lingered over Garrett's torso a little longer than they should have.

"Yes, two, by the window," Garrett declared, nodding.

"Not a problem."

Grabbing two black menus, the lithe hostess showed us across the royal blue and white dining room. On the walls were paintings of the park, while set about the floor were dark wooden chairs with dusky blue cushions placed next to white linen-covered tables. In a corner, away from the crowded center of the room, we were shown to a table by a french window that overlooked the park across the street.

When I went to take my chair, Garrett pulled it out for me. Instead of starting an argument, I just took my seat.

After our hostess had handed us each a menu, she spotted more diners gathering at the entrance and quickly scurried away.

"What is good here?" Garrett asked, opening his menu.

I scanned my menu. "Don't know. I've never eaten here."

He lowered his menu and glared at me. "I thought you said this was your favorite restaurant?"

I shrugged without raising my eyes from my menu. "It is, because it overlooks the park. That doesn't mean I've ever eaten here."

He shook his head. "There is no logic to that statement, Lexie."

I regarded his slight frown over the top of my menu. "Can't a restaurant be your favorite because of where it is and not for the food?" I put my menu down. "I bet if you asked a ten-year-old about their favorite restaurant it would be because of where it is. Like McDonald's. They like to eat there because of the playground."

"You're a grown up, not a ten-year-old."

I sniffed with indignation. "We're all ten-year-olds on the inside."

"Okay, I'll give you that one." He put his menu to the side. "What else do you like, besides restaurants next to City Park?"

I sighed and picked up my menu again, thinking. Why was it when people asked me questions I was torn between telling them what they wanted to hear, and telling them the truth?

"I like ducks," I stated in a matter-of-fact tone, wanting to stick to a simple subject I did not have to lie about. "Ducks, hedgehogs, squirrels, dogs, and otters."

He leaned over the table, resting his arms along the edge of the tablecloth. I was not sure if the slight smile on his lips was for me, or was a result of some comical thought he was having about me.

"What else?" he badgered.

"You're full of questions." I continued to glean the menu, debating between the BBQ Gulf shrimp and the gnocchi.

"If I'm going to introduce you to my world, we should know something about each other, Lexie. What else?"

A young, curly-haired blond waiter wearing a white apron and white, long-sleeved shirt came up to our table. "Good evening, I'm Tim and I will be your server tonight. Can I get you some drinks to start?"

I was about to order a glass of white wine when Garrett spoke up. "Just two iced teas."

Tim bobbed his head. "Sure thing. I'll get your drinks and come back for your order."

After Tim had retreated from our table, I scowled at Garrett. "I want wine."

He picked up his menu, ignoring me. "No alcohol tonight. I need you sober."

"Why? It's not like this is an FBI sting operation, Garrett. We're just going to some club. What's the big deal?"

His eyes remained on his menu. "The big deal is you need to be convincing as my new sub. To do that you need to pay attention to what I'm about to say, and remember everything I tell you. You can't do that when you're tipsy."

Fuming, I did not argue. He had a point, and despite really wanting a glass of wine to calm my nerves, I decided to abide by his wishes.

When Tim returned with our iced teas, Garrett snatched the menu from my hands. "We'll have the fried oysters as an appetizer. The lady will have the gnocchi main course, and I'll have the seared rib-eye filet. Thousand Island on our dinner salads, and a side of oven roasted potatoes."

Tim scribbled the order on his pad, took our menus, and left our table.

My anger was gaining ground. As I sat back in my chair, finding the right words to rip into him, Garrett calmly removed his rolled up white napkin from the plate and spread it on his lap.

"What I just did is something any Dom worth his weight would do. My job, as a Dom, is to predict your needs and see to them. I am expected to be a protector, teacher, and lover to my sub."

"I can order dinner for myself, Garrett. I don't need you to—"

"What were you going to order?"

I squirmed in my chair. Did I have to tell him I had decided on the gnocchi?

He gazed steadily into my eyes, waiting for my answer.

"All right," I confessed, unable to take his continued scrutiny. "I was going to order the gnocchi, but not the oysters. I don't like oysters."

"The oysters are for me." He grinned, arching an eyebrow. "I may not be the best, Lexie, but I'm very good at what I do. You need to listen to me."

Sagging into my chair, I hated the idea of listening to him. However, I really needed this story. I had to just remember that this book would be worth it. *Think only of the book.*

"What else?" I grumbled, playing with the silver fork set beside my plate.

"You're right. You are a ten-year-old." He shook his head, took my hand away from the fork, and placed it in my lap. "When we are together at this club, there will be others watching how you interact with me. You have to be convincing. If you're not, they will get suspicious, and you will never be able to speak with anyone."

"What others? Other Doms?"

"Yes." His eyes drew together, appearing slightly worried.

"What do I have to do?"

"I thought that was obvious. You must do whatever I say."

I was between a rock and a hard place. I had to go along. If I wanted to get anywhere, I had to do as he demanded, no matter how much it infuriated me.

"Just remember that this," I motioned between us, "is not real. I'm in this for my book and only my book. So don't think I'm going to wear black leather boots and handcuffs or any of that stuff."

"Wouldn't dream of it." He sat back and took in the small gathering of diners at the other tables about us.

Studying his strong profile, I was slightly disappointed that there could not be more. Any other woman would have done everything she could to possess such a man. For me, he was a means to an end. I had given up on finding someone. Instead, I found the relationships I longed for in the men I wrote about in my books. It may not have been very satisfying, but it was a whole lot easier on my heart.

"When are you going to tell me more about your experiences?" I asked after a time.

His eyes wheeled back to me. "Where did I leave off?"

"Ruth, the one you met in college." I reached for the white linen napkin on my plate. "She made you her sub and you didn't like it."

"It wasn't that I didn't like it." He smiled coyly, making the corners of his eyes crinkle up in the most alluring way. "It just wasn't for me. Not long after Ruth, I met Mary Lynn." He paused and cast his eyes to his plate. "She was in school with me, taking design classes. We started out like a regular vanilla couple. She was the one who wanted more. I would do things to her, here and there, to see if she liked it, and our relationship evolved. After a time, Mary Lynn asked me to be her Dom. That is when everything changed for me. I discovered I liked being in control of her every desire." He grew silent, and his smile slipped away.

The coldness returned to his gaze, stirring my curiosity. "What happened to her?"

He tilted his head casually to the side as he crossed his legs beneath the table. "She started to demand rougher play. Things I would not do to a woman, so I ended it."

"Rougher play? What do you mean?"

"Play is a term we use to refer to the time we actually practice our art, inside and outside of the bedroom. Inside the bedroom, Mary Lynn wanted to go more and more into rough sex. Choking, hitting…the whips and chains end of BDSM. That is not what I do."

"Did she find someone who was into that?"

He readjusted his napkin in his lap. "I'm sure she did. I never saw her again after we ended it."

"Who was next?"

He reached for three packets of sugar from a ceramic bowl in the center of the table. "That's enough, for now." He dropped one of the packets by my glass of tea. "Let's talk about something else."

"Jeez, you can dish it out, but you sure can't take it." I picked up my packet of sugar and dumped it into my tea. "So what is this club we are going to?"

He stirred his tea with his long spoon. "A place I found soon after I arrived in New Orleans. It's pretty generic as BDSM clubs go. It's mostly women interested in being subs with a few vanilla groupies thrown in."

"What's a vanilla groupie?" I lifted my glass to my lips.

"Fans of that book I can't stand, who think they want a BDSM lifestyle. Once exposed to it, they run like scared rabbits." He chuckled.

"Do any of those elite masters you talked about go there?"

The question instantly made him appear uncomfortable. He shifted in his chair and lifted his tea. "Sometimes."

"How do you know when anyone is an elite master? Do they wear green blazers or something?" I started giggling at my joke, and had the air let out of my sails when I saw him drawing a complete blank.

"The Masters Golf Tournament. The winner gets a green blazer....get it?" I rolled my hand in front of him, trying to add emphasis to my joke.

His chiseled features were unmoved. "No, they don't wear green jackets."

God, this guy needed to lighten up. Was everyone that was into this stuff so serious? I placed my hands in my lap. "Okay, so how do you know if someone is one of those elite masters?"

"Experience. And you can't see that unless you know what to look for. Spotting a Dom is another story."

"How is that?"

"In some clubs you can tell by the way members wear a handkerchief. A certain color worn to the left indicates a dominant, to the right a submissive. I can tell by the control they have over their sub." His eyes took a turn of the room. "You see the older gentleman, at the table by the door, with the pretty young brunette?"

I eased to the side in my chair and caught a glimpse of the couple he was alluding to. The older man had gray hair and was dressed in a very nice blue suit with a fastidiously knotted yellow tie. His hair was neatly combed to the side, and everything about him, from the cut of his suit to the gold watch on his wrist, screamed money. The young woman was very slender, with pale, almost gaunt features, perfectly applied makeup, and not a brown hair out of place in her swept up coif. I noticed her diamond necklace and matching teardrop earrings, and figured that was just compensation for what she had to endure.

"What am I looking for?"

He reached over and pushed me back in my chair. "First, don't be so obvious. Next, watch the way he hands her things, the way she is seated perfectly erect in the chair and never moves. He speaks to her as an aside, never directly. When he does say anything to her, then and only then, do you see her move."

I tried to get an unencumbered view over his wide shoulder by raising my butt a little in my chair. The woman did seem awfully stiff, and then a waiter brought a basket of bread to their table. I watched, fascinated, as the man retrieved a roll from the basket, buttered it while the woman never moved, and then placed it on her bread plate. He said something to her, and then her hand reached for the roll.

"That's sick!" I spat out.

"That's a Dom at work. The total control he has over her defines him as a Dom."

I pointed back to the older man's table. "That turns you on? Buttering someone's bread for them, telling them when to eat it?"

He shook his head, snickering at my display. "Every Dom is different; some require absolute obedience in all things, and some only require it in a few things."

I eyed him suspiciously. "Where do you fall in that range?"

Tim returned to our table, carrying a bread basket in his hands along with a plate of butter slices. "Here you go, guys, fresh out of the oven."

I waited for Tim to walk away, and then my eyes went instantly to Garrett. He was grinning at me, daring me with his gaze. That was enough for me. I grabbed a roll from the basket and banged it down on my bread plate.

"Don't even think about it," I grumbled. "The last time anyone buttered anything for me I was three."

He reached for a roll. "As far as I can tell, you're still three."

"Oh, ha-ha." I knifed a pat of butter.

"Look, Lexie." He placed his roll on his bread plate. "We're going to have to work together if you want to be convincing." He sat back, adjusting the sleeve of his jacket. "Being a Dom isn't about being turned on by having some sort of slave. It's about having a person surrender their desire to me. Giving me the treasure of absolute trust. That's what turns me on. Trust, not power."

I put my knife down and plopped my roll on my bread plate. "So in other words, you want me to trust you."

"To be convincing as my sub, yes, you must trust me." He picked up his roll. "Have you ever trusted anyone implicitly?"

I wanted to shout out, "Hell no," but I stopped and sat back in my chair, thinking. Had I ever really trusted anyone before? Let someone have the kind of control over me that Garrett alluded to? Maybe that was what came from spending so much time on my own as a kid. I learned early on that people could not be trusted. If you could not trust your parent to be there for you, who could you trust?

"I gave up trusting a long time ago. But I promise to make a better effort at this." Snatching up my bread, I took a bite.

I was chewing ferociously, swallowing back my disgust with every mouthful. I knew that he was observing me, but I didn't care. I sat in silence, brooding and chewing. After I had finished the entire roll, he reached into the breadbasket and placed another on my plate.

"Perhaps you might actually taste this one. They're very good."

Snapped out of my trance by his voice, I glanced over to see him enjoying a bite from his bread. Maybe I was making too much of this. I should just shut my mouth and play along with his game. Hopefully, after tonight I would have enough to come up with some ideas for a story. Nodding to the roll, I smiled for him.

"Wanna butter it for me?"

His hearty chuckle instantly made me feel better. Funny how the man had that effect on me.

* * *

The club Garrett took me to was nothing more than seedy bar in a square, gray-bricked building on Prytania Street. One of the less popular bars that I had never been to before, The Edge had a reputation of luring a rough crowd. I had always believed that kind of crowd to be made up of bikers and gang members. Garrett insisted otherwise.

"It's well known as a place for recruiting willing subs," he explained, motioning to the red neon sign above a plain wooden door.

"Recruiting? That's rather a strange way to put it."

He glimpsed the full parking lot around us. "Not really. If you think about it, that is what we do, recruit individuals to join in our play."

"Were you dropped on your head a lot as a kid? I just can't get around the fact that a man like you, successful, intelligent, and…aren't normal women enough?"

"What is normal, Lexie?" He placed his hands behind his back, arching his shoulders slightly. "Is living cloistered away in your apartment writing novels about strong, sullen, and unhappy doctors falling in love with assertive and vivacious women normal?"

I was floored by his comment. "You've read my books?"

"All four of them." He nodded. "You said if I was to get to know you as a writer, I should read your books. After our lunch yesterday, I purchased the e-books and spent the night studying you through your writing."

"You read all four of my books in one night?"

"I'm a fast reader."

I had not expected this. Men didn't read romance novels. Even if they attempted to, they usually never finished and wrote off the entire book as a woman's fantasy.

"Should I even ask what you thought of them?"

His hand went to my back and gently nudged me toward the bar entrance. "You're a very good writer, but your heart was not in those books. The woman I've been with is not the woman who wrote those novels."

Our feet crunched on the shell-covered parking lot beneath us. "I don't understand. What do you mean, it's not me?"

"It's not your voice," he clarified, as we came to the wooden door. "You have a distinctive character, and if you put that in your books…well, I think you would be more successful." When he reached for the large brass handle on the door, he stopped and glanced over at me. "Remember, you are my sub. Don't talk unless I speak to you, and if anyone comes up to you and starts a conversation, you look to me for permission. Got it?"

I tugged nervously at my black purse strap. "I got it. I don't like it, but I got it."

He pulled the door open. "Just keep looking to me if you don't know what to do."

The thump, thump, thump of the loud music coming from inside hit me, and I hesitated. "What if I have to go to the bathroom?" I asked, as he stood beside me.

He lowered his head to my right ear. "You are never to leave my side. If you want to get out of here, tap on my arm." He held the door open for me. "That will be our signal."

Smoke covered the entrance like a mist, and as we passed through it I coughed. The lights were dim, but at the far end of the rectangular room there was a brightly lit dance floor with flashing orbs and strobe lights, reminding me of a chintzy disco. I wondered if Doms and subs were allowed to dance together, or did the subs have to dance with subs, and Doms with Doms? I needed to remember to put a scene like that in my book. I could see it now, a bunch of masters dancing in green blazers.

We were working our way toward the long wooden bar, with a mirrored back, that sat against the far wall. The bar was crowded with an interesting mix of women wearing slinky dresses, black leather, and a few in jeans and T-shirts. All the men were in business suits, every single one of them, which struck me as very odd. Halfway to the bar, I felt Garrett's hand on my shoulder. I figured that was a gentle reminder to act more sub-like. I caught his angry scowl and quickly lowered my eyes, hunched my shoulders forward, and in general tried to look miserable.

"Stop frowning," he whispered to me. "You enjoy being with me, remember?"

"What do you suggest? Do you want me to be a Stepford Wife like in the restaurant?"

"Just avoid making eye contact with people, for Christ's sake." His hand squeezed my shoulder.

When we made it to the bar, Garrett pulled out a red vinyl-covered stool for me that was ripped and had foam sticking out of it. I didn't want to sit on that thing. When he saw me second-guessing the stool, he squeezed even harder on my shoulder.

Wincing, I took the stool, placed my purse in my lap, and waited. He stood beside me, taking in the room.

"You need to watch the interaction between people," he muttered out of the corner of his mouth. "Watch how they approach each other. Look for subtle signs. Remember the body language I saw in you in the park? Look for that in the subs. Doms will stand erect, tower over their sub, assert their dominance."

"Like you?" I mumbled.

"Yes, like me." His breath was against my cheek. "I'm your Dom, so act like it."

There was something about the way he said those words, and the feel of his breath, that ignited a tiny spark in a dormant part of my gut. I had thought myself immune to feeling anything remotely resembling desire since my days with Sid. But this tickle, this inkling was unmistakable. Closing my eyes against the sensation, I willed it away. Such thoughts about Garrett Hughes were not only irresponsible, they were dangerous.

Searching for a distraction, I became intrigued by a couple not far from our spot next to the bar. She was a leggy blonde, decked out in a short beaded black dress and high black heels. He was an older gentleman in a suit with black hair, peppered gray. It was not so much their looks that aroused my curiosity, but the way they were interacting with each other. The blonde was not flirting, as I would have expected of an attractive woman with a man she had taken a fancy to. Instead, she was avoiding eye contact with the man, dipping her head to the ground. Her hands were at her sides, not playing with her hair or face like a woman trying to draw a man's attention. She was listening intently to what the older gentleman had to say, almost mesmerized. When the man abruptly turned away, I was confused. I saw the blonde follow him, staying back a few feet, but definitely allowing him to walk ahead. He went to the dance floor and waited as she came up to him. Standing before the man, the blonde listened as he spoke to her, then raised her arms around his shoulders, and began seductively swaying her slim hips beneath her beaded black dress.

I turned to Garrett, wanting to share my observation with him. Without thinking, I was about to open my mouth to speak when his angry voice was in my ear.

"Remember what I told you."

Shutting my mouth, I sheepishly scanned the bar to see if I had been discovered. For a few uneasy seconds, I waited to see if we were going to be run out of the bar, but no one seemed to notice.

"Heads up," he mumbled to me. "Here comes Colin."

I wanted to ask Colin who, but didn't.

"You met Colin the other day at the park with me," Garrett stated, reading my thoughts.

How did he do that? Before I could even begin to address Garrett's psychic abilities, Colin was standing before my stool, grinning from ear to ear.

The attractive man with the piercing blue eyes and handsomely carved features was dressed in a fitted brown suit like all the other men in the bar. Colin had removed his tie and unbuttoned the top two buttons on his cream dress shirt. His fine, light brown hair was slightly windblown, and his faint five o'clock shadow deepened the curve of his square jaw. I thought his gaze on me a bit too intense, but then he directed his eyes to Garrett.

"You work fast," Colin remarked, as he came forward.

Garrett leaned against the bar behind me. "I told you what I saw in her."

"Is she compliant?" Colin asked with a little too much excitement in his voice.

"We're working on that," Garrett replied with the hint of a snicker.

Colin turned to face me. "Nice to see you again, Lexie."

My stomach shrank, and I swerved my eyes to Garrett, not sure what to do.

"Say hello, Lexie," Garrett offered, and placed his hand on my shoulder.

His comforting touch reassured me. "Hello, Colin. Nice to see you again," I said, trying to sound as monotone as possible.

Had I said too much, not sounded believable? Would he suspect something was up? Christ, how did these subs do it? I had been a sub for less than five minutes, and already I felt like I was developing a complex. I stared ahead, trying to look as passive as possible. God, I needed a drink.

"Very good," Colin cooed. "I didn't think she was right for you, but you've proved me wrong, yet again. How do you do it?"

Again? Oh, wait till I got him in the car and grilled him about that!

"Colin, where is Missy?" Garrett inquired.

"Home, flu." Colin shrugged his wide shoulders. "She couldn't play tonight, so I'm out alone."

I was glad that they, at least, gave sick time to their subs. Was there vacation time, too?

"Are you going to bring her to the club?" Colin asked, pointing to me.

Garrett's hand squeezed my shoulder, encouraging me to stay quiet. "I haven't decided. We have a lot of work to do."

Colin's face dipped in front of me. His eyes darted back and forth between mine, then he stood up again.

"You should bring her," he finally said. "The empress will want to get a look at her. You know how she feels about outsiders."

The empress? Who was that? More topics of discussion for the car ride home.

"Let me know what you decide. I would like to be there when she is introduced to the other members." Colin veered in front of me. "See you later, Lexie." Without waiting for my reply—or not expecting one—he stood again and nodded to Garrett. "We need to talk."

Colin set out across the bar, and was only a few feet away when I felt Garrett's hand ease up on my shoulder. I wanted to release a long sigh of relief, but thought better of it. I didn't want to let Garrett down.

"That was very good," Garrett whispered to me. "I know just how much it killed you to keep your mouth shut."

"You have no idea," I grumbled.

"You stay here," he curtly ordered. "Don't talk to anyone while I'm gone."

"Where are you going?" I asked, panic-stricken.

"I need to speak with Colin."

"What about the club he mentioned? And who is this empress, Garrett?"

"Save the interrogation for when we are out of here, Lexie." He came closer, tempting my skin with his hot breath. "Once you get started asking questions, I'll never get you to stop."

He went off after Colin. Trying to follow him with my eyes, I lost him behind a crowd of men, blocking my view of the dance floor. Normally, I would have just stood from my stool and adjusted my view. I could not do that here. Like Garrett had said earlier at dinner, people were watching.

Sighing slightly, I shifted my butt a little on the stool and waited. It didn't take long for the next challenge to present itself when two young women wearing jeans and T-shirts approached the bar, giggling between them.

"Did you see that gorgeous one with the dreamy eyes?" a redhead said beside my stool. "He would do."

"No way," her friend, a perky brunette with too much makeup replied. "We came here to find a Mr. Grey, and we aren't leaving until we've met one."

"Are you sure there are men like that here?" the redhead fussed.

"That's what the guy at the door said. They come here with their subs."

The redhead tossed back her long locks with her pale hand. "I sure would love to be somebody's sub for one night."

The brunette glanced over at me. "I'm not sure I could be like these girls." She motioned to me. "How do they sit there like zombies?"

"That's not what happened in *FSOG*."

"None of this is like what happened in *FSOG*," the brunette countered. "I just want the hot sex; the other stuff, not so much."

The women moved away, and my eyes searched the room for Garrett. All about, men and women were paired off; some of the women were talking, the others were passive and quiet. I had not noticed so much in the beginning, but now everywhere I looked I saw evidence of dominant-submissive relationships. Two women were even sporting black leather collars with rhinestones.

"Time to go," Garrett murmured, taking my arm.

Practically lifting me from the stool, I noticed the way his lips were smashed together and the deep worry lines marring his brow. "What's wrong?"

"In the car...not here." He then pulled me across the crowded bar to the entrance.

Once outside, we headed straight for his black BMW. This time he opened the door for me and waited until I was safely in my seat before slamming the door shut. Glancing back at the bar, I saw Colin standing by the entrance, watching us. The man's suspicious eyes never wavered from our car. As Garrett started the engine, I kept my sights on Colin. There was something menacing about the way he was gawking at our car.

"You mind telling me what that was about?" I shouted, as soon as we had left the parking lot. "And what was all that shit Colin was spouting about clubs and empresses?"

"Colin and I belong to a special club. The De Sade Club." His hands gripped the steering wheel. I could see how his knuckles shone white against the black leather. "It's for high-end Doms wanting subs; a place where you can go to meet women who have a desire to be subs. Every member is carefully screened, and admission to the club requires a lot of references and money."

"How did you hear about this club?"

"Through Colin. I contacted him when I arrived in the city. He introduced me. The empress is the woman who runs the club. She arranges meetings, handles any disputes between subs and Doms, and offers a place where we can play without any unwanted attention."

I was shocked. This was something you would see in the movies, or read in racy novels. "Are you talking about a whorehouse?"

"No, nothing like that." He shook his head. "More like a matchmaking service."

"I don't understand. Why would you join a club like that?"

He wiped his hand over his brow. "Because I wanted to meet like-minded women I didn't have to train. There are a lot of bars like that one to meet women. Then you have to train them, find their limits, and set boundaries. It can be time-consuming and tedious for someone like me. I don't have time to devote to such a relationship with starting up the new office, so I joined the De Sade Club to have ready access to women already well-trained."

"Christ, Garrett, it sounds so…I don't know what to call it."

The eyebrows went up. "It's no different than your Mardi Gras crews, Lexie. Those are special clubs where members meet like-minded individuals and share secret parties. It's the same thing, yet geared toward BDSM gamers."

"Yeah, but members of a carnival club don't get together to have sex," I insisted.

"How do you know that?" He chuckled. "From what I've seen of Mardi Gras that is about all that does go on."

The whole notion of such a club infuriated me. "Come on, Garrett. You know what I'm talking about."

"It's just a meeting place, Lexie. That's all. Sex between two consenting adults can happen anywhere, in any circumstance. What are you so angry about?"

I slammed back in my car seat, sulking. "That shit just sounds creepy, that's all."

His lips spread into a condescending sneer, making his face appear darker. "You really shouldn't curse like that. It doesn't become you."

"Become me?" I folded my arms and snickered. "Fuck that."

His eyes returned to the traffic ahead on Prytania Street. "I think I liked you better back in the bar."

"You would. Don't push me, Garrett," I snarled.

"Wouldn't dream of it, Lexie."

The rest of the ride back to my place I said nothing, just tried to digest everything I had witnessed. I had to admit I wasn't that surprised by the revelation about his club. This was New Orleans, after all, and I had grown up mired in weirdness. I had hoped Garrett to be above such foolishness. I guess the real shock was finding out that he wasn't that much different than the rest of us.

When his BMW eased into a parking spot in front of the old Victorian Gothic house where I lived, I had replaced my anger with a calming dose of reality. It was his business, not mine, what he did with his life. If he chose to belong to weird clubs where he met others of his kind, then so be it. I had never been judgmental of anyone's sexual preferences. As long as it was consensual between two individuals over the age of eighteen, and didn't involve animals, I was fine with it.

"Are you going to take me to your club?" I asked, as he walked me up the herringbone path to the front doors.

"No," he answered sharply. "It's not for you."

I pivoted around to him. "Why not?"

"Lexie, what you experienced tonight was the tamer end of BDSM. There will be consequences if you get in much deeper. I'm not sure you're ready for that. The De Sade Club can be…intense for those not trained in the art."

"How intense?"

He placed his hand behind my back, encouraging me toward the porch steps. "Make me some coffee and we'll discuss it."

"Do you ever say please?"

He smirked at me. "No."

Shaking my head, I let him usher me up the steps. "Does your mother know you're into these clubs?"

That made him laugh out loud, and his booming laughter disturbed the tranquility around the grand home. "No, and I hope to God she never finds out."

I pulled my keys out of my black purse. "Why, what would she think?"

"Probably where did she go wrong." He wiped his hand over his forehead. "She's a very mild-mannered

Southern woman. Goes to church on Sundays and makes a pot roast every Saturday for dinner. My tastes would be more than disturbing to her."

I put the key in the lock. "She ever ask about the women in your life?" The deadbolt clicked open.

"Frequently. I tell her I just haven't found the right woman, yet." He pushed the heavy doors open, and we walked inside.

We headed up the grand staircase to my apartment.

"This is magnificent," he mumbled, admiring the carved bannister.

"Your mother is going to get suspicious, Garrett. You're how old…thirty-two, thirty-three? She's going to start asking about grandchildren in a few years."

His eyes wandered up the flight of stairs. "Actually I'm thirty-five, and she has already mentioned that." He ran his long hand along the carved banister, caressing the wood like a lover's skin.

I envied that banister briefly, to be touched like that…whoa, what was I thinking? I knew it had been a long time since I had been with a man, but…back to business.

"So why won't you bring me to your club?" I persisted once we had reached the top of the stairs.

He came up behind me as I stood before my apartment door. "Lexie, faking it in that bar was nothing compared to what you would have to do in that club. There are rules, conduct for behavior, things you would have to learn."

I opened my front door and glanced back at him. "What would I have to learn?"

His eyes volleyed between mine. The ripple of excitement that tore through me was so intense, I wanted to look away, but couldn't.

"If you were to go with me to that club you would have to be trained," he whispered.

"Trained to do what?" I asked, my voice a little unsteady.

His lips came closer to mine. "Trained to submit to me."

Okay, that did it. My knees wobbled slightly, and for a spilt second I thought I was going to fall into his arms. I regained control of my faculties, raised my head, and proudly met his eyes head on.

"I'm not afraid of you, Garrett. I will do whatever I have to for my book." I kept my eyes steadily gazing into his, showing him that I was the stalwart woman I pretended to be, even if I didn't believe it. "Do you think there is a story in this club?" I voiced, sharing my thoughts with him.

He backed away from me. "You can't use the club in your book, Lexie." He strolled in my front door.

I gawked at his broad back as he stepped into my living room and flipped on the recessed lights. "Why not?" I rushed in the door behind him and shut it with a bang.

"Because if word got out about the club, they would suspect one of their members. If I was ever discovered…these are powerful people. They could hurt me financially, ruin the firm, or drive me out of the circle." He removed his jacket.

"What circle?"

"I would be blackballed out of every BDSM bar, club, or gathering. I would have to venture out on my own to find subs, and that poses more problems than it's worth." He tossed his jacket to my antique sofa, his eyes going over the furniture with more than a casual interest.

"Why would going on your own pose a problem? I would think being free of some club and its rules would be better."

He went to the love seat and ran his hand over the yellow velvet cushion. "Where did you get this furniture? It's exquisite."

"It was a wedding gift from my mother." I walked into the center of my living room, enamored by the way he was stroking the love seat. Damn those hands.

"She has exceptional taste," he clucked, and then stood back from the love seat.

"You didn't answer my question, Garrett. Why is it a problem to go out on your own?"

He clapped his hands together. "I would have to gamble on the sub I found, possibly have to do a lot of training, and then there is no guarantee that it would work." He moved away from the love seat and came toward me. "Ever since that book came out, there have been a lot of pretenders to this game, making clubs almost a necessity for the true practitioner. Many of us like to remain hidden from the general public."

I nodded my head, remembering the two women in the bar. "I think I overheard some pretenders back at the bar. They kept talking about that book and wanting to hook up with a Mr. Grey type."

Garrett hesitated before giving me a weak smile. "I'm afraid what they will end up with is a bad experience with someone who is not a true Dom."

"Hell of a lifestyle you have, Garrett. How many people get hurt by what you're involved in?" Chucking my purse to the sofa next to his jacket, I motioned to the kitchen. "How do you like your coffee?"

He came up, pausing inches away from me. "You're right. We really do need to set the record straight about my way of life." He furrowed his brow. "How far would you go for this book of yours, Lexie?"

Was he kidding me? I threw my hands up. "The book is everything, Garrett. I would do just about anything to get a good story."

His eyes stayed locked on mine. "Prove it."

"What?"

"If you want to go with me to the club, you're going to have to be trained to be my sub. Learn ways to treat me and how to take punishment and reward from me."

"What are you talking about?"

"In the club, you're under a great deal of scrutiny. Submissive behavior to your Dom is expected at all times. Your loyalty to me might even be tested by other Doms. Are you prepared for that?"

"Yes," I blurted out. "Absolutely. If it gets me into that club and affords me an intimate view of what you do, then I'll do anything. What would I have to do?"

"First, let's see if you can do it." He came around behind me. "Stand perfectly still."

"What are you going to do?" I was about to turn around to him when his hands came down hard on my shoulders, keeping me in place.

"For the next ten minutes, you are my sub. Everything I tell you to do, you must do. Any want I have, you must fulfill. Do you understand? Answer yes or no only."

When he mentioned his wants being fulfilled, I debated stopping him and setting some conditions. Then again, this was a very attractive man who wanted to spend time with me. If something more came of it…maybe I shouldn't worry about conditions.

"Yes," I sighed.

"Good. Then close your eyes."

That did not help make me feel any more comfortable with the situation, but I did as I was told. Wasn't I being a good sub already?

"Part of the duty of a sub is to be familiar with her master's touch. I have to be able to touch you in any way I please. You cannot flinch or appear afraid." His hands moved slowly down my back, his fingers pressing against my flesh. "Your body is mine to control."

I pictured his hand on the bannister of the stairs; the way he had caressed the wood. I let go of my apprehension and tried to concentrate on his hands.

"You only want to please me." His voice was steady and firm in my ear. "Letting me touch you, any part of you, pleases me. You need to please me, Lexie." His hands glided down my back and over the curve of my backside.

Alarm shot through me. He was kneading my butt with his fingers, and I wanted to turn around and slap him. I forced myself to let go. Taking in a deep breath, I let the air out between my gritted teeth, hissing like a snake cornered by a predator.

"That's it," he murmured to me. "You're letting me take control. I will not hurt you. I want only to gain your trust. Trust me, Lexie." His hands moved around my hips to the valley between my legs as his body curled into my back.

The scent of his cologne mixed with the warmth of his arms enveloping me was very distracting. When his hand cupped my groin, a sudden swell of lust surprised me. The feel of his hand was highly erotic, making me yearn for him to go deeper. His fingers dug into my crotch, and I arched my back, sucking in an excited breath.

"There you go." His voice was breaking down my resistance. "Give in to me."

The throbbing started between my legs and slowly rose up my back, causing a rush of desire to overtake me. Without warning, he let me go. The sudden loss of his body heat made me shiver, as if the coldest winds of winter had embraced me. I stumbled slightly forward and he caught my arm.

"That was very good."

Turning to him, I was not sure how to react. I wanted this, needed this to write my book, but what he had done had been so intimate and unexpected.

"Why did you do that?"

"To see if you could handle it." He went to the sofa and picked up his jacket. "Now picture me doing that to you in a room full of people, perhaps with your clothes on, perhaps off. There are no limits at this club." He paused and arched a dark eyebrow at me. "Are you sure you're ready for this?"

"But you said…." I stumbled, and wiped my hand over my forehead, feeling flushed. "I thought this wasn't always about the sex. You said at dinner—"

"I lied." He shrugged on his jacket. "It's always about sex, because sex is the ultimate act of submission for a Dom."

"I'm not going to have sex with you, Garrett, and I—"

"I don't want to have sex with you, Lexie." He adjusted the jacket around his shoulders. "Nevertheless, if you're determined to go to the club with me, we will have to practice being a couple. You must look comfortable with me, as if we know each other…intimately." He moved toward my apartment door. "I'll come by for lunch tomorrow, and we will practice some more."

"You mean you'll grope me some more."

"Your role, as a sub, is to appear as my companion, student, and lover. You must never fear me, and make it look as if everything you do is to provide me pleasure. To do that, we're going to have to get close to each other, very close. Do you understand what I'm saying?"

At that point, I should have told him to go to hell. My mind was shouting at me to do just that, but my body was having other ideas. If I ended it now, I was guaranteed never to see him again. That was something I was not yet willing to do. That was why I found my voice and answered, "Yes, Garrett, I understand."

His smile was one of triumph. Getting me to go along with his plan was in some small way a victory for him. After all, he had called me another Dom, and taming me would be his greatest challenge.

He opened my apartment door and his smile fell away. "I'll pick you up at twelve thirty for lunch. This time I will pick the restaurant."

I folded my arms over my chest and nodded, slowing walking up to the door. "You're enjoying this, aren't you?"

His eyes on me, he waited until I was right in front of him. "The question is, Lexie, are you?"

Without another word, he turned away and headed along the landing to the stairs. After shutting the door, I drove the deadbolt home. Resting my head against the thick cypress door, I felt drained. Snapshots of the entire evening flashed across my mind, and I knew I needed to make some notes. The image of Garrett fondling me in the living room made me push away from the door.

The things he had said to me whirled around in my head, and an idea hit me.

Spying my laptop on the desk in the corner of my living room, I went and flipped up the lid. As the screen flashed to life, I pulled out my chair and opened a new file.

The curser blinked on and off in front of me, and then I reached up to the keyboard and typed a title. "Taming Me."

"Shit," I mumbled. "This might be just what I'm looking for."

Day 4

When noon rolled around, I was not able to get out of bed. The previous night, I had discovered that the apparent reason for my warm flushes during my time with Garrett was not related to passion, but to the flu. After getting a first chapter down on my computer, a sudden rush of nausea sent me to the bathroom. There I had stayed for the next three hours, lying on the cool white-tiled floor and praying to God someone would shoot me.

With the light of day I found my nausea, and trips to the bathroom, had eased and I was able to get a little sleep. That was until the pounding began. I checked the time on the alarm clock next to my bed, and groaned. I realized Garrett was probably standing outside my door, prepared to inflict some new torture on me.

Grabbing at the ratty white cotton robe on the end of my queen-sized trundle bed, I stood and stumbled toward the front door. I had barely pulled the robe about my long nightshirt—the one with the picture of Jackson Square on it—when I flung back the deadbolt.

"What in the hell, Lexie?" His dark eyes ran up and down my robe. "Why aren't you dressed? I said twelve thirty."

I leaned heavily on the door for support, wishing he would go away. The gray suit he had on was neatly pressed, and his deep blue tie was perfectly knotted. Did the guy ever appear rumpled?

"Leave me alone, Garrett. I had a shitty night."

"What's wrong?" His hand went to my forehead, and his cool touch felt marvelous against my brow. "You're burning up." He came in the door and took my arm.

"I think it was the gnocchi," I offered, as he shut the door behind him.

"I doubt that." He ushered me toward the sofa. "When did this start?"

"I was writing after you left last night. Then around midnight, I felt really sick." He set me on the sofa. "I spent the night on the bathroom floor."

"Why didn't you call me?" He stood back from the sofa, his eyes all over me.

"About lunch?" I rested against the sofa, exhausted. "I didn't have your cell phone number. I guess I could have looked up your office number, but I—"

"Where's your purse?" he inquired, scanning the living room.

"Why?" I pointed to the modest pine bench next to the front door. "I put it there."

He went to the bench I had bought at a secondhand store and opened the black purse I had used the night before. When he found my black iPhone, he dropped my purse and came back to the sofa with the phone in his hand.

"I'm putting my numbers in here for future reference." He tapped his numbers into my phone, as he took a seat next to me. "Anything happens…you get sick in the middle of the night, or you get busted for drug trafficking...you call me."

I watched his profile, as he inputted his cell and home numbers. "Is that a joke...from you...Mr. Serious?"

He glanced up at me. His eyes scoured my face. "Have you eaten today?"

The thought of food almost sent me rushing back to the bathroom. "Now I know you're being funny." As I sat up, my hand brushed his thigh.

Garrett recoiled from me, scooting a few inches away. His reaction confused me. After the way he had touched me the night before, I thought we had been making progress.

"You cannot touch me unless I invite you to do so," he explained. "You are my sub, and any physical contact we have has to be allowed by me." He placed the cell phone next to me and stood up.

"Fine, sorry. Look, I'm really not in the mood for more of your lessons today, Garrett." I stood up, feeling a little queasy.

"Lexie, sit down, you can't—"

He never got to finish his command before I went running from the living room toward my bathroom, my hand covering my mouth. I barely made it to the toilet before the vomiting began again.

I didn't recall seeing him enter my bathroom. I only felt his hands rubbing my back, as the violent heaving shook my body.

"You're okay," he said, holding my hair. "I'm right here."

When I could finally sit back on my knees, he retrieved a hand towel from a shelf next to my small vanity and wet it. Coming to my side, he began wiping my mouth and chin.

"You've really got some bug there, little Lexie."

The cool towel felt so good against my face. When I could finally focus again, I saw him sitting next to me, wedged between me and my vanity. The bathroom was barely big enough for me. Somehow, he had managed to squeeze his over six-foot frame inside.

"Little Lexie?" I smiled, wavering slightly. "My mother used to call me that when I was a girl."

"What does she call you now?"

The thought of my mother woke me from my lethargy. "It doesn't matter." I went to stand, but he stopped me.

"Come on. I've got you." He scooped me into his arms and stood from the floor. "Let's get you into bed."

I tried to laugh, but it hurt too much. "Under any other circumstances, Mr. Hughes, I would decline that offer."

He held me to his chest. His arms were strong and he felt so good around me. Without thinking, I closed my eyes and rested my head against him. It was heavenly to have someone take care of me. To just let go and be…. God, I stunk! I got a whiff of my breath, and the first thing that came to mind was how could he stand holding me so close?

"I should really brush my teeth and try to take a shower," I muttered, trying not to breathe on him.

He gently lowered me to my bed. "Later, after you've slept a little. When you wake up, we'll see if you can hold anything down."

I pulled the covers around me, feeling a chill. "We?"

He tucked the covers around my shoulders. "I'll be in the living room if you need anything."

"You don't need to stay, Garrett. I'll be fine. You've got your business to run."

"I've got my phone. I can make some calls while you sleep." He moved toward the bedroom door. "I'm not leaving you like this."

I turned on my side, keeping him in my line of sight. "I'm used to being on my own. It's really okay."

He reached for the door handle. "You're not alone anymore, Lexie. I'll be here, from now on."

The click of the door closing was the last thing I heard before falling asleep.

* * *

When I woke I was weak, but very hungry. Sitting up in the bed, I freed my body from the jumble of blankets entangling me, and then wiggled out of my robe. Pulling at my damp nightshirt, I got a whiff of my breath. It smelled like I had spent the night in a garbage dump.

Cursing under my breath, I stumbled to the bathroom. After brushing my teeth, washing my face, and putting on a lot of deodorant, I slipped into my comfy gray sweat suit. Standing at my half-closed bedroom door, I smelled something delicious wafting into my room. When I heard someone moving about my kitchen, I recalled everything Garrett had said before I fell asleep. I was flabbergasted that he had actually hung around.

Gingerly pulling open my door, I peeked outside. The aroma was heavenly, making my stomach rumble. I hesitated, contemplating if I should return to my bathroom and try to improve my appearance for him.

I waved off the notion, rationalizing that he had already seen me at my worst. "Oh, I must be feeling better."

Rounding my bedroom door, I found Garrett in my efficiency kitchen, hovering over my small gas stove and intently peering into a pot. He even cooked with intensity. Gone were his jacket and tie, and he had rolled up his white shirtsleeves, exposing the ropelike muscles in his forearms. If I hadn't been so sick, I might have been turned on by his arms. My eyes edged downward to the curve of his slacks over his round butt, reminding me of the strong body beneath the tailored clothing. I debated if he belonged to a gym to stay in such good shape, or if he was a runner, logging miles on some out of the way path.

"You're up," he said, sounding cheerful. "How do you feel?"

"Hungry." I stepped into my bright yellow kitchen, which I had spent one summer's day painting not long after moving in. "What's in the pot?" I pointed to the white stove.

"Chicken soup." He went to the unfinished pine cabinets lining one side of the kitchen. "You didn't have much here in the way of food, so I went to the grocery store up the street and bought some things for you." He pulled out one of my plain white soup bowls from the cabinet.

"Garrett, you really didn't have to go to all that trouble. I'm fine."

He turned off the burner on the stove. "You're sick, Lexie. You need someone to take care of you."

As he ladled some of the soup into the bowl, I wondered how much of what he was doing was for me, and how much was for his new sub.

"Is this part of your training?" I motioned to the soup. "You make a woman feel safe and taken care of, so she will do your bidding?"

The cold hard stare he gave me cut right through me. I knew I had said the wrong thing. "I guess you're feeling better. You're back to your old bitchy self."

I was an ass. Here he was being nice to me and I attacked him. "I'm sorry, I shouldn't have said that." I wrapped my arms about my body. "I'm just not used to people...doing things for me."

"Would you feel better if I lied to you and screwed around on you like your ex-husband? Is that how you want me to be?" He tossed the bowl on the counter, splashing some of the soup on his pants. "Shit!"

I had never heard him curse before. Rushing to his side, I removed a handful of paper towels from a roll next to my sink and began wiping the stain on his pants. He immediately jumped back and snatched the paper towels from me.

"Leave it."

I leaned back against the white Formica countertop behind me. "What is it with you and being touched? I'm not one of your subs, Garrett."

"Then what are you, Lexie?" he snapped. Dropping the paper towels on the countertop, he held up his hands and backed out of the kitchen.

I went after him. When I reached the living room, he was already rolling down his sleeves while reaching for his jacket on the sofa.

"I'm not good with people. What I said was wrong, I know that. I'm just trying to figure you out, Garrett. You stay here with me, take care of me when I'm sick, but when I—"

"I stayed because you needed someone, Lexie." He slipped the jacket over his shoulders. "You're not the tower of strength you make yourself out to be. You can ask for help every now and then. It won't make you weak."

A million unhappy memories came rushing back to me, and my gut burned with bitterness. "That's exactly what it will make me. Don't you get it?" I shook my head, as he stopped fixing his jacket and glanced over at me. "When you need help, when you have to ask people to help you, you're weak. You have to be able to stand on your own in this world. When you can't, you'll be ripped apart. No one wants a weak, worthless girl around to...." I covered my hand over my mouth, ashamed of the intimacy of emotion I had shared with him. I thought I was able to keep it inside...I had been wrong.

His features softened, and his brown eyes rounded with concern. "Who told you this?"

"No one told me." I folded my arms over my chest, fighting to keep from trembling. "I learned it first hand when I was a kid. Nothing like having a mother who was never around, to teach you to be self-sufficient."

"Who raised you?"

"Nobody really. My grandmother for a while, but she died when I was six. After that, I was on my own. "

"What about friends or other family? There had to be someone."

I shook my head and went to the sofa, feeling weak. I flopped down on the soft velvet. "We didn't have any family. Until I was eight, she paid a babysitter to stay with me. After that, all I had were the neighbors around us in the Quarter who would help me. They would make me dinner, go over my homework, and keep me company until she came home...if she came home. Some nights I was all alone."

"I can see why you have a hard time trusting anyone...including me." He took a seat next to me on the sofa.

I tilted my head back, feeling a little lightheaded. "My mother used to always tell me not to whine about anything. If I wanted something I had to make it happen, me and no one else. I guess what she taught me stuck." I closed my eyes. "I think I need to go back to bed."

His fingers combed through my hair. "You need to eat."

The way his fingers brushed against my scalp was so soothing. I just wanted to stay like that for a little while longer, before I had to move again. I don't know if he sensed I needed to feel him next to me, or if he wanted it too, but he pulled me to him and kept running his fingers through my hair.

"I want you to trust me, Lexie. I need you to trust me. Can you do that?"

I sighed and opened my eyes. "I'm working on it, Garrett."

"That's all I ask." He sat me up and nodded. "Let's get you something to eat, and then I want to try an experiment."

My heart skipped a beat. "What experiment?"

* * *

Thankfully, I was able to keep down the chicken soup Garrett had made for me. After he had taken the bowl into the kitchen, he returned to the sofa where I was propped up on two pillows and held his hand out to me.

"Come with me," he cooed in his silky voice.

I was immediately suspicious and hesitated before asking, "What are you doing?"

He stooped down on his knees, holding my gaze. "Remember what I said about trusting me?"

I warily bobbed my head.

"Then you need to do it, now." He picked me up and carried me to my bedroom.

Being a romance writer, this was the part of the story when you knew what was going to happen next. With Garrett all bets were off. It was safe to say he was not taking me to bed for sex, especially since he'd just seen me retching my guts out earlier. I smelled, and was no one's idea of a dream lover. So what exactly did he have in mind?

When he deposited me in front of my bathroom door, he put his hand to my forehead. "Looks like your fever is gone, and your color has come back."

"Yeah, I feel better." I waved into the bathroom. "What are we doing?"

"Take off your clothes," he ordered, gazing down my sweats.

My eyebrows shot up. "Excuse me?"

He towered over my figure, arching his shoulders toward me. "You're going to take a shower with me. It's time to get back to your training. This will show you that I can be trusted, no matter how vulnerable you may feel. And secondly," he grinned, "you smell."

"I'm sick," I argued, put off by his comment about my offensive odor.

"You're better." He began to unbutton his white shirt.

I waited, stunned into silence, as he undid his shirt and eased it from around his shoulders. His naked chest was more than I had expected with his well-defined shoulders, carved pecs, and ripped abs…definitely not a runner. He probably spent a lot of time in the gym.

He motioned to my sweat suit. "Take off your top."

I stubbornly folded my arms over my chest. "Are you out of your mind?"

Unzipping his pants, he glared at me. "Don't you want to finish *Taming Me*?"

My mouth dropped. "You son of a bitch. You read my book?" I backed out the bathroom door. I never liked to share my work with anyone, until it was finished. For him to go into my computer, and read the beginnings of my book, was even more of a violation than standing naked in front of him.

"You have a great idea for a story, Lexie, even if you did name the main character Ralph." He rested his hand on the wall next to me. "I could see the book coming alive after just the first chapter. It would be a shame to give up now."

He was right. I hated that he was right. The first chapter the night before had poured out of me. Until I had been overcome with nausea, the story had just flowed. I could only get so far with what I had learned from Garrett. I needed more. I needed to go deeper into his world.

"If you want more to put in this book, then take off your clothes," he commanded, reading my thoughts, yet again.

Spitting nails, I glowered at him. This mind reading bullshit was getting on my nerves. I reached for the bottom of my sweatshirt, cursing my career choice. "Fine, but if you—"

"If you trust me, Lexie, you'll do as I say and never question."

Wrenching the sweatshirt over my head, the cool temperature of the bedroom hit my skin. His eyes were taking in my small breasts while I lowered my sweat pants and underwear to the floor. After stepping out of the pants, I walked into the bathroom.

At my small shower stall, I was about to turn on the faucet when his hand reached out, stopping me. "I'll do it."

Lowering my hand, I could feel his naked chest against my back. Slowly, he turned on the water and waited. We stood like that, his body pressing into me as the water warmed. He tested the temperature with his hand and then whispered, "Get in."

I stepped below the cascade of water and slowly pivoted around to Garrett. He was standing in the open glass door, unzipping his gray pants and watching me. I wanted to cover my naked body with my hands, but I fought back against my modesty and kept my hands at my sides. Methodically, his eyes took in every detail of my slim figure. From my throat, down over my firm breasts, to my slender waist, his eyes roamed. When he came to the triangle of dark hair between my legs, I felt self-conscious about not having shaved. Then again, I had not planned on taking a shower with anyone, let alone Garrett.

When he was done examining me, he dropped his pants to the bathroom floor. I was convinced things were going to go too far. As I took in his body, I was surprised to find that he was not erect. I had always believed that even the sight of a naked woman would get a man hard, but not Garrett.

The steam from the hot water was rising up when he came under the shower. At first, I was too nervous to look him in the eye. Keeping my focus on his chest, I waited for him to tell me what to do.

"Turn around," he directed, running the water on his hands and then through his hair.

I faced the wall behind me and closed my eyes as the water hit my face. His hands were on my shoulders, gliding down the length of my arms. "Relax for me," he murmured in my ear, his body easing into my back. "Give in to me, Lexie."

As he lifted my hands I didn't resist, and placed them on the tiled wall in front of me. Inclining my head forward, his hands went to my shoulders. He gently massaged the muscles in my neck, shoulders, and back. I would tighten up when he hit a tender spot, then he would remind me to relax and continue on with his gentle prodding.

Between the warm water and the way his massage soothed my sore muscles, I was clinging to the shower wall with my eyes closed, trying to stay upright. As his fingers moved down my back, working out the stiffness as they went, I became more comfortable with his touch. His hands were like velvet next to my skin; soft, tender, yet determined. When he gripped my butt, all the tension in my body returned and my eyes flew open.

"You're tensing up. You have to believe that I will never hurt you when I touch you." His mouth was right at my ear and his voice was hypnotic. "You will allow me to touch every inch of you and never doubt my intentions." His hands kneaded my butt cheeks, hard. "Tell me you are mine to touch. Say it."

I swallowed back my nervousness. "I'm yours to touch," I repeated in a shaky voice.

"I didn't hear you, Lexie."

"I'm yours to touch," I firmly stated.

"Anywhere?" he sighed into my ear.

I reluctantly nodded. "Yes, anywhere, Garrett."

"Master. You must call me Master."

"Master," I echoed.

As soon as I said the word, his hand slipped between my legs and rubbed along my folds. "This is where I want to touch you."

I instantly tried to push his hand away.

"No," he declared behind me. "Don't fight me. Never fight me."

He turned me around. When I stared into his face, I didn't hide my anger. He had manipulated me, and in the process humiliated me.

"Ah, now you're angry with me. I can see it in your eyes, Lexie."

I wiped the water from my face. "That was dirty."

He let me go and stood back from me. "That was nothing compared to what is to come. You wanted access to my world, so you'd better get ready."

When he left the shower, I caught a glimpse of his erection. Manipulating me, making me call him master, had excited him, while my naked body had not. In that moment, I understood something about Garrett. For him it was not about sex, it was about control. Until he could control me completely, he would never take me as a lover. That was the one thing I knew I had to hold on to, my will.

After quickly putting on my sweat suit, I found Garrett in my living room adjusting his blue tie. His wet hair was sleeked back and his always pressed clothes were now slightly wrinkled.

"Tomorrow night I'm going to bring you to the De Sade Club," he announced.

Pulling back my wet hair, I leaned against the doorframe to my bedroom. "That soon? You think I'm ready?"

"I prefer not to wait too long. Knowing Colin, he has already told the empress about you, and she will want to meet you." He picked up his jacket from my sofa. "I think you can handle it."

"What else did fondling me in the shower prove, Garrett?"

Slipping on the jacket, he glanced back at me, frowning. "That you're comfortable with me." He tugged at his right sleeve. "And I didn't fondle you, Lexie. I was proving a point."

"What? That you're my master?"

Ignoring me, he picked some lint from his jacket. "I'll pick you up tomorrow night at seven. Wear a simple black cocktail dress, no sequins, rhinestones, or bows, high black heels, and put your hair up, with very little makeup and only red lipstick." He went to the door and turned back to me. "Tomorrow night, from the moment we leave this apartment until we come back, you had better call me Master."

"Or what, Garrett? Are you going to punish me?"

"Only if you deserve it." Grinning, he stepped into the hall. "Get some sleep. I'll call you in the morning." Then, he quietly shut the door.

Day 5

Tired, but feeling much stronger, I spent the day at home working on my book. I kept thinking back to our shower. The entire incident had left me more confused about Garrett than comfortable. Seemingly overnight, a relationship I had thought to be businesslike and platonic had become muddled by the question of sex. Yes, he was sexy as hell, and there was some kind of chemistry between us. Yet, the way he kept his distance from me, and his aversion to being touched, baffled me.

The only thing that had not suffered from our time together was my book. The words were flying out of me. I could not type fast enough, and felt inspired by what I was learning about Garrett's strange world. I had already written two more chapters, and was well on the way to creating the sexual tension needed between my hero and heroine, when my noisy stomach insisted I take a break.

Heading to my tiny kitchen, I opened the refrigerator to see what I could put together for lunch when I was greeted by a welcomed surprise. I remembered Garrett saying he had gone to the grocery store for me. Until that moment, I had not realized the extent of his shopping. The refrigerator was crammed full with an assortment of fruits, vegetables, cold cuts, cheeses, and even a pint of chocolate Hagan-Daz ice cream in the freezer. I was stunned by the gesture. Here I thought I was just some experiment to him. The contents of my refrigerator made me feel like I was something more.

After finding the loaf of sourdough bread Garrett had placed in my microwave oven, I celebrated my virtual cornucopia of food by sampling a bit of everything. As I ate I felt my strength returning, and the last remnants of whatever virus that had struck me vanished from my insides. I even had a few bites of ice cream to top off my meal.

My stomach full, I turned my eyes to my laptop in the living room, keen to get back to my book. Getting comfortable at my desk, I was just about to start another chapter when my cell's Jay Z ringtone broke through the air. Reaching for my phone, Garrett's name flashed before me. I thought about not answering his call, but a pang of guilt won out over my anger, and I edged my finger across the iPhone screen.

"Hello, Garrett."

"How are you feeling today?"

His voice sounded the same way his hands had felt caressing my skin. I forced my concentration back to the call. "Better, much better. I, ah, want to thank you for yesterday. I found all the food you bought for me a little while ago. You really didn't have to do that."

"You need to eat better. All you had in your fridge was an old wheel of cheese and leftover Chinese food."

"Well, I don't shop much."

"Why not?" he probed.

"What I buy depends on how big my royalty check is. Plus, I was never a big eater." I squirmed in my chair, as the sound of his voice kept bringing me back to our time together in my shower.

"You need to take better care of yourself, Lexie."

My eyes returned to my manuscript. I needed to get back to my book. "Are we still on for tonight?" I quickly asked, changing the subject.

"Yes. Do you remember what I told you to wear?" He was sounding sarcastic again.

I rolled my eyes. "I'm not deaf, Garrett. I remember."

"Do you own a simple black cocktail dress, or should I bring one with me?"

The question surprised me. "Where would you get such a dress?"

"I frequently buy clothes for my subs. From my estimate, you're about a size two, petite. I can bring something with me if you need it."

My grip on the phone tightened, as I pictured his eyes going-over my naked body. "I have a dress."

"Be ready at seven. I don't like to be kept waiting." He hung up, and the cold indifference in his voice stayed with me.

I stared at my phone, mulling over the man's mood swings. There were times when he could be so gentle and caring, and then times he could be a real son of a bitch. I wasn't sure which one I liked more. The son of a bitch I could keep at a distance. The caring, gentle Garrett was starting to grow on me.

"The book, Lexie," I muttered, putting down my phone. "Just stay focused on the book."

* * *

At seven on the dot, while I was pacing the hardwood floors of my living room, the downstairs doorbell scared the life out of me. Clasping my chest, I took a moment to calm down. After a deep breath, my hands ran nervously down the front of my sleeveless, black satin cocktail dress. A little dated, but simple with an oval neckline and high hemline, it was neither flashy nor overstated. I only hoped it would meet Garrett's standards; otherwise, this was going to be a long night. Shaking my head at the level I had sunk to just to get a story, I went to the speaker by my door and buzzed him in.

Seconds later, I heard heavy footsteps trotting up the staircase. When I opened my front door, he was standing before me like a Greek statue. Attired in a black suit with a crisp white shirt and perfectly knotted gray tie, he radiated confidence. The dark suit deepened his sculpted features, accentuating his deep brown eyes, chiseled cheekbones, and square jaw. Damn, he looked good.

Hovering outside of my door, he scanned my outfit, and his wide brow crinkled when he came to my low-heeled black shoes. "Do you have another pair of black heels, higher than those?"

I was about to tell him that the high heels would hurt like hell after twenty minutes, but I bit my tongue. I had learned enough about the man to know that there was no point in arguing.

"Sure, let me go and get them."

He followed me inside, shutting the door behind him. "I like the dress," he complemented, as I reached my bedroom door.

"It's not too old-fashioned?"

"No." His eyes felt as if they were looking through my dress and not at it. "It's perfect…for a submissive," he coyly added.

After switching to the stiletto-heeled black pumps I had saved for a special occasion, I returned to the living room.

"Much better," he asserted with a nod. He came across my small living room to my side and pulled something from his jacket pocket. "Put this on."

In his hand was a white leather collar. The buckle was silver, and there were silver D-rings attached to it. Staring at the collar, I thought he was joking.

"You've got to be nuts, Garrett. I'm not putting that on." I pointed to the offensive object, snorting slightly.

"If you don't put this on, you will not be allowed in the club as my sub. In addition, not being connected to a Dom like me could be very dangerous for you," he protested.

"Dangerous how?"

"Lexie, I don't think you realize how hard core these people are. They take submission very seriously. If they think you're not mine, they will...." He held up the collar to me. "Just put it on."

I snatched the collar from his hand. "What kind of club is this, Garrett?"

"A very exclusive club that took a hell of a lot of pull to get into. I can't risk anything going wrong."

I fit the collar about my neck. "Why not? Can't you find another club?"

He stepped behind me and helped fix the buckle. "Not like this one. Many of the members are very affluent and politically connected. In this town, to get anywhere in business, you need their help."

I turned to him. "So this all comes down to business connections for you. It's not about the submission, is it? It's about money."

"Everything comes down to sex or money, Lexie, especially where men are concerned." He lowered his hands to his sides. "Some of the things that go on in the club, I don't necessarily agree with. I'm there because I'm a businessman who also happens to love the art of seduction."

I had a new insight into his character, and I didn't like what I was seeing.

"That suits you." He motioned to the collar.

I raised my hand to the snug fitting strap of leather. "It's uncomfortable."

He took my arm. "It's only for tonight."

Guiding me toward the apartment entrance, he reached for my black satin handbag waiting on the bench by the door. I removed my keys from the lock and waited, as he opened the door for me. Just when I was about to step out into the hall, he placed his arm across the threshold.

"From now on, until we return to this apartment, I'm to be called Master or Sir. You are never to call me by my given name in front of these people. The slightest misstep and they will be suspicious of you. I cannot allow you to jeopardize what I have spent months building. Do you understand?"

I pushed his arm out of the way. "I've got it, Master."

He moved aside, smiling at me. "I like the way you say it."

"Yeah? Well, don't get too used to it, because after tonight, I'm hoping I have everything I need for my book." I shut my door and set the deadbolt.

"We'll see, Lexie." He waited as I dropped my keys into my purse. "I have a feeling there is much more to come for us."

I refrained from telling him what I thought of his feeling. I was to be his sub for the evening, and figured I had better start playing my part. Once our evening had concluded, however, I would make sure I took off my little white collar and told him exactly where to shove it.

* * *

The De Sade Club was not a club, but a private residence in the Garden District of the city. Nestled among the live oaks, blossoming crepe myrtles, and historic homes of First Street, the pink, two-story, double gallery mansion did not appear to be the menacing structure I had envisioned.

Detailed iron railings ran the length of the first and second-floor galleries, with additional wide archways of black ironwork framing the long french windows situated along the home's façade. Gardens of azaleas and gardenias rose on either side of the oak door at the entrance, while two huge, black cast-iron lanterns hung from beneath the second-floor balcony. Trimming the edge of the property was a short, black iron fence, accentuating the heavy use of black iron in and around the structure.

"So this is your club," I stated, as Garrett shut my car door.

"Enough talk." He hit the alarm on his remote and the yellow lights of his black BMW flashed twice. "Don't speak unless I ask you to. If someone asks you any questions, look to me before you answer. When I nod, then you have my permission to speak." He took my elbow and we started down the uneven sidewalk toward the front gate. "And above all, always refer to me as Master or Sir."

"Yes, Master," I said mockingly, fighting to keep my balance on the cracked and broken walkway.

"You need to be on your best behavior, Lexie. Screw this up and I will be very angry with you." His hand closed around my arm. "Remember, you're always being watched."

I simply nodded my head, as he pulled me through the gate and up the stone path to the front door. Standing on the grand porch, I glimpsed the dark street behind us and noted the array of very expensive cars park in front of the home. From fine German automobiles like Garrett's, to Porsches and even two Ferraris, I was beginning to get a feel for the kind of people I would be meeting inside.

The front door opened behind me, and when I turned an older woman wearing a white maid's uniform was smiling at me. Her coffee-colored face was quite beautiful, with fine features and silver hair. When she saw Garrett, her smile deepened.

"Good to see you again, Mr. Hughes."

"Treba." Garrett dipped his head. "How are you tonight?"

"Fine, sir, just fine." Treba moved away from the door, allowing us inside.

The small foyer was tastefully decorated in bright yellow wallpaper dotted with small white flowers. A two-tiered brass chandelier hung from the high ceiling and shined down on the old oak hardwood floors. A deep walnut Napoleon settee and bench lining the wall of the entrance caught my eye. The pieces had to be antiques and were undoubtedly very expensive.

"Ms. Mabel's in the parlor with the other guests, Mr. Hughes. You know the way." Treba shut the door and waved us deeper into the home.

Garrett took my hand. "Thank you, Treba."

Leaving the foyer, we moved into a short hallway decorated with assorted framed photographs. A few were of children playing on beaches, or visiting Disneyworld. As we progressed, the children got older, ending with high school graduation portraits, and one large formal wedding photograph. I glimpsed the assorted pictures, perplexed at how anyone could go from the Disney World to Bondage World.

"Mabel Bergeron is the first person you're going to meet when we enter the next doorway up ahead." Garrett gestured to the end of the hallway. "She is the empress that Colin referred to. She owns this house, monitors the club, and makes sure everyone abides by a code of conduct during our play." My heart began to pound. "She will ask you how we met, how long we have been together, and if I'm a good master." He stopped before the last tall door along the hall. "You have to impress her in order to be admitted to the club, so make it look good. Mabel can spot a fake a mile away." He put his hand on the crystal doorknob, giving me one last encouraging smile. "Relax; and remember, you are mine."

As he pushed the door open, it took everything I had to stay upright on my pointy heels. What in the hell had I been thinking? I was a writer, not some spy meant to infiltrate an underground network of tie me up, tie me down fanatics. Regrets started piling up when I realized exactly where my hunger for a bestseller had brought me. If I made it through this night, I vowed I was going to start drinking, heavily.

"Are you ready?" Garrett whispered to me through the corner of his mouth.

I wasn't sure if I was supposed to answer, so I just squeezed the hell out of his hand.

"I'll be right by your side the entire time." He started into the room. "Not to worry."

The parlor was actually a long, windowless room with an assortment of small wooden tables and green cushioned chairs set up as a sort of bistro. Colorful framed portraits of women tied or handcuffed in various provocative poses covered the walls. The paintings were quite extraordinary. As I admired the portraits, I reflected on the mind that had created them, and if the artist was also a member of the club. Set between the pictures were various whips, black hoods, and pairs of handcuffs; even the chandelier above was made out of handcuffs. At one end of the dark green painted room was a walnut bar with a bartender dressed in black, tending to a few guests wearing similar black cocktail dresses and black suits. In fact, everyone in the room was in black. A few of the women dressed like me were wearing black leather collars. I touched the white collar about my neck, wondering why mine was a different color. Behind the bar, carved into a mirrored wall, a circle with three tadpole-like shapes coming together caught my eye.

"It's the Ring of O," Garrett whispered beside me, mind reading again. "It's a symbol associated with the bondage culture."

"There's my handsome Dom," a harsh voice declared from the corner of the room.

"That is Mabel Bergeron," Garrett muttered.

When I followed the voice to its source, Garrett tugged on my hand, probably reminding me to behave. Reclining on an exquisitely carved red velvet chaise, wearing a bright crimson dress and dripping with long gold chains, was the owner of that grating voice. Round, with deathly white skin and fiery red hair, the older woman looked nothing like an empress. She was more akin to a Storyville madam, well past her prime. Despite an absurdly thick application of makeup, she appeared to be in her mid-sixties. Her invasive green eyes alluded to a formidable and cunning individual beneath the caricature.

"What have you brought me, my boy?" Mabel called across the room.

Escorting me to her red velvet chaise, Garrett slipped his hand behind my back while Mabel's bright eyes perused every inch of me. I thought what initially flared in her small eyes was jealousy. Then the light changed, and her intense focus became one of profound interest.

Mabel stood, grunting slightly as she pulled her weight up from the low seat. "Colin warned me you had found a new playmate," Mabel said to Garrett, never taking her eyes off me. "Pretty little thing. I thought you would have preferred someone…taller."

"Her name is Alexandra Palmer," Garrett told her. Letting go of my hand, he took a few steps back from me.

Mabel came up to me, circling me like a wolf debating on how to kill its prey. Dipping her head to the right, she let her eyes wander over every inch of my face. "How did you meet Garrett Hughes?" She waved a plump hand at me. "Your Dom will give you permission to speak to me."

I looked to Garrett, and he nodded his head to Mabel.

"We met at Woldenberg Park." I kept my answer short, not wanting to offer too much information.

"How long have you been his?"

I had to do some quick math, adding up the days since we had first met. "Since…four days. I've been his for four days."

Mabel peered over to her right. "Is that correct, Colin?"

Colin emerged from behind a small blonde, smiling for Mabel. His black suit accentuated his broad shoulders and athletic build.

"That's right. It began the day after they met by the river."

I glared at Colin. How the hell would he know anything about us? The way the man's blue eyes were drinking in my figure made my flesh crawl.

Mabel eyed Garrett, as she spoke to me. "Is he good to you, your Dom? Does he see to your needs?"

"Yes," I answered. "He has taught me well."

Garrett raised his hand to his mouth, hiding a grin from the mistress of the house.

"Well then," Mabel motioned Garrett back to my side, "you are welcome to join our club, Alexandra, but you must adhere to our rules in order to remain. First, you are here as a guest of your Dom. You are not a member until you have been given a black collar by him in a ceremony. After that, if your Dom is done with you, he can pass you off to the group. When that happens, another Dom may collar you for his own. You cannot be with any other Doms in this club until you have been collared, and only one Dom per sub. I do not allow harems in this club, despite the numerous objections of my Doms." A slight dissent of deep chuckling could be heard from the men around the room. She grinned, flashing a glimpse of her yellow-stained teeth. "All members must attend meetings once a month, and attendance for special functions is required," she continued. "Dues are paid by your Dom. Subs never pay to be part of the club. What members chose to do in this club is private and shall never go beyond the walls of this home. I have had subs try to blackmail members in the past, and they have been harshly dealt with. All subs in this club are to be obedient. If for any reason you're not happy with your Dom, or if he does things to you without your consent, then you can come to me and we will discuss terms for dissolving the union. Everything done in this club must be done with your consent. We do not tolerate cruelty, torture, or infliction of pain. If that's what you're into, then it must be done off these premises." Mabel's eyes stared into mine. "Do you understand, and will you abide by our rules, Alexandra?"

Not sure if I should speak, I simply nodded my head.

"Good, that's settled." Mabel was about to take a step away when she leaned over to Garrett and said something I could not hear. Trepidation roared through me. Had I screwed up? Was she disappointed in my performance? When Garrett clasped my hand, giving it a reassuring squeeze, I took a calming breath.

"I'm impressed," he whispered to me.

Colin and the blonde he was with were the first to come up to us after Mabel walked away. Colin's eyes were eating me up. Little alarm bells went off in my head. This guy was going to be trouble. I was not sure why I suspected it, but I did.

"Well, that will make the old girl happy." Colin shook Garrett's hand. "You must make it official soon."

My eyes darted from Garrett to Colin.

"Mabel doesn't like her Doms taking up with subs from outside of the club," Colin explained to me. "You'll need to be collared like the rest of the subs."

I could tell Garrett was acutely aware of how Colin was ogling me.

"It's just a simple ceremony all subs must perform, Lexie," Colin went on. "We pay a pretty penny to belong to this club. Once you receive your black collar, the others will feel more at ease."

I shifted my attention away from Colin to the mousy blonde next to him. Her head was turned downward and I could not make out her features. She was petite and wearing a simple black cocktail dress. The hem was trimmed in black lace and there was even a black lace bracelet about her tiny left wrist. The collar about her neck was made of black leather.

"We should get a drink," Garrett affirmed, and hastily pulled me away.

On the way to the bar, he lowered his head closer to my ear. "Stay away from him."

I wanted to tell him that wouldn't be a problem—the guy gave me the creeps—but I just nodded my head in agreement.

While Garrett ordered a drink at the bar, I recognized the prominent local businessman, Nathan Cole, clasping the arm of a leggy brunette with another black leather collar. Known about the city for his real estate developments, the man's bedroom brown eyes gave me a hasty examination. Beside him, I spotted the notorious attorney, Gerard Bence, whose commercials were always a staple with the local five o'clock news. Clinging to him was a very slender blonde with the most clear blue eyes I had ever seen. She was devastatingly beautiful and should have been gracing the cover of a fashion magazine, and not hanging on the arm of an ambulance chaser. At the corner of the bar, there was an elegant man without a date; tall and lean with blond, curly hair, and deep green eyes.

When he glanced my way, I thought he seemed familiar, yet could not place his name.

"Ren Plancharde," Garrett murmured in my ear, anticipating my thoughts. "He's the artist who did the portraits on the wall. Very well-known among our kind, and growing in popularity in the vanilla culture."

I soon discovered the entire club was composed of the movers and shakers from the city: politicians, businessmen, with a renowned heart surgeon and an actor thrown in. Each man had their arm about a woman with a black leather collar. All the women had the same vacuous look that I was trying to imitate. It did not take me long to feel sorry for these women. At the end of the night, I could walk away from this charade; they had to continue on with it for as long as they could.

"Garrett." A tall, skinny man with blond-gray hair came forward, extending his hand. "How is my house coming?"

"Judge McCord, it's coming along nicely." Garrett took the man's hand. "We should have the preliminary plans to your builder within the week, so he can start clearing the property."

"That's good," the judge returned in a slow drawl. "The wife's hot to get started on the house."

Wife? I eyed the very thin blonde standing behind him, noting that there was no ring on the third finger of her left hand.

"She has been bugging me to build in Lakeview since before that wretched storm. Only after Katrina could we afford to buy three lots in that neighborhood."

"Yes," Garrett agreed, shifting his eyes to me. "I have five houses in various stages of planning out there, with orders for four more."

"I take it business is good." The judge patted Garrett's arm. "The benefits of belonging to Mabel's little group." He smiled, showing off his large capped teeth, reminding me of a horse. "We'll talk soon."

Garrett gave a curt nod of his head. "Of course, Judge."

After the garish man and his diminutive blonde had walked away, Garrett leaned over to me. "His wife is one of the social elite in this city, Allison Wagner, part of Wagner and Billings shipping company."

I had heard the name before. Anyone who had grown up in the city knew of Wagner and Billings. They owned most of the port of New Orleans.

"She has the money and lets him do what he wants, as long as it is out of the public eye." Garrett peered around the room. "Many of the men here are in similar situations. They have wealthy or politically important wives who don't want to know of their affairs. That's why clubs like this are so important, and why many of these men pay handsomely for the privilege of belonging."

I glared at him, thinking, *Then why are you here?*

He chuckled, amused by my face. "Yes, you're asking why I am here? I don't have a wife or girlfriend to appease." He leaned over, resting his elbow on the polished copper top of the bar. "I have a business to get off the ground. Sometimes joining such clubs can have financial benefits, as well as...," his eyes traveled over my body, "extracurricular ones."

I snorted with disgust.

He put his hand about my waist. "Your eyes give you away, Lexie. I can look into them and know your every thought."

I put my hand over his to push it away.

"Don't," he warned. "Several of the men here are checking you out as fresh meat. I need to show them that you are mine." He pulled me closer. "Whatever I do, go along with it."

I wanted so much to scream at him, but I could almost feel the eyes of the room on me. His hand ran along my hip, cupping my ass. Then he pulled away and picked up his glass of scotch from the bar.

"Let's get a table and you can see what happens next." While holding his drink with one hand, he took my elbow with the other. "This will be quite an education for you."

While we cruised across the room, Garrett's hand slipped to my butt, patting it right as we passed before a trio of men. I wanted to lash out at him. Instead, I kept my head down and swallowed my pride as the men chuckled.

At the table, he sat down first and left me to pull out my chair. Taking my seat, he lowered his head, hiding his words from the rest of the room. "Remember, I'm the one in charge and we must put on a good show. So don't get that face." His eyes swerved to me. "That look you get when you're angry. Your forehead furrows, your cheeks turn pink, and your mouth turns down into an adorable pout." He raised his head. "No matter what you see, keep your emotions hidden. They're watching you to see how you will react. It's a test."

Not a minute after he spoke, a very fat baldheaded man at a table to our left stood from his chair. He hooked his finger through the D-ring on the collar of the redhead seated next to him and urged her to stand. Her face remained impassive as he lowered her head over the table, placing her hips in front of him. Hiking up her black dress, he exposed her black silk underwear. When his hands began tugging the panties down her legs, my stomach lurched.

"Stay calm," Garrett instructed in a low voice. "The play is beginning. They will each take their subs in different ways. Just remember to keep your face relaxed. They can't see this upsetting you."

Around the room, the other men took note and began groping and undressing their subs. I watched the faces of the various women. Some remained indifferent to their Dom's attention, while others were enjoying it.

In a corner of the room, I saw Colin with his petite blonde. He had her on her knees before him, her hands working the zipper of his pants. Her blonde hair was secured in his fists, and he was pulling her head closer to his crotch.

The room soon filled with the sounds of heaving breathing, giggling, and assorted moans. I fought like hell to keep a straight face, as I saw women in various stages of undress being strewn over tables, kneeling in front of men, or on all fours on the green carpet. Presiding over the entire affair was Mabel, observing the activities from her red velvet chaise. When she connected with my eyes, I immediately lowered them to the table.

"She's waiting to see how you handle this," Garrett whispered, holding his glass in front of his mouth to hide his words. "She always watches new subs, very closely." He drank from his scotch and returned it to the table. "What are you thinking?"

"You want me to talk…now?" I whispered.

"Yes, just keep your voice down."

"I think this is disgusting," I mumbled.

"'I think this is disgusting,' Master," he corrected.

"You asshole."

"Not funny, Lexie."

The fat, baldheaded man to the side of us had removed every strip of his sub's clothing and was kneeling behind her, his mouth kissing her round white butt. The redhead was swinging her hips side to side, teasing him.

"Stand up," Garrett ordered next to me.

My eyes flew to him.

"Remember your place," he hissed.

I dropped my head and stood from the chair. He came around to my side and turned me toward Mabel's chaise.

"She has to see us doing something, Lexie." He rested his hands on my shoulders. "I want you to close your eyes and block out the other noises in the room." His breath tickled the back of my neck. "I'm going to touch you, like we practiced in the shower. Just relax."

His hands slowly edged down my shoulders, his fingers tickling my skin as they swept along my upper arms. Garrett's firm chest pressed into my back, and I relaxed against him. When his hands moved in front of me and gently fondled my breasts, my nipples tingled with excitement. Sensing my arousal, Garrett began moving his thumbs methodically back and forth over my erect nipples in the most tantalizing way.

"You're doing fine," he softly said. "She's watching us, so pretend you are enjoying this."

The problem was, despite the company in the room, I was enjoying his touch. His hands were so compelling that when they caressed me, it did block out everything else around us. He moved from my breasts, crept over my stomach and around my hips, until his hands came to rest at the valley between my legs.

"I do adore touching you," he breathed into my cheek. "A shame it's all for show."

A fire sparked to life in my gut, as his hands fondled my crotch, and I arched into him. Hiking up the hem of my dress, his hand slid upward to my black underwear. I should have been mortified, but I wasn't. The feel of him next to me, the caress of his hand, was so distracting. He curled his fingers into me, pressing into my folds. I closed my eyes and struggled not to moan. The sheer delight of his touch was overpowering.

Unexpectedly, he let me go. "We've done enough."

I opened my eyes and saw the judge, who Garrett had spoken to earlier, on the floor in front of us, kneeling behind his blonde and thrusting into her. His black suit pants were down around his ankles, and his saggy ass was pumping back and forth. The baldheaded man next to us had his redhead spread out on the table with his head buried between her legs. She was gasping and clutching the table, undulating as he pleasured her. Off in the corner, Colin was rocking his hips back and forth as his sub's mouth moved up and down his visible erection.

"Have you seen enough?" Garrett asked, as I observed other couples in the room in similar sex acts.

Disgusted, I lowered my eyes to the floor.

He came around to my side and fastidiously adjusted his suit jacket. "Let's get out of here."

* * *

After a quick drive across town, Garrett and I were climbing the wide staircase to my apartment door. I wasn't sure if it was the aftereffects of my flu or the stress of the entire evening, but I was exhausted.

"You were very good tonight," he praised, taking my keys from my hand.

"You should have warned me it was going to be an orgy."

"How was I to prepare you for that, Lexie?" He opened my door for me. "No amount of training could have made you ready for tonight. All in all, I think you did well."

I took my keys from him. "What did you think I would do? Run screaming from the room?"

"Some women might have, but you behaved accordingly." He unclasped the collar from about my neck.

"It doesn't take much of a brain to say nothing or not appear appalled, Garrett." Rubbing my neck, I pushed my front door open. "Makes me curious about the kind of woman you really want."

"Kind of woman?" His raised his nose in the air, glaring down at me. "What is that supposed to mean?"

"Do you want someone like the women in that club?" I dropped my black satin purse and keys on the bench by the door. "Did you see those women? They were dead inside."

He shut my front door. "They looked just like you. It's how they're expected to act at the club. When they are alone with their Doms, I know for a fact they are very different." He removed his jacket. "For instance, the woman Colin was with, Missy, drives him crazy. He's been wanting to end their relationship for some time." After tossing his jacket to my sofa, he walked into the kitchen and opened the cabinet below my sink.

"What happens to her then?" I queried.

Garrett pulled out a bottle of Johnny Walker Black Label from under the sink. "She goes up for selection by another Dom in the club."

"Where did that come from?" I pointed to the bottle.

"I bought it at the grocery store the other day." He held the bottle up, smirking. "Got to love New Orleans. I can't quite get used to the concept of buying liquor at the grocery store. In Dallas, you can only purchase alcohol at a liquor store. In some parts of the city, you can't buy it at all."

He reached for two old-fashioned glasses in the cabinet above my stove. Walking past me, he went back to the living room and placed the glasses on my coffee table.

"Now, we can relax," he remarked, and poured out three fingers of the scotch into each of the glasses.

I kicked off my heels. "I don't think I can ever relax around you."

He lifted a glass from the coffee table and brought it to me. "Why not?"

"I never know if I'm being tested or trained, or just made real damned uncomfortable in general." I took the glass from his hand and kicked back a deep swig of scotch.

"I'm sorry I've been hard on you. I warned you in the beginning this wasn't going to be easy."

I winced as the alcohol burned the back of my throat. "Hell, Garrett, a root canal is a walk in the park next to an evening with you."

His eyebrows scrunched together, making him look uncharacteristically concerned. "I had hoped that at least some of our time together had been pleasurable for you." He turned away and went to the coffee table.

Oh, major guilt trip. "No, that's not what I meant." I went after him and stood by his side as he picked up his glass. "It's just that you can be so...."

"Intimidating?"

"More like a general pain in my ass."

"Lovely, Lexie. And very descriptive, too." He hoisted his glass in the air, toasting me, and then tossed back a portion of the dark golden liquid.

Watching his lips, I was overcome with a desire to taste the scotch on them, lick away the traces of alcohol, and then let my mouth travel slowly down his chin, neck, and chest, to his—

"I'm surprised you haven't found another husband with that attitude," he said, interrupting my fantasy.

"What makes you think I want another one of those?" I went around to the sofa and sank into the soft velvet cushion.

"I know your first attempt wasn't successful, but I'm sure there is another man out there who can make you happy." He sat down next to me, setting his drink on the coffee table.

Placing my glass beside his, I curled my feet beneath me and rubbed my sore right insole. Damned high heels. "Men don't make women happy, Garrett. We only need them to approve of us. It's all about someone else telling us that we're beautiful, or smart, or wanted. Women have a hard time believing that for themselves."

He pulled my right leg out from under me and placed it over his lap. Taking my foot, he began to massage it with his delectable hands. I almost fell off the sofa, as he worked his thumbs deep into my tender insole.

"It's the same way for men, Lexie. We aren't born confident, it has to be instilled in us."

His hands felt so good. I wanted to moan out loud, as his thumbs rubbed small circles deep into the sole of my foot. Instead, I tried my best to focus on our conversation. "Yes, but I think society is a bit more indulgent of your sex than of mine. A woman who gets ahead is a bitch or ruthless; a man is just regarded as successful." As he massaged the ball of my foot, I swore I was going to have an orgasm.

"I agree, but a woman can also be gentle and caring, tearful and soft. If a man were to act that way, he would be shunned," Garrett countered.

"God, you're good at that." I motioned to my foot.

He shrugged. "I'm better at back massages. I love touching a woman's body. It's something I always try to do with my subs…when they're good."

"What do you do when they're bad?" tumbled out of my mouth, before I could stop it.

He paused, pondering the question. "It depends on the sub. Each punishment is tailored to their needs."

I reached for my scotch, needing something to cool me off. "How do you tailor punishment to someone's needs?"

Garrett slid my other leg over his lap and began rubbing my left foot. "Punishment is meant as a way to teach pleasure and displeasure to a sub. When I hand out a punishment, it's to show that they have displeased me, and I do not wish to see the behavior repeated. It's not intended to harm or hurt them. It's to make them heed my wishes."

"You lost me." I pulled my legs from his lap, feeling uncomfortable again.

He wiped his hands together and then unknotted his tie. "When I punish a sub, I want to make the punishment memorable. In another way, I want to make it reinforce their submission to me." He removed his tie, curling it about his long fingers." Punishment is about withholding pleasure; tempting, promising, but never giving."

I was mesmerized by the way the cool gray silk was laced in and around his fingers. I hurriedly gazed down at the drink in my hand. "So what do you do, spank them, tie them up, what?"

He took my glass and put it on the table. "Would you like a demonstration?"

"No." I shimmied away, picturing being held over his lap and spanked like a child.

He leaned toward me, holding up his tie. "If you want to truly learn about my world, Lexie, you must experience it." His face inched ever so close to mine. "I promise I will not hurt you."

His thin lips hovered in front of me as I mulled over his offer. He had a point; perhaps I needed to experience what he did to his subs in order to be able to write about it. As his dark brown eyes seared into me, my resistance slipped away.

"All right, fine." I sat back against the sofa. "I'm only agreeing to do this for the sake of the book."

"Of course. It's all about the book." He stood from the sofa and went to the middle of the room. "Come here."

Taking in a deep breath, I stood up and approached him. Without my heels, I came right under his chin and noticed a slight dimple I had never seen before.

"Turn around," he commanded.

Sighing at the insistence in his voice, I did as he asked, wishing he could just ask nicely for once. When his hands went to the zipper on the back of my dress, I almost pulled away. Then I recalled his words from previous encounters. I had to relax, and I had to trust him.

"You didn't pull away," he whispered, as the zipper slowly eased downward. "You're learning."

"I'm getting—"

"No talking. You never talk when I'm punishing you."

I snorted. Silly me.

After he had pushed my black cocktail dress off my shoulders, I waited calmly, as the fabric slid down my body and gathered about my ankles. Standing before him in my underwear and strapless bra didn't seem like such a feat anymore. Perhaps I was getting the hang of this. Then another thought hit me; maybe I wanted to be naked in front of him.

His fingers lightly stroked along my shoulders and then his deep voice said, "Put your hands behind your back."

Not sure what to expect, I complied. I felt the silk tie being wrapped about my wrists and secured tightly. At this point, I should have been getting concerned. Every instinct I had was screaming at me not to go along with his plans. Even so, there comes a time in a relationship when belief in another person outweighs reason. We want to believe someone will be kind to us, love us, or take care of us; no matter how many times our past has taught us otherwise. This was that moment for me. I believed Garrett would not hurt me. I knew then that I trusted him.

When his hands left my wrists, they began working their way down my back until his fingers hooked the top of my black silk panties. He eased the panties down my hips and all the way to my ankles. Lifting my right foot and then my left, he removed the underwear and dress from about my feet.

The cool air in my apartment was making my flesh dance with goose bumps, and when he patted my naked behind, the chill turned into a rush of heat.

"On your knees," he said behind me.

With a little awkward effort, I got down on my knees. I prepared myself for a few slaps on my butt, thinking that was what he had in mind for my punishment. When he kneeled behind me, pushing my head over to the hardwood floor, my stomach clenched. Feeling so exposed caused a rush of adrenaline to race through me. My heart was pounding and my breath was coming in nervous gasps. I stayed like that for a few minutes, waiting for him to touch me, spank me…do something.

Then his hand slipped between my legs, and I bit down on my lower lip. At first, he lightly traced his fingertips over my folds, sending a shiver through me.

"You're wet. That means I do excite you," he murmured. "That's very good."

I hated to admit it, he did excite me. The more time we spent together, the harder it was getting to try and remain objective. Now he knew that I was attracted to him, making me feel even more emotionally vulnerable.

His fingers began to work slowly up and down, rubbing my clit, stroking my folds, and driving me insane. The play had gone too far, and I should have stopped him, but I didn't. It had been a long time since a man had touched me like that. Hell, no man had ever touched me like that! Garrett knew just where to place his fingers, and how hard and how fast to move along my most sensitive spots. It was like he was reading my thoughts, knowing how to bring me the utmost pleasure. Suddenly, I did not care that it was Garrett doing these things to me, or that it was part of some silly punishment. All that mattered was his desire to make me come.

"Are you going to come, Lexie?"

"Oh, God," I shouted, as I could feel my body getting ready to climax. "Yes."

He tapped my clit. "Are you close?"

"Yes, please just do it," I cried out, as my body tensed and twisted, on the verge of letting go.

Garrett abruptly pulled his hand away, and I almost crashed to the floor. "Don't stop," I groaned.

"I didn't tell you to speak," he growled.

I careened my head to the side, as he moved out from behind me and went to the coffee table. Lifting his drink, he then drained the glass.

I watched in disbelief that he could stand there so calmly, slamming back his scotch, as I lay on the floor panting for him. What kind of man was this?

He came back to me, and I thought we were going to have another go, but he simply untied my hands, adding to my confusion.

"To not know satisfaction is punishment, Lexie."

I rolled over and glared up at him. This wasn't punishment, this was agony. To want someone so completely, and then have them refuse you…my humiliation was now complete. I sat up on the floor, too shocked to stand.

Returning to the sofa, he retrieved his jacket and slipped it on. "I will call you tomorrow."

I reached for my underwear. "Don't bother."

He dropped his tie in his side pocket. "You wanted a demonstration. Now you understand more about what I do."

"What you do?" I stood from the floor and pulled up my black underwear. If I was going to let into the son of a bitch, I at least needed to be partially dressed. "Do you enjoy humiliating me?"

Tilting his head slightly to the side, he took a few seconds to think about the question. "Did I coerce you into taking part in our play? So how did I humiliate you? You wanted that. You wanted me."

I grabbed my dress from the floor, not wanting to discuss why or how much I had wanted him. "Get out, Garrett, and don't come back."

"I'll be back, Lexie." He took a step closer to me. "You and I have come too far to turn back now."

"I have enough for my book." I clutched my dress to my body, covering myself. "We don't need to see each other anymore."

"Your book?" he chuckled. It was a cold sound that I had never heard from him before. "My dear woman, this is about much more than your book." He waved his hand at me. "We'll talk some more when you're in a better mood." He strode toward the door.

"I don't want to see you again," I adamantly declared, as he reached for the doorknob.

"We both know that's not true," he stated, without turning back to me. He opened my apartment door and walked out.

By the time he closed the door behind him, I was already cursing my desire to see him again. He had me all figured out. I listened to his footfalls heading toward the staircase and yearned to break through the elusive walls Garrett Hughes had built around his heart. I needed to know the real man beneath the calculated exterior. It was time to turn the tables on him. The only question was how?

Day 6

Despite the constant stab of anger with Garrett, I spent the morning pouring all my frustrations into my book. The story was beginning to take shape and the main character, Ralph—yes, I kept the name to piss off Garrett—was turning out to be as much of a son of a bitch as the man who he was based on. I put everything into those first few chapters. Our dinner date, the time we had spent together at The Edge bar, and even my introduction to the De Sade Club.

Eight chapters in and the story was progressing nicely. How would it end? Did Ralph and my lovely heroine, Elise, end up happily ever after with a baby and a house in the suburbs? Unfortunately, I didn't see that kind of life for Garrett. If anything, I pictured him as an old man, attempting to train subs who had more sense than he did. Shaking my head, I pushed such disturbing images away. I did not want to picture Garrett old or weak. I could only see him as the man he was.

The jarring interruption of my cell phone made me look away from my laptop. Normally, I didn't answer the phone when I was working, but I thought it might be

Garrett. God, I had it bad. Picking up the phone, I sighed heavily when I spotted Al's name on my caller ID.

"Hello, Al," I said, with all the enthusiasm of a woman heading into her gynecologist's office.

"Lexie, I don't know what kind of shit you've tapped into to write this new book, but it's fucking great." The excitement in his voice was unsettling. Agents never got excited unless they were getting paid.

"Yeah, well, I've been doing a lot of research for this one, and it's paying off." My fingers itched to get back to my manuscript.

"You all right, Lexie?" The concern in his voice sounded sincere. I knew better.

"I'm fine, Al." I attempted to sound upbeat.

"You're not in trouble, are you?"

Trouble? The taunting word danced around my head like a circus bear with an umbrella. I was a little like that bear, broken and humiliated.

"No, Al. I've just been doing a lot of…research."

"Hope you're not getting into that sick shit. It's fine to put all of that submission crap in a book. It don't work in real life."

"Not to worry, Al. I haven't lost my objectivity," I lied.

"That's good. Keep e-mailing me the chapters. I can't wait to find out what happens next," Al chuckled into the phone speaker.

"Neither can I," I mouthed, not wanting him to hear me.

"This could be a great series, Lexie. I know you've got Ralph hooked up with this one broad in this book, but the way this bondage crap sells, you should be thinking of doing more with this character. He's really interesting, and the women readers would eat him up."

"I never thought about a series, Al. You're right, maybe bringing in a new woman with each book would be something new."

"New sells, Lexie, and new sex stuff with bondage really sells. Be thinking of that when you write the ending. You could even introduce the next woman in the series at the end of the previous book. With any luck, you could get several books out of this."

I was invigorated with the new angle for my book. "Thanks, Al. I knew I kept you around as my agent for some reason."

"Here if you need me, Lexie, and watch your back. I don't know where you're getting all of your research, and I don't want to know. Just be careful. If there is a real Ralph out there, he's one sick son of a bitch."

After he hung up, I put my phone to the side when it rang again. This time it was the sick son of a bitch. Watching his name and number flash across my phone screen, I contemplated letting it go to voicemail. On the fourth ring, his intense dark eyes came to mind. I answered the call.

"Are you in a better mood?" His luscious voice poured into my ear, arousing my hunger for him.

"I'm not speaking to you."

"Then don't speak. Listen. I'll be coming by to take you to an early dinner. Dress casually."

"You asshole. Do you honestly think I want to—?"

"We both know what you honestly think, Lexie. I'll see you at six."

Slamming the phone down on my desk, I vowed I would in no way, shape, or form, go out to dinner with the man. I was done. Enough was enough.

For ten minutes I sat at my desk, stewing. Then I rose from my chair and went to my bedroom. I had to find an outfit for dinner.

* * *

When Garrett arrived at my door, he had removed his brown suit jacket and rolled up his pale yellow shirtsleeves, exposing his strong arms. His wavy, dark brown hair was a little disheveled, and his pants had the hint of a few wrinkles in them.

"You look rumpled," I announced after leaning against my doorframe, not sure if I was going to let him in. "What happened? Did your dry cleaner go on strike?"

He motioned to my extra tight skinny jeans and very snug dress top. I had left my hair down, teased it to add some sexy volume—what every woman's magazine told me I needed—and put on a liberal amount of red lipstick, mascara, and dark eyeliner.

"You look like you're trying too hard." He walked into my apartment. "Is that outfit for my benefit?"

"No." I slammed the door closed. "I felt like dressing like this. It has got nothing to do with you."

He nodded, folded his arms over his chest, and stared at me. "Wash your face, and put on something you'll be more comfortable in. May I suggest pulling your hair back? Where we're going there might be a lot of wind."

"Wind? What are you talking about?"

He spun me around, placed his hands on my shoulders, pointed me to my bedroom door, and then playfully slapped my behind. "Go on, or we'll miss the sunset."

I headed toward my bedroom door and glanced back at him. "Why didn't you just do that last night?"

"Do what?"

"Spank me," I replied, entering my bedroom.

I went to my dresser and pulled out a favorite pair of blue jeans that were out of style, faded, but so soft that when I wore them, I felt as if they were a part of me.

"Because I did not want to spank you," he said, standing in my bedroom doorway. "That would never have proven my point."

"What point?" I walked over to my queen-sized trundle bed and put down my jeans.

"Withholding pleasure is punishment. Spanking you would not have been pleasurable for you," a cocky grin crossed his lips, "or for me."

That grin spoke volumes to me. I had been getting through his heavy defenses after all. Shaking my head, I gestured to the door. "Shut that while I change."

He never budged. "Undress in front of me."

The low insistent sound of his voice enticed me. Five days ago, I would have protested adamantly against taking off my clothes in front of him. Now, I relished it. Somehow in the space of a few days, I had gone from a modest good girl to a wanton wicked woman. Taking up the challenge in his eyes, I faced him and slowly began unzipping my jeans. It took a little bit of effort to get the tight jeans down my hips. I think I looked more like a contractor hanging sheetrock than a woman trying to enticingly remove her clothing. When I finally got the too snug top over my head and stood before him in my bra and panties, the look of longing in his eyes made my heart soar. I knew then that he wanted me, had always wanted me, just as much as I wanted him.

His eyes once again turned frigid. "Get dressed," he barked, breaking the spell. "Dinner is getting cold."

* * *

Dinner actually turned out to be a picnic, but it was the setting that had impressed me more than the meal. As a surprise, he took me to City Park just as the tip of the sun was touching the horizon. He found a spot for our picnic beside an odd-shaped lagoon filled with ducks, and surrounded by oaks with their hanging branches brushing against the surface of the water. Garrett had even brought four extra loaves of french bread for me to feed the quacking mallard ducks and assorted swans taking an early evening swim next to us.

I eyed the dark wicker picnic basket and long brown bag of french bread placed on the red blanket. "You've really outdone yourself."

"Martin's Wine Cellar did the food," he said, reaching into the basket. "They usually cater most of our office lunches when I have meetings with my staff." He pulled out a clear plastic container of fried chicken and handed it to me.

I put the container on the blanket, as Garrett retrieved a bottle of white wine from the picnic basket. "Where is your office?"

He popped the cork on the wine and acquired a crystal glass from the basket. "On Camp Street. Not far from my apartment in the Warehouse District. Why do you ask?"

"You just never talk about your job."

"Nothing to tell. You already know I'm an architect." He poured the pale yellow wine into the glass.

"Why did you become an architect?"

Garrett handed me the glass. "I always liked watching buildings go up when I was a kid." He reached into the basket for another crystal glass. "Office buildings, homes, strip malls. It didn't matter. Just the idea of dreaming something in your head, and then seeing it come to life, was always the ideal job for me."

"This new firm you're starting, is it doing well?" I took a sip from my wine.

"Yes, surprisingly so." After filling his glass with wine, he returned the bottle to the picnic basket. "Several big contracts have already been signed, with a few more in the works."

"You think this is because of that De Sade Club, don't you?"

His eyes grew somber and he peered into his wine. "What's your point, Lexie?"

"Maybe it's you, and not the club, making your business successful."

He swallowed some of his wine and turned his eyes to the lagoon next to us. "Being a member of the club helps, especially in this town. The business community here is very close-knit. I needed something to help me break in quickly. Without the club, it might have taken me years to get ahead."

I had more questions I wanted to ask about his life and past, but I found myself tongue-tied.

"Will you tell me why coming here with your mother was your best childhood memory?" His voice was soft and pleasing.

I sat back on the blanket and crossed my legs while attempting not to spill a drop of wine. "I don't know. Maybe because she paid attention to me here." I put my glass down on the blanket and snapped up a loaf of french bread. "It was one of the few times I remember laughing with her. My mother never laughed...at least not with me." I ripped a few pieces from the loaf and threw it into the water.

A furor of quacking waterfowl swam toward our spot. Garrett put down his wineglass and grabbed for another loaf of bread. "I think they're going to attack," he laughed.

We frantically began pitching pieces of bread to the ducks heading our way. Several climbed out of the water and came right up to us, quacking for more bread.

"Was it like this when you were a kid?" he asked, tossing piece after piece of bread to the ducks gathered about our blanket.

"I don't think there were this many."

When the bread came to an end, at least twenty ducks of various colors and one lone black swan sat at the shoreline next to us, staring.

"Should we throw them the chicken?" Garrett posed with a half-grin.

I wiped the crumbs of bread from my hands. "No, that's for us." I picked up my wineglass and gazed out over the lagoon. "What was your best memory growing up?" I glanced back at him. "You know…something that made you happy, something you miss."

He lifted the container of fried chicken from the blanket. "Dinner with my family. We used to sit around our big dinner table and talk. My two sisters would talk more than me, but I remember how much I liked listening to their stories. It made me want to have a family of my own one day. Sit around the dinner table and talk with my kids, like my parents talked with us."

I got comfortable next to him. "You want kids?"

"Wanted, past tense." He selected a chicken wing from the container. "I was idealistic growing up. Now, I think I'm more realistic."

"It's not idealistic to want a family, Garrett."

"No, I agree. It's just that the more I see of the world, the less I want to bring a child into it."

I eased over and inspected the friend chicken in the container. "Your world isn't the real world."

"It's my world, Lexie, and I'm not going to change it."

He took a bite of his wing and as he chewed, I was reminded of the image I had created of an old and gray Garrett still training his subs.

"How is the book coming?" he inquired.

I picked a thigh from the container. "Good. I sent the first few chapters to my agent this morning, and he loved it. He said he can sell the...." I paused, recalling Al's exact words. "Crap out of it."

"Is Ralph going to get Elise in the end, like a good little romance, or are you going to keep him searching for his ideal mistress of domination?"

I frowned at him. I swore I didn't know how the man did it. He was always reading my thoughts. "Funny that you mention it, but today I got an idea for a second book. I've been thinking all afternoon about a series. Every book could be a new woman and how Ralph tames her."

"You'll have to change the title. Perhaps *Taming*...someone. You can insert the new woman's name in with each book." Reclining on the blanket, he tossed the bones of his chicken to the ducks gathering at the water's edge.

Two brown mallards, with brilliant blue stripes on their wings, went after the bones, diving to the bottom of the shallow shore. Garrett chuckled as he watched the birds rummaging for the bones. "See, they do like chicken." He returned his eyes to me. "The women in these stories, who will you base them on?"

"You haven't told me about all of your adventures, yet. I seem to remember we left off with Mary Lynn. She started liking it rough and you ended it." I took a bite of my chicken thigh. "Who was next?"

"Do you really want an accounting of all the women I've known?"

I hiked my eyebrows up, smirking. "All? Are there that many?"

"It could be a very long series," he joked. Sitting up on his elbow, he reached for his wineglass. "The next woman I met was Kimberly. She had a love of horses, very rare steak, and an obsession with having sex in public." He sipped his wine. "Taming her was a risky proposition for me."

"Why?" I took another bite of chicken.

"She was my professor in my senior year of undergraduate school."

"And you became the teacher's pet, I take it."

"No, I became the teacher's punisher. Kimberly just loved to be punished." He smiled as if lost in his memories.

I flashed back to how he had punished me and understood why Kimberly probably loved his punishments. They were memorable. "What happened to her?"

He lightly shrugged his shoulders. "She went back to her husband after me, worked out her marriage."

"She had an affair with you?"

"No, she had a fling. They were all flings. I knew when I started with each of the women I've been with, that it would never last. I don't have relationships."

I wanted to ask if that rule applied to us. I didn't. As long as he never told me the truth, I could hold on to my fantasy of having a future with him. I knew it was childish to harbor such hopes, but when a man started to eke his way into your heart, you were powerless to stop it. Summoning the courage to drive him out wasn't something I wanted to do, just yet.

Garrett pointed to the partially eaten thigh in my hand. "Are you going to finish that?"

I shook my head. "No."

He took the leftover chicken from me, and threw it to the few ducks waiting at the edge of the lagoon. His eyes burned a little brighter as he observed the ducks scrounging for the scraps. Maybe Al was right, maybe he was a "sick son of a bitch" I needed to stay away from. Problem was the more time we spent together, the less convinced I became that I would ever be strong enough to simply walk away.

* * *

Having been entertained by the ducks, eaten our fill of the chicken, and emptied the bottle of wine, Garrett took me back to my apartment. By the time we headed up the steps to the arched front doors of the subdivided mansion, darkness had taken over the sky and twinkling stars were popping out all over.

"I have a dinner meeting with clients tomorrow night," he told me, while I opened the heavy double doors. "I won't be able to come by."

I gave him an encouraging smile. "You don't have to explain, Garrett." I stepped inside the foyer of the home. "You don't have to tell me where you're going every night. I'm not your wife."

"True, but I don't want to keep any secrets from you." He banged the doors closed. "A night off from me will give you the opportunity to work on your book."

A ripple of disappointment twisted in my gut. "The book, of course. Yes, that is the most important thing in my life, right now." I began to sluggishly climb the steps, all my energy instantly drained from me.

We walked in silence up the rest of the stairs. When I crossed the landing to my front door, Garrett stayed right behind me. Putting my key in the lock, I debated if he was going to come inside, or if he had another session planned for me.

"I'll call you tomorrow around lunchtime to check in," he said, as I eased my front door open.

I looked back at him, noting how he remained rooted to the landing. "Aren't you coming in?"

"No." He took a step back. "Good night, Lexie."

"Good night, Garrett." I leaned forward, without thinking, to give him a peck on the check.

He stiffened and then recoiled from me. The irate glint in his eyes reinforced his disapproval.

I was so tired of the second-guessing and games with him, I didn't bother to hide my disgust. Sighing heavily, I waved my hand at him. "What is it? I can't give you a kiss on the cheek? After everything we—"

"I determine what you can and cannot do, Lexie. You can kiss me when I say I want you to kiss me." The cruel intonation in his voice was not what I needed to hear at that particular instant. If anything, his haughty arrogance pushed me over the edge.

"You sick, self-centered, stupid bastard!"

He grinned, really grinned, looking so pleased that it made me even angrier. "How long have you been keeping that bottled up inside?"

I raised my hand, and curled it into a fist. I was about to punch his chest when he grabbed my arm and slammed me back against the dark paneling next to my open front door. He pressed his body into me, pinning me to the wall. I wriggled beneath him, but he held me fast.

"You are never to raise a hand to me," he snarled in my ear. "I tell you what to do, when to do it, and you had better damn well listen to me, or the next time my punishment won't be as kind."

While he held me against the wall, a flurry of techniques I had learned in assorted self-defense classes came back to me. Instinctively, I raised my knee to his groin. I missed and only hit his inner thigh. The pain inflicted by the blow was enough to cause him to hunch over, allowing me an opportunity to escape. I was just inside my front door when he grabbed for me. I tried to free my arm of his grasp, but he was too strong for me.

"You're going to pay for that." The fury in his eyes scared me.

Garrett flung his arms about me, and after kicking my front door closed, he dragged me into my living room. I struggled against him. He held me so tight I could barely breathe, as he carried me to the center of the room. Knocking the coffee table aside, he dumped me on the sofa. I flipped around on the soft yellow velvet cushion in time to see him removing the thin brown leather belt from his pants. The fear in me escalated. I was scrambling to my feet, ready to run away. He was on me again, shoving me face down into the sofa.

"I'm stronger than you, Lexie. You can't fight me." He wrenched my hands behind my back. "I will always win."

I turned my head to the side, wanting to cry out. I gasped for breath, as tears gathered in my eyes, and then he tied my hands with the leather belt. My hands secured, he sat back on my legs and began working my jeans and underwear down my hips.

"Let me go, Garrett," I shouted.

"Oh, no," he laughed. "You've had this coming for a while now. You need to know, once and for all, that you must do as I say." After pulling my jeans and underwear to the middle of my thighs, he ran his hands over my bare butt, kneading his fingers deep into my flesh.

The thrill of lust his hands created astounded me. I thought I would be repulsed. Instead, my body reacted to his touch with the most intense surge of longing. Biting down on the cushion next to my face, I refused to let him know how much he was affecting me.

"Time to play," he murmured into my back. His lips were on my ass, kissing me; his teeth were nipping at my skin. A deep groan was working its way up my throat when he slipped his fingers between my legs and flicked my clit.

"Garrett, please," I moaned.

"You like this." He leaned over my head. "You're already wet for me."

The thwack of a slap resounded throughout my apartment. My eyes flew open, and then the sting on my behind awakened a sickening sense of dread.

"Do you like that?" he teased in my ear.

I squirmed beneath him, but the weight of his body was too much, and I soon grew exhausted. When I settled against the couch, he dipped his fingers between my legs again. This time he slid inside of me.

I gasped as he worked his fingers in and out. I closed my eyes again, as the heat rose from my belly. When he removed his fingers I opened my eyes, wary of what he would do next. Another slap sliced through the air. This time I cried out and my eyes watered.

"You have a very lovely ass," he purred, rubbing his hand over where he had spanked me.

The touch of his hand immediately erased the sting. His fingers once more worked their way toward my groin, eased into my folds, and mercilessly stroked me, making me moan. His fingers labored diligently to bring me to climax, and just before I could let go, he pulled out and slapped my butt, hard.

I tensed, and this time I screamed with frustration and pain. It was as if the intensity of my excitement only increased my sensitivity. I was panting into the sofa, the saliva dripping from the side of my mouth.

His hand once more rubbed over the spot where he had spanked me, soothing my discomfort. "I can do this all night, Lexie. I am the master, and you are my slave."

Slave. He had never used that word before, and the sound of it sickened me. Was that what I was to him? Was this what had become of me?

He kissed the spot on my butt where he had hit me, as if trying to alleviate my pain. When his fingers once again hooked inside of me, I cursed him. He stimulated me without mercy and brought me even closer to the edge. After I was denied the relief of orgasm, he would slap my behind, rub it tenderly, and start the whole process over again.

I don't know how long I lay beneath him, taking his punishment. Eventually, when I was drenched in sweat and exhausted from the alternating bursts of pleasure and pain, he sat up, untied my hands, and stood from the sofa.

I didn't move at first, I was stunned by what had happened. Garrett reached for my arm and pulled me up on the sofa. Wincing when my sore rear rubbed against the cushion, I felt ashamed. I sat there with my jeans around my ankles, glaring at the point where his wrinkled yellow shirt tucked into the waist of his brown suit pants, too afraid to raise my eyes.

"You deserved that," he coolly stated.

"Nobody deserves that, Garrett."

He leaned down, placing his face in front of mine. "You liked it, didn't you?"

"No I didn't. How could anyone like that?"

I wanted to turn away from his disturbing gaze, but couldn't. What was happening to me? I used to be so strong, and could turn down any man I found the least bit unappealing. Yet, I could not turn away from him, and the reason I couldn't horrified me. I wanted him too damn much.

"One day soon, I'm going to make you come over and over again, Lexie. When you scream, begging me for more, you will be mine…completely."

Revulsion roared through me like a river of fire. I stood from the sofa. "That day will never come." I hurriedly pulled up my underwear and jeans. "This is over."

He appeared amused as I zipped up my pants. "Walk me to the door."

I couldn't decide if I wanted to punch him or shred him with a knife. "Get out, Garrett!"

He took my elbow. "Come with me."

I tried to slap his hand away, and he threw his arms about me, holding me against him. I gave up fighting him at that point. I was too exasperated. I just wanted him out of my apartment, to block his numbers from my cell phone, and to never speak to him again.

"Work on the book tomorrow. I will pick up dinner Friday night, and then we can stay in and work on it together."

"How do you do that?" I asked, pulling away from him.

"Do what?" he innocently responded.

I motioned to the sofa. "You attack me, tie me up, torture me, and then you can stand here and talk about bringing over dinner and working on my book. Are you completely deranged?"

The delightful smile that crept across his lips was captivating. I should have been furious with the man, clawing his eyes out; instead I stood there, enamored by him. When he nudged forward, wrapped me in his arms, and slowly lowered his lips to mine, I was downright shocked.

His kiss was unlike any other I had ever received. His lips tempted me, brushed against mine with such tenderness that I could not believe they belonged to such a fiendish man. I had thought that Garrett's hands were wonderful, but his lips were a whole lot better. His arms held me tighter, as his kiss became more demanding. When he urged my lips apart, I was helpless to resist. He delicately caressed the edges of my tongue, encouraging me to accept him. My arms slipped around his neck and I surrendered to him, sighing with contentment. I was the first to pull away, afraid of the intimacy of that kiss. Despite having my body naked and vulnerable beneath him, nothing we had shared prior to this had felt as close.

"Sleep well, my little Lexie." He kissed my forehead.

Letting me go, he turned away, and opened my apartment door. As he went through the door, I thought he would steal one more glance. He didn't. I was beginning to understand that Garrett Hughes did not give too much of himself in one meeting. He only offered snippets of the man he was beneath all the domination and subterfuge. His kiss was the first real glimpse I had ever seen of his true self. From that moment on, I was determined to uncover more, because what I had experienced in that brief kiss was worth a lifetime of exploration.

Day 7

Waiting...that best described my day. I was waiting for my cell phone to ring, and to hear his seductive voice on the other end of the line. I tried to concentrate on my book, even banged out another two chapters. As the morning sun beamed in through my french windows, stretching across my hardwood floors, I was beginning to fret over not hearing from him.

Had I forgotten the previous night and what he had done to me? Absolutely not! Was I still angry? Yes, but I was also fascinated by the way he was able to make me want him, even more. Garrett had called me his slave, and I was beginning to believe him. I had always reckoned a slave to be someone who was a servant, someone who did anything their master desired. I was learning that being a slave was not so much a physical state, but an emotional one. Being a slave to me, meant keeping Garrett happy. Despite all the things he had done to me, I still had a desire to please him.

After filling my coffee mug for the fourth time, I returned to my book. At least my escapades with Garrett were making for some compelling reading. Even I was having a tough time believing that I had actually gone through some of the things I had written about.

I was going over the latest scene, where Ralph had tied up Elise and was alternating between sexually exciting her and spanking her butt. They say you should write about what you know. I planned to put everything I experienced with Garrett into my story, and then some.

Right when I was getting to the best part, my cell phone rang next to me on my desk. I jumped at the sound of my Jay Z ringtone and grabbed for my phone. My heart beat faster when I saw his name flashing back on the caller ID.

"How are you feeling today?" The sarcasm in his voice was not wasted on me.

I sat back in my desk chair. "My ass hurts."

"You were bad. I had to show you I mean business when it comes to heeding me."

The sound of his smooth voice in my ear was appeasing me. I needed to stay angry. "Don't ever do that again, or I'll file charges, buddy."

His roaring laughter filtered through my phone speaker. "The last of my subs who threatened that, I ended up getting a restraining order against. She became obsessed with me."

I sat up in my chair, pulling on my sweatshirt. "Which sub was this?"

He sighed into the phone, and then I heard voices in the background. "One I haven't told you about, yet."

"Are you at work?"

"Just shutting the door to my office. I don't want everyone knowing my personal business."

A thought struck me. "Do any of the people you work with know about your lifestyle?"

"My boss does. Hayden Parr was in my fraternity at UT Arlington and shares my…interests."

"Interests?" I laughed, playing with the frayed bottom of my sweatshirt. "What's he like? Your boss?"

"Why do you ask?" His tone changed from playful to suspicious.

"Is he like you? Does he have subs?"

"No. Hayden dabbles in the art. He was never serious like me. He's divorced, but recently has settled down with another woman." Garrett paused, and I heard a phone ringing in the background. "They're calling me for a meeting. I've got to get back to work."

"Of course," I whispered, disappointed he had to go.

"I wanted to tell you, I have news. Our presence has been requested at the club this Saturday night."

"Requested?" I didn't like the sound of that.

"Mabel called me a few minutes ago. She's having a special party for all the members and wants us both there."

"Why does she want us to go to a party?" I didn't think my brief meeting had made that much of an impression.

"It's a club function and attendance is required. You'll need a gown, Lexie. It's a formal affair."

My heart sank. Owning a ball gown had never been on my list of things to purchase. He was lucky I had a cocktail dress. "I don't own a gown, Garrett," I confessed.

The ringing of a phone started up again. "I've got to go. I'll get you a gown and bring it over when I come by tomorrow night."

"You don't know my—"

"I'll see you tomorrow night." And then he was gone.

Clutching my iPhone, a whirlwind of apprehension seized me. Why did we have to attend a party at his club?

Did I really want to go? After our last visit, reason told me I needed to stay away from the De Sade Club. Then that nagging voice of curiosity began to grow louder. What if something happened at this party that I could use in my book?

Shaking my head, I knew I would go. That was the problem with being a writer. You may be able to write yourself into precarious situations with ease, but it was getting out of them that required the real talent. I just hoped I didn't end up regretting my decision.

Putting my cell phone down on my desk, I returned to my book. After I finished reviewing the last scene I had written, visions of women swirling in gowns and men donning tuxedos began to materialize in my mind.

"Could be interesting," I mused, as I glanced over my notes on a yellow legal pad to my right. "I wonder if Ralph and Elise should go to a fancy dress ball."

Day 8

With Garrett's impending visit that evening, I decided to get a little housework out of the way after a morning session of frenzied writing. It was also a way for me to work off some of my nervous energy. Thinking ahead to our evening together, my imagination got carried away with different possibilities, the greatest one being, would tonight be the night?

Reflecting on what I knew of him, I suspected something might happen. We had been leading up to this point. Sleeping together seemed quite probable...or did it? What was the usual waiting time between Doms and subs? Was there a protocol one had to follow? I even Googled the idea, but nothing showed up. By the time I pulled out my old, trusty vacuum to snatch up the accumulating dust bunnies that I had been intentionally ignoring, I had worked myself into a state, debating about whether or not we would do the deed.

As my vacuum cleaner sucked up the dirt from my hardwood floors, I mulled over my feelings for the man. Was this semi-twisted obsession I had for Garrett Hughes love? Or was this a carefully manipulated obsessive response of a sub to her Dom? Sure all love was some form of obsession. When did you know the obsession was going to turn into a lifelong passion? At some point, we all had to wake up to the reality of relationships. They were hard. Obsession was never going to be enough at the end of the day for two people to build a life together.

The questions kept coming like water over Niagara Falls, and I had no answers. By the time I finished putting away the dishes in my sink, mopping my yellow linoleum kitchen floor, and changing the sheets on my bed—just in case—I had not come any closer to understanding the jumble of feelings that rattled about in my heart. Giving up and leaving my fate to the stars, I went to shower for my coming evening with Garrett.

After deciding on jeans and a casual blue top, I was putting the last touches on my light application of makeup when my cell phone ringtone filled the air. Running from my bedroom, I reached for the phone on my desk. I never bothered to see who was calling, assuming it was Garrett checking in before he came over.

"Did you pick up the food, yet? I'm starving," I declared, anxious to hear his voice.

"Alexandra?"

I froze. The woman's high voice cut right to my heart. I had not heard that voice in over a year, but I knew it too well to ever forget the sound.

"Hello, Mom." I let out a long, slow breath. Why was she calling tonight of all nights? It was typical of Lily Palmer, butting in right when I didn't want her.

"How are you, baby?" The sickly sweet quality of her voice was just as fake as it had always been.

"Fine. Why are you calling?" I interrogated, hoping to cut this short.

"As warm as ever, I see. We haven't spoken in over a year and that's all you have to ask? Not a 'how are you, Mother' or 'how have you been'?"

"Jesus, Lily, what do you want?"

"Ah, there she is. I was wondering when the real you was going to appear. Congratulations, you held in all of that animosity about ten seconds longer than the last time we spoke."

My frustrated snort of indignation echoed about me. "You'll never change, will you?"

I heard my mother sighing loudly through the speaker, a sure sign the woman was growing short with me. I could recall so many fights with my mother beginning with just such a sigh.

"I was calling to ask for your help with something. I can assume by the way you answered that you already have plans for the evening, so I won't keep you."

I mouthed a scream and threw my fist into the air. She always did this; played the guilt card. "What is it, Mom?"

"You're busy and I don't—"

"Just tell me for Christ's sake!"

Silence greeted my abrupt plea. After a highly dramatic pause—classic Lily Palmer—she spoke up.

"My garage door opener is stuck again. The last time that happened you came over and fixed it for me. Do you think you could—?"

"I told you to get someone out to repair it last time." I sighed, sounding just like her.

"Well, it's too late to call anyone now, and I need to get my car out of the garage to go somewhere."

I thought of the dozen or so calls that I had received from her over the past few years. From broken water heaters to refrigerators on the fritz, my mother only called when she needed something repaired. Deep down, I knew it was just her way of reaching out to me, and every time she had called I gave in and went to her rescue.

Glancing at the clock on my microwave I toyed with the idea of leaving Garrett a note, and then I pictured his deep brown eyes seething with outrage that I had stood him up.

"Fine, Mom. Just give me—"

A light rap on my apartment door startled me. He was early.

"Ah, hold on, Mom." After putting my phone on mute, I went to the door and opened it. Garrett was waiting with his light blue shirtsleeves rolled up and a heavy five o'clock shadow. In his arms were two large brown bags. The smell of Chinese food drifted in my door, making my stomach growl.

"Take one of these." He shoved one of the paper bags toward me.

"Sure." I took the bag, and after he entered my apartment, I shut the door.

While I set the bag on the bench by the door, Garrett headed to my kitchen. Returning to my phone, I hit the mute button again.

"Look, I'm not going to be able to make it. I have a business meeting and I—"

"Who's that?" Garrett loudly demanded, coming out of the kitchen.

"Is that a man?" my mother asked, her voice taut with curiosity.

"Who is it, Lexie?" Garrett's dark eyes were swimming with irritation.

"Who is he? You know I always hated it when you let people call you that," my mother whined in my ear. "You have a beautiful name. Does he know your real name, Alexandra?"

I glared at Garrett. "Yes, Mom. He knows my real name. I want him to call me Lexie."

Garrett's brown eyes registered a rare look of shock.

"So are you coming to help me?" Lily went on.

He came closer to me, straining to hear my mother's voice over the phone speaker.

"No, Mom. I can't come over right now. I'll call you later. Bye." I hung up before Lily could come back with something I could not say no to.

Dropping the phone on the bench, I reached for the brown paper bag I had set there.

"I thought you didn't speak to your mother," he challenged, blocking my way to the kitchen.

"I don't." I walked around him, carrying the bag. "Every now and then, she calls with these excuses for me to come over. Her dishwasher isn't working or the hot water heater is out."

"What was her excuse this time?"

"The garage door is stuck and she needed to get her car out." I put the bag on my Formica kitchen countertop. "It's silly, but it's the only time we seem to talk."

Garrett came into the kitchen. "She wants to see you."

"I don't want to see her." I opened the bag, and the aroma of fried egg rolls and chicken with vegetables tempted me.

"You need to go and see her, Lexie." His voice had that authoritative edge to it, like when he barked orders at me.

"Please, Garrett. Stay out of this. Everything between me and my mother is...." I ran my hand over my forehead, as the knots in my stomach twisted tighter. They were the same knots I always got whenever I dealt with Lily.

"Why don't you let me drive you to her place? We can fix her garage door. Then come back here and eat our dinner."

I held my hands up emphatically. "No way. I could never explain…whatever we are to her, and you don't need to be exposed to my mother's scrutiny. She'd rip you apart and ask a million questions about us and—"

"Us?" He folded his arms over his wide chest. "What about 'us'?"

I was only making things worse for myself. "I just meant that she would want to know what we are. That's all. I did not imply that you and me are anything more than…friends."

He laughed, filling the small kitchen with his booming voice. "Friends don't do what we have done together, Lexie. Just tell her the truth; that I'm your Dom and you are my sub."

"No, we can't tell her that. And when did I ever say I was your sub? I thought this was for the sake of the book. I never consented to be anything to you other than a writer of your story."

"Do you really think that's what we are doing together?" His face lifted into a playfully grin. "Research?"

I shrugged, not sure if I was ready to tackle that question. What had started out as a simple business arrangement was getting complicated, and I was quickly losing my objectivity. "I don't know what to think of…whatever we are," I eventually mumbled.

"I'm glad you're confused. It means I'm making headway." He began unpacking the Chinese food from the bag. "Let's put this in the fridge and then I'll drive you to your mother's. We can figure out what to tell her when we get there."

"You don't have to do this, Garrett."

"Yes, I do." He handed me a carton of fried rice. "Part of being your Dom means that I protect you from all tribulations...and that includes overbearing mothers."

* * *

My mother's home, in the affluent suburb of Lakeview, overlooked a circular grassy park with sporadic oak trees, and was surrounded by wide, winding streets that boasted newly renovated homes. This part of the city had been decimated by Katrina; even though the national media preferred to concentrate their camera lenses on the poorer sections of the city, the black water did not discriminate. It would seem Mother Nature did not harbor any prejudice when she annihilated a city. Rich and poor, black and white, everyone suffered, making every resident of that city equal in their misery.

Parking his black, sleek car in front of my mother's one-story, California-style bungalow, Garrett glanced over at me as he turned off the ignition. My foot was tapping nervously on the floor of the car, and I was chewing on my nails like a starved dog.

"Are you all right?"

When I saw the concern in his face, I sat up and wiped my hands over the legs of my jeans. "I think I'm gonna puke."

He smiled briefly and then patted my thigh. "She's your mother, Lexie. How bad can it be?"

"Ever had surgery without anesthesia?"

He chuckled, shaking his head. "No, of course not."

"Then you have no idea what you're in for." My hand went to the car door. "Look, no matter what she says, what questions she asks you, just remember Lily is like a computer. She stores away everything you say as ammunition to use on you later. So don't give her any."

"Duly noted." He reached over and undid my seat belt, carefully freeing me of the black strap. "You forget, Lexie, I'm an experienced manipulator. I can handle your mother."

I rolled my eyes. "You are so in trouble."

I directed my attention to my mother's soft yellow house with its half-stucco, half-brick exterior. The home had a casual feel to it, with an L-shaped porch that had exposed beams above and a hanging porch light shaped like a Chinese lantern. Garden beds around the porch were dotted with overgrown palms, adding a tropical vibe to the entrance.

"How long has your mother lived here?" Garrett asked, as we ambled along the long walkway to the porch.

"About fifteen years." I pulled my mammoth brown leather purse closer to my body. "She bought it about a year before she retired from nursing."

"Your mother's a nurse?"

"Yep." I climbed the steps, still feeling sick to my stomach. "Bugged the crap out of me to be a nurse, but there was no way I was going to follow in her footsteps."

"It's not so bad shadowing a parent. I followed my old man and became an architect like him."

I glanced up at his strong profile and noticed that even from this angle, the intensity in his eyes remained. Maybe it was the slight ridge above his brow that made him appear that way, or perhaps it was the person he was: intense, focused, and commanding.

My shaking hands stretched for the doorbell, and then I felt his hand on my shoulder.

"Relax. You're not the scared little girl you once were, Lexie."

"I'm not?" I pressed the doorbell.

He squeezed my shoulder. "You've been with me. Now you're stronger."

I snickered at him. "Stronger for putting up with you, or weaker for submitting to you? It's a matter of perspective."

The slight smile that lifted the edges of his mouth stoked the queasy feeling in my stomach. "You've submitted to me?"

I swallowed hard and turned back to the door. "You're right...I'm stronger."

He was still chuckling as the door opened.

When I first saw her sinister brown eyes and teased brown hair, I didn't know what I was expecting. I guess I had hoped that she had aged, or grown some maturity in the year since we had last seen each other. However, the clingy red, rayon dress, high black heels, and slathering of makeup told me Lily Palmer was never going to gracefully accept middle age.

We looked a lot alike, with the same oval face, creamy complexion, round cheeks, and full, red lips. Lily's features were rounder than mine with an upturned nose, flat chin, and slightly sunken cheekbones. She had always said I resembled my father—a Ukrainian merchant seaman that she had met in a bar in the French Quarter. I had spent many a night thanking God for that one small saving grace.

"Well, aren't you a strapping man?" Lily lilted, sounding like a hooker enticing a John.

"Jesus, Mom!" I exclaimed, as I barreled in the front door, slouching my shoulders—an automatic physical response to my mother's usual inappropriate comments.

"Mrs. Palmer," Garrett purred in that seductive voice he only used when torturing me. "I'm Garrett Hughes. Lexie's boyfriend."

That word made me reel around and gawk at him.

"Boyfriend?" Lily was undone. She patted her surgically enhanced bosom, smiled as if she had just eaten the pet canary, and giggled, sounding like an out of tune piano. *Could this get any worse?*

"Alexandra never speaks to me about any of the men she's dating." My mother avidly waved him inside. "We'll have to compare notes on my daughter's bad habits, Garrett."

"Mom, enough." I surveyed the living room with its array of antique furniture and my mother's collection of paintings. "We're just here to fix your garage door, and then we can go," I asserted.

Garrett's eyes were drinking in the mixture of darkly finished, heavily carved, American Empire antique furniture. "You have some exquisite pieces. I've admired the furniture you got for Lexie in her apartment. I have to admit, I don't think I've ever seen such a collection."

Mom's tittering made my stomach curdle. "Aren't you sweet?" She sounded like Scarlett O'Hara on crack. "I dated a buyer for Christie's Auction House for years. Larry taught me the benefit of investing in antiques. I learned a great deal from him."

"Uncle Larry was also married with three kids, Mom." The dig felt good.

"Separated," Lily countered. "He could not help it if the silly little cow he was married to wouldn't give him a divorce."

Garrett cleared his throat and motioned to a painting on the eggshell-painted stucco wall next to the front door. "Is that a Wonner?"

I studied the abstract, still-life painting of a nude woman next to a lake. How in the hell did he know what that was?

"Yes, a gift from a former admirer who collected art." My mother sounded unusually demure. "You know Paul Wonner?"

Garrett nodded, studying the painting. "I had a friend who was an art historian. She taught me all about the abstract impressionists, such as Wonner. It was her favorite style."

I figured this had to be a former sub of his and made a mental note to ask him about this one later in the evening. I could already envision another book featuring an art historian, sex in assorted museums, trips to Paris…I really needed to focus.

"I'm impressed, Garrett." She turned to me, her mouth twisted in a funny smile. "How exactly did a man like you end up with my Alexandra?"

"Thanks for the vote of confidence, Mom." I headed over to the connecting dining room and plopped my purse down on the claw-footed Chippendale table.

"Well, after your marriage to that dirtbag musician, I've worried about your taste in men, Alexandra. You need a man to uplift you. You never saw me running around with men below my station."

I glared at her. "You have a station? You were the daughter of a grocery store owner from the Seventh Ward."

"I raised myself up from my humble beginnings," she cooed, smiling back at Garrett.

"Not from where I'm standing," I quipped.

"Mrs. Palmer," Garrett jumped in, giving me a sour frown. "We should see to your garage door. Lexie mentioned something about your needing to go somewhere."

"Please call me Lily, Garrett." She ran her hands down her revealing dress. "Yes, I'm meeting a friend for drinks."

I put my hands on my hips. "What's this one's name?"

My mother shot me an impatient smirk. "Charles Langerly, owner of the Langerly Restaurant on St. Charles Avenue."

"What are you going to do now, Mom, collect recipes?"

"What is that supposed to mean?" She raised her nose in the air, reminding me of a rat terrier.

"Just that every new man always coincides with a new collection of things. There was Elliot, the jeweler. Then Dan, the clothes buyer for a major department store who improved your wardrobe. Steve the art collector." I motioned to the Wonner painting. "Mark the plastic surgeon." I did not bother to remind her of his contributions.

"That's enough, young lady." She pivoted on her high heels to Garrett. "The garage is this way." Ignoring me, she marched past me and into the kitchen.

Garrett came up to me and took my elbow. "Play nice," he murmured.

"Not with her," I grumbled, and allowed him to escort me into the kitchen.

After showing Garrett through the open kitchen with her updated Viking appliances, and into the cypress-paneled den with its extra wide plasma television and high-tech media system, we walked into the rear of the home and to the one-car garage that housed my mother's prized red 1987 Mercedes-Benz 560SL roadster.

"Wow, haven't seen one of these in a while," Garrett admitted, studying the perfectly preserved car.

"Lyle, the antique car dealer," I proclaimed.

My mother nervous laughter echoed about the garage. "Really, Alexandra, what kind of impression are you trying to give Garrett about me?"

"A bad one," I flatly answered.

Garrett clapped his hands together. "Let me see if I can find the problem." He went to the console for the garage door in the middle of the low-hanging ceiling and pulled off the plastic housing over the motor.

While Garrett was preoccupied, my mother eased up to my side. "Where in the hell did you find him?" Her eyes were going over the curve of his round backside like a praying mantis sizing up a mate. "He's gorgeous."

"Mom, do you think you can turn down your hormones, for once?"

She elbowed me. "Come on, Alexandra. Tell me about him…and you."

I rubbed my arm where her bony elbow had poked me. "No. Nothing you need to know. We're seeing each other."

"Have you slept with him?"

My mouth dropped open. "Jesus, are you drunk?"

Garrett glanced over his shoulder at us. I thought he wanted to make sure we weren't killing each other.

"No, I'm not drunk. If you haven't slept with him, do it soon...and you'd better be worth the wait." My mother motioned to him with a bejeweled hand. "One thing I know is men, and that man gets what he wants. You can tell by the way he handles himself. He's a thinker."

"What are you talking about?"

She shifted her round, brown eyes to me. "He's plotting out his next move, his next words. A man like that is always thinking ahead."

I didn't bother to tell her how right she was.

"I found your problem," Garrett announced. "You have a loose wire." He wiggled his hand inside the gearbox and the garage door began to open.

My mother happily clapped her hands. "Thank God."

Garrett replaced the plastic housing over the motor, and wiping his hands together came back to my side. "Not terribly complicated."

"Another reason why a woman always needs a man around," Lily declared, elbowing me once more.

I just shook my head and went back inside the house.

Once I had collected my purse, Garrett and I headed to the front door as my mother followed us.

"Make sure you come back for a visit, Garrett, so we can have a nice long chat."

I gave my mother an "ain't gonna happen" stare.

She ignored me, naturally. "It was so nice meeting you." She then reached out for his hand. I expected him to pull away from her, but instead he took her hand and gave it a friendly shake.

I found the behavior somewhat unsettling. Why was my mother given the normal treatment, while I was seen as the one carrying some sort of contagious disease?

"A pleasure to meet you, Lily." He sounded as fake as she did. "I look forward to our meeting again."

"Anytime, Garrett." Lily then opened the front door and showed us out.

On the way back to his car I kept sneaking sideglances at his profile, searching for some hint about what he was thinking.

"After five minutes with your mother, I can see why you are the way you are," he commented, opening my car door.

"You were exceptionally polite. I was beginning to think the real you had been abducted by aliens." I glanced back at the bungalow home before I slipped into the car. "She'll be impossible now, having met you." I took my seat.

He pulled my seat belt over my shoulder, leaning across me to buckle it. "Or she'll leave you alone from now on, knowing you have a man to take care of you."

His face was inches from mine. I so wanted to kiss his lips, yet I refrained from giving into my impulse, knowing how he would react. Instead, I sat in my seat, waiting for him to do something. Seconds ticked by as he continued to hover inches from me.

"You're learning," he finally voiced, with a sly smile.

I fidgeted in my seat. "Why did you let her touch you? You never let me touch you."

"She's not my sub…you are." He stood from the car and shut the door.

Watching his strong body move around the front of the car, a tingle of desire rose between my legs. Wanting him was becoming a normal response with me. Like Pavlov's dogs, I would get hot and bothered every time he drew near.

When he climbed into the driver's seat, I turned to him. "You do realize that I can't be your sub, or slave, or whatever you want to call me. I never signed up for that. We've never discussed contracts or had an agreement to have that kind of relationship. This is about research and my book or books, as it's turning into."

He placed his key in the ignition and turned over the engine. "Then we should discuss terms. What do you want to be my sub?"

I was taken aback by the question. I wanted Garrett; there was no question about that. Was I ready to be a part of his world?

"You want me to be your sub?"

"I haven't been training you for the fun of it, Lexie." He pulled into the street. "I want you to be mine."

His. The word sent a shiver through me. "Which means what exactly?"

"You submit to me, submit to my desires, my needs, want only to please me, and offer to be at my beck and call. The only thing that will matter to you, from now on, is me. All I need is for you to agree."

"No," I adamantly replied. "Not a possibility. I'm a writer, Garrett, and my writing will always come first. If I'm in the middle of a book, I will not stop to cater to your needs."

"It's just a book, Lexie."

I was dumbfounded. "But it's my book, my idea, my story, and it will not be swept aside for you or any other man!"

I could see the coldness taking over his features, which meant he was playing hardball.

"This is not negotiable," he griped.

"My creativity is not subject to your demands, Garrett. I'm a free thinker, and I'm not going to be pushed around. You want me, you get all of me; that includes the parts you have no control over." I doggedly folded my arms over my chest. "Don't ask me to choose between you and my writing. You'll lose."

He stared at me for a moment then returned his eyes to the road. I got the impression that he had never come across such a dilemma. My mother was right...he was a thinker, and had been plotting out his next move with me. To keep me under his thumb and hold me to him was his plan, but he had forgotten the one thing about a writer...we can never be stifled.

"When I make a contract with a sub the only contingencies that are allowed are for emergencies, family, and in some situations the women I have been with have been on call and had to leave during our play."

"Who was the woman who taught you about that painter?"

"Melody. We'll discuss her another time. I guess I could allow for your creative endeavors. Especially since you will be telling my story, but I will need some guarantees that you will set aside a certain amount of time for me."

I carefully considered his proposal. "If I agree to all of your terms, how do you usually seal the deal? With a handshake, or is something more involved?"

The car motored down Wisner Boulevard along the outskirts of City Park, heading back toward Esplanade

Avenue. "We can talk about that later. For now, let's just work on the details of us."

Us. It had an odd ring to it, yet somewhere in my gut it felt right. Would handing myself completely over to Garrett make me happy? I figured I had the same chance as any other girl. Besides, it wasn't the rules of a relationship that lifted your heart, it was the man.

"There are some things I need to know. Intimacies, we must settle," he continued.

Intimacies? I braced myself. That did not sound good.

"Birth control for starters. Are you on any, or do I need to take care of that?"

I twisted my hands together. This was getting serious. "My doctor put me on the pill last year. My periods were real irregular. He said it would help."

He slowly nodded. "Have you ever been tested? AIDS, hepatitis, venereal diseases?"

An uncomfortable shudder ripped through me. "After my marriage ended, and I found out that Sid was screwing around, I got tested for everything."

"How many men have there been since Sid?"

That question got to me. I wasn't ashamed of the fact that I had basically lived like a nun since my divorce. Still, telling Garrett that made me nervous as hell.

"Is that really any of your concern?"

"Answer the question, Lexie," he rumbled.

"There was only one guy, not long after the divorce."

"One guy?" He appeared surprised. "I'm glad to see you're not one of those women who go out and sleep with a bunch of men to get back at her ex."

I glanced out the passenger window of the car. "I'm not a whore, Garrett."

"I've never thought you were, Lexie. Far from it." Garrett waved his hand to the back seat. "I almost forgot. There's your gown for the party."

I twisted around and spotted a long black bag hanging from a handle above the back door. "Where did you get it?"

"There's a designer, with a small shop on Prytania Street, I often do business with. I called her yesterday and told her what I wanted. She put a rush on it for me."

"How do you know it will fit?"

He grinned. "It'll fit."

I arched an eyebrow at him. "Was this designer one of your subs?"

He stretched his arm over the black leather steering wheel. "No, Cassidy went to design school with my sister, Becky."

"Your sister?" I sat back in my seat. "Where is Becky now?"

"Dallas. She designs dresses for a few local stores there. She's building quite a brand name." The pride was evident in his smile.

"Does she know about you and your...ways?"

He turned the car onto Esplanade Avenue, crossing the bridge over Bayou St. John. "Becky knows. My oldest sister, Corrine, knows too. Corrine never approved, but Becky was always more open-minded."

"What does Corrine do?"

"She's a professor of fine arts at UT in Austin. Her husband, Jay, teaches history there. They have two daughters, Lindsey and Michelle. They're a handful." He lightly laughed as he peered out to the road ahead. "Every Christmas they always buy me the ugliest ties you've ever seen. I think they enjoy seeing my reaction when I open their gifts."

Hearing him talk about his family only made how he acted at times difficult to understand. There were so many sides to him. Maybe all people were that way. They only allowed snippets of themselves to be revealed, waiting for time and trust to uncover a deeper glimpse into the facets of their souls.

* * *

After returning to my apartment, we retrieved the Chinese food from the refrigerator and sat at my breakfast bar, eating out of the white paper cartons. Garrett was lifting noodles and pork from a carton with chopsticks, appearing quite adept. While I was munching on an egg roll, he motioned to the black dress bag he had draped over my sofa.

"Don't you want to see your dress?"

I glimpsed the bag, not feeling too enthused. I had reservations of what Garrett had picked out for me, with images of black leather draped with silver chains taunting me.

"I'll look at it after I eat." I took another bite from my egg roll.

"I'd prefer for you to look at it now."

I put my egg roll down on a paper towel and wiped my hands together. "Are you insisting or commanding, because it's really hard to tell with you."

"Which one is going to get you to look at the dress?"

Emboldened by his question, I gazed into his riveting eyes. "You really need to work on incorporating please into your vocabulary."

He leaned over to me, grinned, and waited for a second or two before he answered, "Never going to happen. Go and look at the dress...that's an order."

"You...." I let the flurry of obscenities I wanted to hurl at him die on my lips. How could I expect anything less from him? Scooting off my stool, I gave him one last nasty smirk, and then went to the sofa.

As I slowly lowered the zipper on the garment bag, I became intrigued. It wasn't the shine of black leather that peeked out, but the soft and inviting texture of dark hunter green velvet. My excitement rose as I removed the dress from the protective bag, completely overcome by what I found.

The evening gown had a square neckline with wide straps, a raised waistline that sat right below the bust, and was beaded with small crystals that sparkled in the light. The fabric flowed down from the waist and was not heavy like real velvet. It was more like velveteen. Light and airy, the dress held the promise of making me feel graceful.

"Garrett, this is beautiful."

He spun around on his stool, holding his carton of pork and noodles in one hand and his chopsticks in the other. "Put it on. I want to see how it fits."

"It might be a little big. Everything is always big on me," I remarked, figuring it would probably need some adjustments.

He motioned to my bedroom door with his chopsticks. "Just try it on, Lexie."

Skipping to my bedroom, I lovingly carried the gown in my arms. Once inside, I laid the dress on the bed and was about to go back to shut my bedroom door when I stopped. Why bother? The man had seen all there was to see of my body. Returning to the bed, I quickly shimmied out of my jeans and top, slipped off my bra, and reached for the dress. I had just eased up the zipper in the back, and was going to the bathroom to take a look in the mirror, when I realized the gown not only fit, it felt as if it had been fitted to my body.

"I was right," he affirmed from the doorway. Folding his arms over his chest as he leaned against the frame, he added, "It's you."

"Garrett, this dress fits me better than my wedding gown did. How did you? I mean how—?"

"I know your body. I told Cassidy what to do to make it fit you."

Never before had a man said such a thing to me, let alone proved it. Even my marriage to Sid had never been filled with the intimacies I shared with Garrett. I doubted Sid had ever learned what size dress I wore, much less ordered one to fit me like a glove.

Garrett eased into my room. "There is one thing missing."

As he approached, he reached into his dark blue trouser pocket and then held his hand in front of me. There, shimmering in the half-light of my bedroom, was a necklace of diamonds.

"It's a collar. I figured you needed a better one than the white leather." He stood behind me and wrapped the jeweled collar about my neck.

The cool touch of his hands against my neck sent darts of desire plummeting to my groin.

When he stood back, I raised my hand to the stones. "Go take a look," he insisted, gesturing to the bathroom.

Picking up the skirt of the dress, I dashed into my bathroom and gazed at my reflection in the small vanity mirror. The deep green color of the dress contrasted beautifully against my creamy skin, while necklace added a real zing to the whole outfit. I felt like a princess.

"I like it," my prince said from the bathroom doorway.

"It's too much, Garrett."

He tilted his head slightly to the side, inspecting me. "No, you need to be stunning tomorrow night. Everyone needs to believe that you're mine." He paused and lowered his gaze to the white tile on my bathroom floor. "No matter what happens tomorrow night, no matter what you may see, you can never appear shocked or afraid. Everyone must think you are used to such events."

"What's going to happen?"

A speck of worry flashed and then vanished from his eyes. "Nothing. It's just a party."

Garrett walked out of the bedroom, leaving me to change. As I put the gown on my bed, the warning he had given me kept repeating in my head. What should I expect at this party?

When I returned to the living room, Garrett was putting the Chinese food cartons back in my refrigerator. It was then I noticed how his highbrow was scrunched together, as if he was deep in thought.

"I should get going," Garrett proposed, clapping his hands together.

"You're leaving?"

"Of course. You have your book to write, and I have paperwork to do for the office." He went around the breakfast bar and toward my front door.

I quickly followed him. "Okay, I just thought that...."

He turned to me. "That what? We would spend the evening together?"

I shrugged. "Well, yeah."

"That's what couples do, Lexie. We're not a couple. Not yet. If you agree to become my sub, that will change." He opened the door, gazing down at my jeans. "I'll pick you up at eight tomorrow night." Without so much as a kiss or even a second-glance, Garrett walked out my front door.

After locking the door, I leaned against it. "How in the hell do I write myself out of this one?"

Day 9

At precisely eight o'clock the downstairs buzzer to the main entrance clamored throughout my apartment. I hit the button on the speaker by the door and waited to hear Garrett's footfalls on the landing. When I heard him approaching, I pulled my door open right as he stepped in front of me.

His tuxedo was fitted to perfection about his lean waist and wide shoulders. The touch of shiny black silk on his lapels and down the side of his trousers caught the light from the chandelier above. He had slicked back his wavy hair, and the usual dark stubble on his cheeks and jaw were gone. His musky cologne, and the way his tuxedo clung to his body, made my knees go weak.

"I'm glad you put your hair up." He motioned to my juvenile attempt at a twist. "I like your hair up." His eyes perused the rest of my outfit. "The color suits you."

I ran my hands down the ultra-soft velveteen material. "Yes, it's a lovely dress. It will be hard to part with."

"Part with? What are you talking about?" He came in my door.

I watched his back as he walked into my living room. "When you return it to that designer friend of yours. It's a loan, right?"

"The dress is for you, Lexie. We may have other parties to attend at the club, and you'll need something nice."

My hand went to the diamond collar about my neck. "And this?"

"A rental." He grinned at me. "It goes back Monday. I'm an architect, not a millionaire."

I let out a long breath. "Whew, that's good."

"Why? Don't you want diamonds?"

I shook my head. "No. Things have never interested me, and especially not jewelry. I'm not like my mother."

He came up to me. "I never thought you were."

"Sid did." I let out a mocking chuckle. "He always told me that I was just like her because he thought I wanted him to make money. What I really wanted was for him to help pay the bills."

"I think your ex-husband never understood you. If he had, he would never have left."

"Maybe he left because he did understand me. Probably why I'm almost thirty and still alone." I went to the bench by the door and picked up my black purse. "My mother always swore I would end up alone."

"She's wrong, Lexie. You won't be alone."

I gauged the faint light of affection in his eyes. "How can you be so sure?"

He never answered and moved closer. "Do you have a wrap? It's rather chilly out."

I had to think what was in my closet for an instant. Living in jeans and T-shirts had its disadvantages when it came to dressing up. You tended to fall out of practice.

Putting my purse down, I mumbled, "I have something."

Disappearing into my bedroom, I went to the tall dresser next to my bed. It took a few minutes of hunting, but in the bottom drawer, packed away in tissue paper, I found a black lace shawl my mother had given me years ago. It complemented my dress perfectly. Draping the shawl around my shoulders, I walked into the living room and found Garrett sitting at my desk, his eyes glued to my laptop screen.

I came up behind him, peering over his shoulder to see what had put him in such a trance. To my amazement, he was reading my manuscript. From what I could see, he was already well into the second chapter.

"What do you think?" I asked.

He swerved around to me, wide-eyed. "I—I didn't hear you, I was so engrossed in the story," he confessed, gesturing back to the laptop.

That made me smile. "Engrossed is good."

"It's amazing, Lexie." He stood from my desk chair. "I was enthralled from the first few sentences. I want to read more."

His style of ordering, instead of asking, must have been wearing me down. Usually, anyone other than Al wanting to read my manuscripts before they were finished was sent packing. Not Garrett; I wanted to share the book with him.

"Of course you can read more," I told him. "It's your story, after all."

Placing his hands behind his back, he shook his head. "No, it's your story. There may be elements of it that come from me, but the essence of it is you. The way you write, I can hear your voice, not mine."

"Thank you, Garrett. I think that is one of the best reviews I've ever had."

Taking my arm, he escorted me to the front door. "We don't want to be late. The empress frowns on anyone being late to her parties."

I collected my black purse. "It's a party; aren't you supposed to be fashionably late?"

He opened my front door, and then the worry I had seen in his eyes the night before resurfaced. "Not to this, Lexie. Tardiness to special parties is not tolerated at the De Sade Club."

* * *

After Garrett's dire warning, I was relieved when we entered the dark green parlor inside Mabel Bergeron's home a few minutes before a rush of other guests flowed in. The furniture in the long, windowless room had been rearranged, with the wooden tables lined up against a far wall and the green-cushioned chairs set up in a circle around a square stage in the center of the room. On top of the stage was a Napoleon red velvet chaise. It was the same one I had seen Mabel seated on when I had first come to the club.

Gazing at the gathering of guests, I noticed all the women were wearing formal gowns. Many had replaced their leather collars with expensive gold, silver, or bejeweled ones like mine. All the men were in tuxedos…some even had tails. I thought the whole charade rather surreal, as we strolled about a room with the paintings of the women tied or handcuffed on the walls staring down on us. The silver handcuffs in the huge chandelier above caught my eye, and I wondered what kind of life the members of this club lived after they returned home.

"Let's get some champagne," Garrett suggested. He placed his hand in the small of my back and encouraged me toward the walnut bar across the room.

"What about staying on our toes?" I mumbled out of the side of my mouth, trying not to attract attention.

We approached the bar and Garrett leaned in closer to me. "Keep the same glass with you all night, and drink only a few sips," he whispered in my ear.

"Garrett," an attractive blond man called, strutting toward the bar.

"Ren, how are you?" Garrett waved his hand to me. "Ren Plancharde, this is Alexandra Palmer."

I recognized his blond, curly hair and deep green eyes from the last time I had come to the club. He was the painter Garrett had mentioned.

Ren Plancharde dipped his head to me. "Ms. Palmer, it's a pleasure."

"Surprised to see you at this party, Ren. Not working?" Garrett slipped a possessive arm about my waist.

"Always working," the refined artist admitted. "Mabel insisted I come." His eyes took a turn of the crowd milling about the room. "You know I hate these things." He gave Garrett a painful smile. "We'll talk soon, my friend." Clasping a flute of golden liquid in his hand, Ren Plancharde walked away.

As we waited by the bar with a few other couples, a young bartender dressed in a tuxedo came up to us and set two flutes of champagne before us without taking our order. While Garrett handed me a glass, I noted that the other guests at the bar were also served champagne.

"Mabel only allows champagne at these events, and will ask questions if we don't drink," he clarified.

Nodding my head in understanding, we then moved away from the bar.

"My, what a fine pair you make," Mabel clucked in her harsh voice. "She looks good with you, Garrett." The round woman came up to us.

Sporting another deep burgundy gown, her red hair was pinned up in assorted curls, and about her shoulders was a red feather boa. Her green eyes were all over me. When she spied the collar around my neck, she smirked.

"That's quite a piece." She gestured to my collar. "You have a very rare master, my dear, to decorate you with such an expensive bauble. It is a very elite gesture." She emphasized the word elite, as her eyes shifted to Garrett.

He cleared his throat and took in the other guests in the room. "Wonderful party, Mabel." He lifted his drink to his lips and took a sip of champagne.

Mabel nodded to the side of the room. "We have a certain matter to discuss."

Garrett lowered his glass, and my stomach cramped with worry.

"Of course." He directed his attention to me. "Wait here," he instructed.

I stood by as they went to a corner of the room, their heads together. Mabel cackled once, drawing a few interested glances from the other guests, and then returned to her intense discussion with Garrett. Now what in the hell was I supposed to do? Standing in the middle of that absurd room, gripping my flute of champagne—too damned afraid to drink it—I decided to focus on the chairs arranged in a circle about the square stage. As I was pondering a list of possible reasons that the small stage had been set up in such a spot, someone brushed against my arm.

When I turned, I expected to see Garrett next to me. Instead of Garrett's intense brown eyes, I was greeted by the invasive leer of Colin.

"You look beautiful in that dress," he chirped.

His hand waved down the length of my gown, and I immediately searched the room for Garrett. What was I to do?

"You can talk to me, I won't tell." He shimmied closer to me. "I know how strict your master can be, but he's not here right now. It's just the two of us."

Wanting to choke the living shit of him with his black tuxedo tie, I was forced to smile sweetly and bite my tongue.

His traced his finger down the top of my left forearm. "I'm free of my sub. It was time…she got boring. I bet you'll never get boring."

This was killing me. To smile and say nothing was not in my nature. I was more an open fire, collect the shell casings, and then bury the body kind of girl.

"Do you think you would be interested in having me for a master, Lexie?" His finger began to draw circles on my forearm. "I promise, I never punish. I'm only interested in giving my subs the utmost pleasure."

I lowered my face slightly, wanting to hide what I was about to say. "Colin," I softly growled, "touch me again, and I will cut off your balls, and shove them up your ass."

The delight in his blue eyes was not what I expected. "I knew you had a fiery side. He doesn't let you show it, does he?" Colin's hand clasped my wrist, spilling some champagne from my glass. "I could make you very happy. Allow me to claim you for myself."

"What's going on?" Garrett's booming voice broke in.

Colin let go of me just as Garrett yanked me to his side. I wanted to tell him everything. When I saw how all eyes in the room were taking in the confrontation, I knew I couldn't. I had a part to play.

"Leave her alone, Colin." Garrett held my arm.

"Just making casual conversation, Garrett." Colin cockily shoved his hands in his tuxedo pants and rocked on his toes. "I thought, perhaps, she had grown tired of your bullshit and wanted to try a master who prefers real pleasure to your games."

"She's mine," Garrett snarled.

"Need I remind you, that you haven't claimed her in the presence of the other members," Colin argued. "I have every right to ask for her, according to the rules of the club."

Garrett took an angry step toward Colin, as my mind reeled. What in the hell was he talking about?

"Colin, Garrett, enough," Mabel spoke out, coming up to our party. "Such things are not decided using your fists in this establishment." She leveled her green eyes on Colin. "You know better than that. Take your chair, we're about to begin."

Colin was not happy about the reprimand, but he backed off and bowed his head graciously to Mabel. Once he had gone to the circle of chairs, Mabel took my hand.

"You must sit beside me. I want to see what you think of our festivities, Alexandra."

I allowed her to guide me and was instructed to sit to the right of a high backed, dark mahogany chair. With my champagne positioned on my lap, I watched as other couples came toward the circle. Garrett stood behind me, placing his hand on my right shoulder. The other men in the room with female partners stood in a similar fashion behind the chairs of their women. Colin was several chairs down to my left, standing behind an empty chair and staring ahead to the stage in front of us. Out of the corner of my eye I saw the artist, Ren Plancharde, hovering close to the bar, his thin lips turned downward in a disapproving scowl.

Not knowing what to expect, I kept my gaze focused on the stage like the other women around me. Garrett's hand felt comforting. When I took in a deep breath, he squeezed my shoulder.

"I'm sure you have never witnessed a collaring ceremony, my dear," Mabel said beside me. "It's something special to our club. A way to bind subs to their Doms, so there can be no disputes among the men. I've found it best, when dealing with men, that they make a public claim to a sub, thereby ensuring others will stay away. Having witnesses to such an event is so worthwhile." She clapped her hands. "Let's begin."

From the entrance to the room a man came forward. Wearing a sharp tuxedo, he carried a black leather collar in his hand. He was older, somewhere in his mid-fifties, attractive, had a slight paunch, and receding hairline. He was vaguely familiar to me. I realized where I had seen his face. A judge in the parish courthouse, his television commercials had flooded the airways when he had run for re-election a few months prior.

Behind him, walked a woman wearing a hooded white robe. Her feet were bare and her face was partially covered. I did not recognize her until she entered the circle. It was Heather, the mousy blonde I had seen with Colin.

"We leave it to the sub to decide the man she wishes to have as her Dom," Mabel explained. "How she makes that decision is up to her. Everything in this club is done with the consent of both parties." Mabel waved toward the man as he removed his tuxedo jacket. "Once she consents, she must prove her loyalty to her Dom by consummating her choice before the group in a ceremony."

My heart began to beat a little faster, as my eyes remained glued to the man on the stage before me. Having removed his jacket and flung it aside, he was rolling up his shirtsleeves as Heather waited in front of the red velvet chaise.

Mabel stood up. "Remember this is for the rights to this woman," she spoke out in a clear voice. "Heather Vreeland has freely chosen Avery Gautier to be her master, and consents to everything that will take place tonight." She motioned to Colin. "Colin Bergeron, do you consent to give up this woman?"

Colin nodded his head. "I do."

Mabel returned her gaze to the stage. "Heather Vreeland, do you consent to this ceremony?"

Heather's timid voice rang out. "I consent."

Mabel motioned to the man standing on the platform. "You may begin."

Avery approached Heather and lowered the hood from around her face, then pushed the robe over her shoulders, letting it fall to the floor. She was completely nude. I watched the man inspect Heather's body, and an uncomfortable pang caught in my gut. As she stood before him, Avery Gautier fastened the black leather collar in his hand about Heather's neck. My grip tightened on my champagne glass, hoping that was the extent of it.

"My son is a fool," Mabel whispered beside me. "Giving up such a prize. Ah, but men are fickle beasts."

My eyes darted to Colin. *Her son?* God, I needed a sip of my champagne.

As Colin ogled Heather's naked body he licked his lips, prompting me turn away. Hiding my revulsion, I was diverting my eyes to the main attraction when I felt Garrett's thumb begin to, ever so lightly, rub back and forth over my shoulder. The steady motion calmed me. I closed my eyes for a second and concentrated on his touch. Heather's giggling made me open my eyes. While naked before the red velvet chaise, her appointed Dom was fondling her, running his hands along her slender hips, stroking her small breasts, and to my amazement, the woman was enjoying it.

I was a voyeur; ashamed that I was having any part of this. At the same time, I was fascinated by what was taking place. While Avery's groping became more insistent, Garrett's thumb pressed harder into my skin. The constant reminder of his presence, the enticing way his thumb caressed me, made it difficult to concentrate. When Heather moaned, Avery's hand eased between her legs.

"She was always such a tease," Mabel muttered. "I'm not surprised that she's up on that platform again. It's the second time this year." Mabel shifted in her chair and leaned over to me. "If you ask me, she likes doing it in public."

I could not believe what I was hearing.

"Of course, not everyone is like her," Mabel went on. "Some subs don't care for the ceremony in the beginning. They are the modest ones. In the end, they all come around."

Heather gasped as Avery tossed her face down on the chaise. I flinched and Garrett's thumb drove even deeper into my flesh.

Mabel sighed, looking bored. "I hope they don't take too long."

When Avery positioned his hips behind Heather's round ass, my body tensed. Garrett's thumb began to move faster back and forth, pressing harder into me. While Avery unzipped his pants, my breath caught in my throat, and Garrett dragged his thumbnail across my skin. As Avery rammed into Heather, Garrett pushed his thumb deep into my shoulder. Heather cried out when Avery began mercilessly pounding into her. I bit my lower lip as Garrett's thumb began mimicking Avery's every thrust.

My insides were on fire. I pictured me up on the stage with Garrett behind me, taking me, making me his. Clenching my flute of champagne, I was sure it was going to smash into pieces at any moment. Beads of sweat gathered beneath my dress as Garrett's thumb continued its deep probing.

Thankfully, the ordeal ended when Avery groaned and then slumped over Heather's back. A round of applause broke the silence of the room, and Garrett lowered his hand from my shoulder. All around me, other guests were standing from their chairs, cheering enthusiastically.

"Stand up and clap," Garrett barked in my ear.

In a daze, I stood and timidly patted my hand against my champagne glass, not quite sure why we were lauding such a display.

"Thank God that's over with," Mabel complained. "Now we can eat."

I peered over at the woman in astonishment. Perhaps she had seen one too many of these ceremonies and had grown bored with the entire affair. I, on the other hand, was in dire need of a cold shower.

"You can never truly belong to your handsome master, Alexandra, until you set foot on that stage and have him make you his." She glanced back at me, her green eyes threatening. "Otherwise, there will always be questions about your loyalty to your Dom…and to our club."

My heart came to an absolute standstill.

As if just made aware of their audience, Avery collected Heather's white robe and covered her naked body. Sitting up on the chaise, she adjusted the robe around her, ran her fingers through her hair, and seemed completely at ease.

"Come, everyone." Mabel twirled a diamond clad hand in the air. "Dinner is being served in the dining room."

Rounds of oohs and aahs replaced the applause, and within seconds everyone was moving toward the entrance. I stood by my chair and waited for Garrett. Mabel was the last to leave, ushering Heather and Avery on to the dining room. When the parlor was finally empty, except for the lone bartender clinking glasses together behind the bar, Garrett came alongside me.

Staring down at his shiny black patent leather shoes, I was too ashamed to raise my eyes. I was not a prude, by any means, but what I had just witnessed would have made a stripper blush.

"Are you all right, Lexie?"

I shook my head. "You should have told me."

He stooped down before me, making me look at him. "What would I have said? You already know what goes on here. How is this different?"

"How is it…? Jesus, Garrett, what kind of shit are you into with these—?"

He placed his fingers over my mouth, silencing me. He dipped his head to the bartender, reminding me that we were not alone. "It's time to go home." He pried the champagne glass from my hand and placed it on the floor.

"What about dinner?" I asked, as he took my arm.

"Dinner is not compulsory. The ceremony was."

We strolled toward the entrance and he placed his arm around my waist. Overcome by the events of the evening, I leaned against him for support. Growing up in New Orleans, I had seen everything. People having sex in public was not a big deal to me. If you have ever been to the French Quarter on Mardi Gras Day, you know that it's everywhere. Seeing it in a private club, in front of some of the city's most esteemed leaders, was something else entirely. This was dangerous, and reputations, as well as lives, could be ruined with this kind of information. Garrett's warnings about the club began to sink in. I realized I had been placed in a precarious position. Not only was my career on the line, so was Garrett's.

After we had settled in his car, I let my eyes wander back to the grand two-story gallery home with its detailed ironwork. I never wanted to return to this place, and for a split second, I wished I had never met Garrett or been exposed to such activities. It was one thing to suspect that there were twisted people in the world; it was quite another to sit in a room filled with them and be privy to their perverse pleasures.

"I had to bring you tonight. If you had not come, they would have asked questions. We cannot afford that kind of scrutiny," Garrett stated, turning the ignition.

"What Mabel said about me having to go through that ceremony...is it true?"

The car veered into the middle of First Street. "In the eyes of the club, yes, but I have no intention of subjecting you to that."

My hands went to the diamond collar about my neck. "What happens if you don't claim me?"

"Until you get a black collar you're not officially a member, only my guest, and any other member of the club could try to claim you as theirs."

"Is that what Colin was suggesting?"

He nodded as the car headed toward St. Charles Avenue. "Yes."

"You forgot to tell me he was Mabel's son."

He squared his shoulders, appearing edgy. "It didn't seem important."

"Important?" I shouted. "You don't think his being the son of that woman will have any influence on him trying to own me?"

"Claim you," he corrected. "And no, it won't. I won't let him claim you. If it comes down to it, I'll claim you first."

"You would make me go through that ceremony we just witnessed? You would humiliate me like that...in public...in front of those sick perverts?"

"I'm one of those sick perverts, Lexie. Remember that." I could see his jaw muscles tensing as he spoke.

"So after you've had sex with me, am I to be your sub?"

Keeping his eyes ahead to the streetlights of St. Charles Avenue, he answered, "Yes, then you would be completely mine."

"What if I don't consent? What if I refuse to be part of your club?"

He turned, giving me a grave and thoughtful look. "You saw the men in there, you know who they are. How long do you think it would be before they would begin to watch you, keep tabs on you, and try to keep you quiet?"

My heart fell to my knees. "What have you gotten me involved with, Garrett?"

"I told you this wasn't about your book anymore. I asked you how far you were willing to go. I warned you there could be consequences."

"Consequences? I thought you were joking. This is the kind of stuff that ends up on the nightly news, not in the middle of my life."

"Welcome to my world, Lexie. No matter what you decide, your life has changed for good."

My life had changed, but not for the reasons Garrett had mentioned. He was the reason everything was different. I shrank into my black leather seat, clutching my shawl. I entertained the possibilities of becoming his, handing myself over to his demands, and joining his club. Then I thought of Heather, and what had happened to her when Colin had grown bored with her. Would my fate be the same if Garrett and I ended? Would I be expected to find another Dom, or would they let me walk away? Somehow, I suspected walking away from the De Sade Club wasn't going to be so easy.

Garrett maneuvered the car along St. Charles Avenue and eventually on to the interstate. A light sprinkle started falling, and by the time we pulled in front of my subdivided house, the rain was coming down in big droplets. I waited for Garrett to turn off the engine, and became curious when he stayed in his driver's seat, staring into his rearview mirror.

"We have a visitor," he commented, never taking his eyes off the mirror.

"What are you talking about?" I glanced out the back window.

"Colin followed us from the club. I noticed his car when we got on the interstate."

"Colin?" I tried to see through the rain covering the back window. "Are you sure?"

"I know his car." Garrett placed his hand on my arm. "When I go around and open your door, don't look back at him."

Garrett opened his door and jumped into the rain. After he collected me, we jogged up the walkway to the front doors. As I fumbled for my keys, I saw him glancing to a black Mercedes-Benz parked two cars back behind his BMW. The engine was running, and the headlights had been turned off.

"What do we do?" I implored, opening the doors.

"We make it look good. I'll stay until he leaves. That should convince him."

After entering my apartment, Garrett removed his tuxedo jacket and dropped it on my antique sofa.

"You might be here a while. Do you want scotch or coffee?" I asked, walking past him.

I was heading toward the kitchen when he came up behind me and enveloped me in his arms. "I don't want anything to drink." His hand then reached for the zipper on the back of my dress. "The whole time we were watching that couple, I kept waiting for you to move, cry out, or stand up. I'm glad you never did."

"You told me not to be surprised by anything."

He unclasped the diamond collar and dropped it to the floor. Kissing the back of my neck, he murmured, "Were you turned on?"

My groin exploded with white heat while his kisses tempted my skin. I tried to spin around, hungry to taste his lips, but he held me firm.

"You have experienced my punishment when you do not obey me." He tugged at the zipper. "Tonight, you will experience my reward for following my directions." He let me go and hooked his fingers beneath the straps of my dress. Slowly, he eased the gown over my shoulders and pushed the fabric down my body. Letting it fall to the floor, he lifted me out of the material and into his arms.

Garrett carried me to my bedroom. I was flushed with excitement of what was to come. Finally, he was going to take me, and I was eager for it. Gently putting me down on the bed, he then pulled my hips to the edge, as he stood over me. I tried to reach for his shirt buttons. He shook his head, stopping me.

"Tonight is about you, Lexie; all about you." Kneeling at the edge of the bed, he lowered the black silk underwear I had put on hoping for just such an outcome. "I plan on pleasing you, over and over again."

After he tossed my underwear aside, he lifted my hips closer to him. I closed my eyes and leaned back against the bed as his lips kissed the inside of my right thigh. God, I was going to explode with longing for him. When his mouth closed over my clit, I almost screamed out loud.

His tongue drew circles, his teeth teased, and he sucked so hard that I arched against the bed and cried out his name. Reaching for my blue bedspread, I held on while my body quivered when that powerful tingling rose from my loins. As the first wave of my orgasm hit, I slammed back against my bed, my body bucking uncontrollably. Somewhere in the distance, I thought I heard someone scream. As my head cleared, I realized it had been me. I was gasping for breath, pulsating with satisfaction, and totally drained.

"Garrett," I gasped. That was...." I tried to catch my breath.

"That was only the beginning." Kissing my inner right thigh and nipping at my flesh, his lips traveled downward. I moaned when his mouth settled over me, and then he began tasting me all over again.

I lost count of how many times he made me come. When he finally climbed onto the bed next to me, I was covered in sweat and unable to move.

"You earned that." He kissed my cheek.

I pulled at his tuxedo shirt. "I want to feel you next to me."

His arms went around me. "Let me just hold you for now."

Sighing with contentment, I closed my eyes and cuddled against him. I had never been so satisfied with any man before, making me question if I would ever feel that way again. Or would Garrett take all my happiness with him when he eventually moved on? I was not stupid enough to believe that we would last, but I did want to enjoy what we had for as long as time would allow.

Day 10

I opened my eyes to discover that the pale light of morning was peeking through my bedroom windows. When I sat up, there was no sign of Garrett next to me. Tossing the covers aside, I immediately went to my dimly lit living room, but he was not there. My green dress was no longer on the floor—neither was the diamond collar. The gown had been neatly draped over the length of the sofa. I was about to reach for the dress when the light from my open laptop caught my attention. Approaching my desk, I spotted the screen open to the last page of my unfinished manuscript. Knowing I had turned off the computer before getting ready for the party, I guessed he had read my book while I was sleeping. Running my fingers over the keyboard, I pictured his long, fine hands dashing across the keys. I went to close my laptop when I saw something written well below the last sentence of my book.

This is better than I could have imagined. You're a great writer.
G

I read his note several times and finally saved it, wanting to keep it for future inspiration. Smiling as I reflected back on our night, especially the moments in my bedroom, I knew things had changed between us...or at least they had changed for me. If he ever asked me again to submit to him, I would not refuse. I was in too deep, and though the book still mattered to me, the man I was writing about was starting to matter more. It would seem that truth had surpassed my fiction.

* * *

After a long hot shower and a cup of black coffee, I returned to my laptop for a day of writing. With the events of the party fresh in my head, I wanted to get as many of the details down as possible. Images of Colin, Heather, Mabel, and Garrett rushed across my mind while my fingers flew across the keyboard, anxious to incorporate everything into the book. As I typed, I thought about the things I had learned the night before about the club, Colin, and my fate if I chose to be claimed by Garrett. Could I live a life like that?

Putting the matter aside, I concentrated on my story. Before decisions had to be made about relationships, before ceremonies were planned, I had to deal with Ralph and Elise. I had to end their tale before I could even think of beginning mine.

As the morning session of writing dragged into early afternoon, I began to check my cell phone for any word from Garrett. At first, I didn't mind not hearing from him. It gave me the opportunity to write undisturbed. However, by the time the late afternoon sun cast its long fingers across my living room floor, I was fretting over why my phone had remained silent.

An unexpected knock on my apartment door distracted me from my worry. I had not heard the buzzer from the downstairs entrance and when I went to the door, I hesitated before stretching for the doorknob.

"Who is it?"

"Lexie, it's Colin."

Colin? I almost shouted out his name with disbelief. What in the hell was he doing here? Turning back the deadbolt, I opened the door.

"How did you get in?"

He thumbed back to the stairs. "Your neighbor let me in."

Dressed in an impeccable gray suit and elegant black and silver silk tie, he appeared fresh from a day at the office. On closer inspection, the light smattering of fatigue circling his blue eyes and the touch of stubble around his jaw made him seem slightly haggard.

His lips stretched into a devious grin. "Can I come in?"

Wary of letting him in my apartment, I stood in the doorway. "What do you want, Colin?"

He slipped his hands in his trouser pockets. "All right, if you want to do this in the hallway…I want to talk to you about claiming you, making you my sub."

I shook my head, waving him into my apartment. The last thing I needed was my neighbors to overhear talk of subs, ceremonies, and bondage. They already thought I was the weirdo writer.

Once inside, he avidly took in my eclectic décor, his eyes honing in on my antique furniture. "Nice place. Small, but nice." He turned to me. "I could get you something nicer."

I shut my front door. "If I let you claim me, is that it?"

"Garrett has made no move to claim you in the club. He has to do so soon; otherwise, another Dom could do it…another Dom like me."

I stayed close to the door, in case I needed to make a hasty retreat. "I'm not interested, Colin. Garrett is my Dom. I don't want another."

"You can't remain in the club without being claimed."

"Maybe I don't want to stay in the club."

He laughed, folding his arms over his chest. "Then I guess you got all the information you needed for your book."

My insides turned to ice. "What are you talking about?"

He came closer to me. "You told me you were a romance writer that day we met at Woldenberg Park. Later, when Garrett told me your full name, I checked you out. I know about your books, your ex, even about your mother. Nowhere did I find any info about your interest in bondage."

"I'm new to the art," I said, my nerves on edge. "Garrett has been training me."

"Training?" he snickered, not sounding very convinced. "Then why did he show up at that bar with you? I even asked him that night why he didn't bring you to the club straightaway. He said he wanted to break you in slowly." He wiped his hand across his mouth while shaking his head. "I know now, he never had any intention of making you his sub. If you were a true sub, you would have never said the things you did to me at the club. When he came back here with you last night, I knew he had never had you. No man would leave your bed in the middle of the night."

I leaned back against my front door, contemplating my options. "What do you want, Colin?"

He nodded, stopping right in front of me. "Good girl. You're smarter than I thought." He paused, his eyes wantonly roaming over my body. "What I want is this…you become mine. I claim you in the ceremony at the club. I say nothing to my mother, or any other members, about you and Garrett, and the book I have no doubt you're writing."

"Why should I go along with that?"

"Because if you don't, I'll have Garrett kicked out of the club, his business shut down, and he'll go back to Dallas with his tail between his legs. I'll make sure he never to sets foot in New Orleans again."

I glared into his icy blue eyes. "Why do you hate him so much?"

"I don't hate him," he said, astonished. "I want you. I've always wanted you since the day we met. I could tell you were no sub, but Garrett refused to see it." He eased his lips closer to me. "Just think of all the fun we will have, and how I will switch you from a Dom to a sub."

The term came back to me. Garrett had told me once the greatest lure for any Dom was turning one of their own into a sub. Suddenly, Colin's aspirations became crystal clear.

"Why should I care what you do to Garrett? Even if you hurt him, you can't force me to do what you want."

"That's true" he agreed. "I can't force you. Nonetheless, wouldn't it be better to submit to me rather than watch Garrett suffer, and watch your friends and mother get squeezed by my connections at city hall? I know a lot of people in this town, Lexie. You can either submit to me and live like a queen, or refuse me and chance losing everything you have."

"That's blackmail," I hissed.

"No, it's an incentive."

"Get out, Colin." I opened the door. "Come back here, and I'll call the cops."

"I know them too, Lexie." He arched over me, trying to appear menacing. "You need time to think about this. I understand. It's a big decision." Reaching for a tendril of my hair hanging from my ponytail, he held it between his fingers. "I'll be in touch."

After he sauntered down the heavy staircase, I quietly shut my door. My mind was reeling with questions about what to do. If I called Garrett, he would go after Colin, and possibly make things worse. I had to think this through. I had to find a way to spare Garrett and me from Colin's desires. There had to be a way out of this.

Returning to my desk, I flopped down in my chair. Leaning my head back, I went over and over a list of possibilities. No matter how I evaluated the situation, only one solution presented itself. I had to submit to Garrett. I had to go through with the collaring ceremony, to protect both of us from Colin. Short of running away, I did not see how I had any other choice. If I had to be claimed, I wanted it to be with Garrett and no one else.

Closing my eyes, I visualized him throwing me over that red velvet chaise and taking me from behind. The eyes of all those around us quickly came into view, and I became queasy as hell. Shaking off the images, I tried to return to my book. I consumed my mind with Elise and Ralph, making their story my own.

As the late afternoon turned into evening, I became acutely aware that I had not heard from Garrett. Had something happened to him, or had he grown tired of me? I was used to hearing from him every day. The sudden silence was confounding. Perhaps I should call him and tell him of Colin's visit. I feared his reaction, and decided I needed to wait for him to call me.

By 10 P.M., I was pacing my living room floor and staring at my cell phone, willing it to ring, so I could hear Garrett's voice on the other end of the line. By 11 P.M., I had stopped pacing, and my anger had kicked in. I was cursing his name and wishing we had never met. Between Colin's threats and Garrett's obvious brush off, I was beside myself. I even went so far as debating on whether or not to delete my manuscript, symbolically deleting both men from my life. It did not take me long to decide that erasing my work was a bad idea. I had to eat.

Finally, worn out with worry, self-recrimination, anger, and disbelief, I climbed into my bed, determined to get some answers in the morning. I would have to talk to Garrett. I was still unsure if he should know of Colin's plans. More importantly, I needed to know why, after a night of intense passion, he had never bothered to call me. So I planned my strategy. I would call him and say I had some questions for the book…and then, I would casually bring up my concerns. Yeah, that would work. It had to.

I laughed at my dilemma. I couldn't write this crap even if I tired. That was the problem with being a storyteller; sometimes a story took on a life of its own.

Day 11

After a restless night's sleep, I got up that Monday morning and chose not to confront Garrett over the phone. The things I needed to say had to be done in person. A quick search on my computer located the address of his office on Camp Street. After donning a respectable pair of blue slacks and a white button-down shirt, I grabbed my leather purse and headed out the door.

In my car on the way to Garrett's office, I practiced different explanations for why I had showed up unannounced. With each scenario, I tried to anticipate his response, and how I would react when I saw him again. No matter how hard I tried to convince myself that I would be able to take the anger he would most certainly hurl at me, the thought of seeing him again was rather daunting.

When I found his modest red-bricked two-story renovated warehouse, I was underwhelmed. I didn't know what I was expecting…maybe a larger building that matched the personality of the man who ran it. The quaint structure had a black awning over a glass front entrance, and a second floor façade covered with long, old-fashioned windows. Written in red over the top of the awning, was the name Parr and Associates.

Parking across the street, I struggled for a few moments at the parking meter, trying to get the correct change to cover one hour. Peering up once more at the building, I took in a deep breath and headed across the street.

As I stepped in the front door, I was greeted by an older, blue-eyed receptionist who had silver wire-rimmed glasses and wore her blonde hair up in a bun. Her friendly smile complimented the congenial beige décor of the reception area. Along the walls were assorted pictures of homes. I assumed they had been designed by Garrett or some member of his company.

"Welcome to Parr and Associates," the blonde declared. "Can I help you?"

Pulling my purse closer, I dropped my eyes to her semi-circular light oak desk. "I would like to see Mr. Garrett Hughes."

"Do you have an appointment?" The blonde reached for a phone on the side of her desk.

"Ah, no. Can you tell him—?"

The loud buzzing noise from the phone cut me off. The receptionist held up her hand as she lifted the receiver.

"Yes, sir."

I waited as she listened to the voice on the other end.

"Yes, sir," she repeated, and then replaced the phone in its cradle. Still smiling, she glanced up at me. "Mr. Hughes will see you, Ms. Palmer." She motioned to a door behind her desk. "You can take the stairs to the second floor. You will find Mr. Hughes's office is the first door on your right."

"Ah, thank you," I remarked without wanting to know how she knew my name. I already guessed who was on the phone with her.

Taking the steps two at a time in the brightly lit stairwell, I quickly emerged on the second floor. A long corridor with deep brown carpet and more beige-painted walls decorated with photographs of homes was waiting. Once I took a few steps into the corridor, I spied a single office door to my right. Placing my hand on the shiny brass doorknob, I held up my head and walked inside.

The first thing I saw in the office was a long row of old-fashioned windows that allowed the full light of day into the rectangular office. The windows had been the same I had noticed from the street. How Garrett had known it was me became obvious.

"Lexie, shut the door," a velvet voice said to my left.

When I turned, he was standing in front of a grand light oak desk with a row of matching bookcases behind it. All my well-intentioned words practiced in the car on the drive over immediately left me. I was fumbling for something to say as my eyes met his. His lips were pursed together, and when he glared at me, I did not know how to react. I ignored that tweak of desire stirring in my gut, fiercely determined not to show him that I was foundering beneath his withering gaze.

"Hello, Garrett." With a little too much dramatic flourish, I slammed the door closed. "We need to talk."

He sighed and leaned back on his desk. "Christ, you're impossible. I knew when I read your book, I...." Pushing away from his desk, he went to the wall of windows that overlooked Camp Street and turned his back to me. "I know why you're here. It's because I didn't call or stop by yesterday, isn't it?" I said nothing, and he folded his hands behind him. "After everything that happened at the club, I would think you would question if we should continue to see each other."

I noticed how his hands curled and uncurled in front of me. "That's not the impression I got after the party when you had your head between my legs," I commented, approaching his side.

Showing me his profile, he coldly replied, "I was rewarding you for your good behavior, nothing more."

"If there was nothing more, Garrett, then why did you read my book?"

He hesitated, and that simple action vanquished all of my doubts. Garrett carefully planned every nuance, every word he uttered. To upset his unflappable disregard meant I was making progress, and perhaps, getting under his skin. At least I hoped so. There were moments I felt as if I were nothing to him.

"After all the time I have invested in you, I was curious to see the outcome of my efforts," he finally admitted. "I understand a lot more after reading your book. More than I needed to know."

I smiled, thinking my book had given him some insight into his chilly disregard. Eyeing his desk, I marveled at how everything was neatly in its place. My desk was always in a state of chaos, with Post-It notes scattered about, bills that needed to be paid, and notebooks of story ideas piled to the side. A writer friend had once told me, "A desk was a reflection of the mind of its owner." In Garrett's case, that was true. Nothing was out of place; even his pens were neatly arranged to the side of his burgundy blotter.

Raising my eyes to the bookcases lining the wall behind his desk, I spotted several framed photographs. In one, a woman with a bright red hat, who had Garrett's eyes and similar features, was smiling for the camera. In another, a man and woman dressed in wedding clothes embraced each other. The picture that intrigued me most was of Garrett smiling happily between two small girls, one of which was giggling. He was not at all like the man standing in front of that window. The ever-present frost in his eyes was gone, revealing a kindhearted, tender man.

"Your family?" I gestured to the photographs.

"Yes." He came up to me. "My sisters and my nieces."

"Sort of makes you a little less intimidating, seeing you with your nieces like that." I pointed to the picture of him with the little girls. "You seem almost human."

He chuckled, and came around in front of me, leaning back against his desk. "When have I not been human with you?"

"I don't know. You've always been larger than life to me." I stared into his eyes and that profound longing for him tugged at my heart. I knew in that instant that I had to do everything I could to protect Garrett from Colin's threats. "You asked me once to submit to you and I refused," I asserted. "What if you were to ask me again?"

His eyes softened, and he stood upright. "You do know what that would mean?"

"I know," I sighed. "If I went through with that collaring ceremony, what exactly would I be to you?"

He dipped his head closer to me, halting inches from my lips. "You would be mine, utterly and completely."

I leaned back from him. "When I'm no longer yours? What then? Do I become like all the other women you have known. Another story?"

"There are no guarantees with me, Lexie."

"I'm not looking for guarantees, Garrett. I didn't have them in my marriage, and I don't expect them from you."

Cocking his head to the side, he asked, "Then what are you looking for?"

"You. The real you." I motioned to the photographs behind his desk. "I want the man in the picture with those two little girls."

"You want too much." He turned away and went back to the windows. "You know what I am, Lexie. I'm not going to change, or give up what I like to do for you. I am a master, and can be no other way."

"What about feelings, Garrett? Don't you ever feel anything for your subs?"

"Feelings are dangerous for a man like me."

I came up behind him and was going to touch him when I remembered how he would always withdraw from me. Something in me wanted to tempt fate, to see if he still felt that way. Reaching up, I rested my hand against his upper back. He flinched, but did not move away. When he spun around, I saw the change in his eyes. It wasn't anger reflecting back at me in his dark orbs, it was desire.

"You should go," he calmly stated, and then the fire vanished from his eyes. "I have a meeting."

Taking a moment to drink in the curves of his face, I resigned myself to my fate. He was inside of me. I would never be free of him until I had all of him. If giving myself to him in a room full of strangers meant we could be together, then so be it.

"I will do whatever you want," I whispered to him. "I don't care anymore."

His brow furrowed, making him appear unsure. "Even knowing what I am, how I am, you would still want this?"

I inched closer to him. "I'll take you any way I can get you."

He backed away as a chill settled between us. "I want you to take some time and really think about this, Lexie." Fastidiously tugging on his grey jacket sleeve, he lowered his eyes to the deep brown carpet. "We have to be practical."

"Practical?" I laughed. "I gave up being practical the day you kissed me."

His eyes shot to mine, and then he quickly turned for his desk. "I need to get to my meeting."

I nodded my head at his abrupt dismissal, knowing there was nothing left to say. I went to his office door, as I placed my hand on his shiny brass doorknob, he stopped me.

"Get back to the book. I want to see how it ends."

I turned the knob. "Ends? What makes you think it's going to end?" I walked out into the corridor beyond.

Exiting the building I felt rejuvenated, and at the same time disgusted with myself. I had kept the truth about Colin from him, something I was sure no sub was supposed to do. I reasoned we were way beyond the clear-cut roles of Dom and sub. What was developing between us was something I prayed would be more long-lasting than a casual fling. Did Garrett feel it, too? If he did, he didn't show it. So how did I get him to admit his feelings? Perhaps performing that ghastly ceremony would show my hardened Dom that true submission was not an act of obedience, but a sacrifice made for the sake of love. He would then take me in his arms and declare his undying devotion. Yeah, I knew it needed a rewrite. I just considered it a work in progress.

Day 12

An uncanny calm pervaded my being when I rose from bed that morning. It was as if I knew my fate and had accepted it. There were no more questions about Garrett, no more uncertainty. My serenity felt as if it had permeated every aspect of my life, even my writing. My head was clear of the clutter of worry, and I was able to get a lot of writing done. The words came like lightning during a wicked summer storm. Before I knew it, the strong afternoon sun had invaded my living room. When I checked the clock on my laptop, I jumped from my desk chair. I had to get to an appointment with Al. He wanted to discuss options for the book and the series.

Stepping into the five-story, nondescript gray office building on Baronne Street, I surveyed the men in suits, and the women in business attire scurrying about. Studying their faces, I wondered which one of them harbored secrets like Garrett. Did the muscle-bound security guard at the entrance to the building prefer to be dominate or submissive? Did the pretty brunette in red, next to me in the elevator, like to be spanked or bitten? Dealing with Garrett had taught me to see the world in layers. Everyone was hiding something, trying to exist in the world of light, but fulfilling their fantasies in the shadows. From housewives with steamy romance novels to politicians with numerous mistresses, everyone was living some kind of alternative existence. An existence where their desires came first and their obligations came second. Stepping out of the elevator on Al's floor, I daydreamed of a world where the shadows we hid behind no longer existed, and desire was expressed openly. What kind of world would that be?

"Damn, Lexie," Al bellowed when I walked through his office door. "You got some great shit here." He pointed to his computer on his cluttered desk. "Great shit."

"I'm not even halfway finished yet, Al." I closed the door and went to the cheap chairs in front of his worn wooden desk. "Imagine how much more you'll like it when it has an ending."

"One of the reasons I wanted you to come in and see me today. We need to talk about that ending, and this series." He had a seat behind his desk, shoving some papers out of the way in front of him. Perusing the mounds of mail, bills, and scraps of paper all over his desk, I felt heartened. It was worse than mine.

"I know you'll probably be pissed with me. I sent your first three chapters on to an editor I know with Donovan Books, out of Atlanta. Her name is Cary Anderson."

I sat back in my chair with a thud. "Al, it wasn't ready for that. What I sent you was—"

He held up his chubby hand, silencing me. "Let me finish before you chew my ass out. Cary loved it. Loved the shit out of it. She wants to offer you a contract for this book, and a series of books. I'd changed the title of the book, though. You could call it *Taming Elise*...that way, for the series you could insert a new woman's name each time. What do you think?" He paused, staring into my eyes, waiting for me to react.

"Al," I said after a few moments of letting the news sink in. "I can't believe this."

He slapped his hand on a few papers piled to his right. "Believe it. I've got a contract coming over in the next few days, and I want you to sign it. They're going to give you an advance, set up a signing tour, and do some heavy promotion for you."

Normally, I would have been jumping up and down with excitement, but I wasn't. I was thinking about what Garrett would say. Would he be pleased?

"Hey, Lexie?" Al snapped his fingers at me. "I just told you you've got a sure fire hit on your hands, and you're staring into space." He stood from his chair and came around the side of his desk, gawking at me with his squinty brown eyes. "Are you high?"

I laughed at him. "Al, you know I don't do drugs."

"Then what's wrong with you? Every other writer I represent would be as happy as a hooker in a fraternity house." He wiped his hand over his red, sweaty face.

Al's similes were always colorful.

"I am happy Al, really," I assured him. "And I appreciate all that you've done. I've just got a lot…well, a lot going on."

His eyebrows rose on his pasty brow. "Lily isn't giving you shit again, is she? Tell that caustic mother of yours to back off. I told you to stay away from her. You always…," he waved his hand at me, "get this way whenever she rides your ass."

"It's not my mother, Al." I shook my head, debating whether or not to tell him about Garrett. There were a lot of intimate details I shared with my agent. He became mother, best friend, worst enemy, and sometimes, the bastard I would hire a hit man to blow away. Al was also pretty good about offering me advice, even when it was unsolicited.

"Is it Ralph?"

I could not believe the man had asked me that question. Christ, was I that obvious?

He shifted his bulk against his desk, and the flimsy furniture slid a little across the yellow-tiled floor. "Hey, I read your book, Lexie. About two chapters in, I knew Ralph was real. I know how you write, and I've never seen such passion in your pages before. Whoever he is, you're smitten."

"Smitten?" I laughed. "Is that even a word anymore?"

"For old Jewish guys it is. So who is he?"

Sighing, I figured what did I have to lose? It wasn't like I had a slew of girlfriends to discuss my troubles with. Al was about the only friend I had. I really needed to get out more.

"His name is Garrett, and yes, he is Ralph. He's a dominant…like in the book?"

Al shrugged his round shoulders. "He likes tying women up, you mean."

"No, not tying, just…dominating. You know, controlling a woman, telling her what to do and so forth."

Al's beady eyes drew together. "How is that different from how most men act? Despite what all the feminists say, Lexie, men are still the dominant sex. It sounds like your guy is no different. Maybe he just has more to prove."

The offhanded remark gave me pause. "What do you mean by 'more to prove'?"

He waved off the question. "You know men, Lexie. Then again, maybe you don't." He stopped and shrugged his round shoulders. "You see, men need to possess...to dominate. It's important to hold a woman captive, keep her close, make her want only for us. It's a rush." He pointed at me. "Your guy sounds the same way."

"No, it's more than that. With him, it's—"

"It's all about power, Lexie. When some men can't be the top dog, they find how to satisfy that urge in other ways. Like Ralph in your book. You have him as an executive in a large engineering firm. He has a boss he has to answer to, so he finds an outlet for his need to be in charge with women."

I had to give Al kudos for his analytical skills. I had never thought of that angle. I had written Ralph as a mirror image of Garrett, and as I mulled over what Al was telling me, it all began to make sense.

"So what's going on with you and Ralph?" Al probed.

I shook my head. "I wish I knew. I'm not sure how to describe it."

"You already did describe it in your book, Lexie. Maybe you should go back and read what you wrote. Seems pretty clear to me how you feel about the guy. Why isn't it to you?"

I remembered Garrett's comment the previous day about reading my book and the insight he had gained from it. I thought that he had been talking about himself. Perhaps he had meant me. Instantly, the reason he had stayed away became obvious.

I stood from my chair. "Thanks, Al. I should get back to my book."

He walked me to his office door. "I'll e-mail you those contracts as soon as I get them. Once you sign, you're going to have to bust ass to get that book finished. Cary wants to move real fast." He opened his office door. "Send me the new chapters and we'll go over it."

I eased into the hallway. "Got it."

"And Lexie, don't worry about your Ralph. He'll come around."

Giving Al one last hopeful grin, I headed down the hallway to the elevator. It was time to get back to work.

Day 13

I had started at sunup on my book, having added two more chapters the day before. Ralph and Elise had been to the party and aroused by the orgy that had been put on display by the demented queen of the elusive Marquis Club. After, they had returned to Ralph's apartment, where Elise had given herself to him. I figured that was what should happen in the story…it was time.

Now my characters were moving toward the next phase in my novel, the conflict. It was that interesting point where their reality came crashing down around them, and they realized that to make a relationship work, they had to be willing to sacrifice part of themselves. It's a shame that real people didn't come to this conclusion as easily as fictional characters. Then again, characters only had a few hundred pages to right a lifetime of wrongs and change; human beings had a whole lot longer and a lot less motivation. No wonder I preferred my characters to people…they were easier to understand.

I was amazed at the speed of my writing. Unlike my other books, this one was pouring out of me. I had already outlined the plot for the next book in the series, about Ralph's adventures with a famous art historian, and had plans for another with Ralph and a Dominatrix name Lucinda. I had other ideas, based on the things Garrett had told me, and some ideas for stories I thought would add to the series.

In the middle of a particularly heated scene between Ralph and Elise, the buzzer from the downstairs door made me jump from my chair. Aggravated at the disturbance—and thinking it was the FedEx guy again, hitting all the buzzers until someone let him in the house—I went to the speaker by my door and pressed the button opening the main entrance.

Back at my desk, I was reading through the last few sentences I had written, getting my train of thought back, when the light rap on my front door surprised me.

Tentatively I approached the door, worried that Colin had returned to terrorize me some more. Instead of Colin, I discovered Garrett standing on the landing. He was holding out a cup of coffee from Café Du Monde and a white paper bag stuffed with beignets.

"We have to talk," was all he said before strutting past me and into my living room.

"Gee, good morning to you, too, Garrett," I muttered, closing my door.

When I faced him, I noticed he was not wearing a suit jacket. His black slacks were sharply pressed while his cream-colored shirt still had those freshly dry-cleaned creases. As he walked by, a whiff of his musky cologne made my toes curl. Then, the aroma of coffee and beignets begged me to follow him into the kitchen.

Standing by the breakfast bar, he handed me the cup of coffee as his eyes took in my outfit. "Did you sleep in that?"

I glanced down at my oversized nightshirt. "Yes, why?"

He dropped the bag of beignets on my white countertop. "Don't you think you should dress?"

I opened the lid on the coffee cup, inhaling the enticing fragrance. "No, I'm a writer. We don't dress for work." I nodded to the beignets. "Why are you bringing me breakfast?" I lifted the coffee to my lips.

He went to the cabinets to the side of my sink. "I can bring you breakfast, if I like, Lexie."

"After our conversation yesterday, I thought you wanted to stay away from me for a while."

He came back to the counter, carrying a white plate. "I got a summons from Mabel last night."

My hand froze, the coffee millimeters from my mouth. "A summons?"

He emptied the bag of beignets onto the plate. "Colin has put in a request to claim you. I was called to the club to respond. I was given a choice to claim you for myself, or let Colin do it for me."

"That sneaky son of a bitch." I slammed my coffee down on the bar. "I didn't want to say anything before. Colin came here the day after the party, threatening me. He knows I'm a writer, and he suspects this has all been about a book. He said if I didn't let him claim me, he would ruin you and me."

Garrett crumpled the white paper bag in his hand. "You should have told me."

"I was trying to protect you," I professed.

He stood before me; his livid eyes probing mine. "Is that why you came to my office yesterday and offered yourself to me? Because of Colin's threats?" He threw the bag across my kitchen.

I shrugged, lowering my eyes to the plate of beignets on the bar. "I knew if I said anything you would have confronted him, and then things would have only escalated. I didn't want things to get out of hand."

"Goddammit, Lexie!" he yelled, making me take a frightened step back. "You should have said something to me."

I threw my hands up. "I thought I could handle it."

He stood before me, his lips slammed together. Turning away, he went to the sink. With his back to me, he clutched the edge of the sink. I watched as his knuckles turned white.

"Garrett, we can fix this. All you have to do is claim me in the ceremony, and then Colin will—"

"I don't want to do that." He slapped his hand against the sink's edge. "Not with you. I never wanted to bring you into this. I thought one time at the club and you could slip away unnoticed. Then we were ordered back, and I knew it was too late." When he turned to me, his face was contorted with anger. "When I take you for the first time, it will not be in a room full of strangers. The first time between a Dom and a sub should be special, and not made into some cheap sex show."

I went around the bar to him. "I don't think we have a choice."

"We have a choice, Lexie. I'm not going to be pressured into taking a sub, and I'm not going to have you go through with that ceremony."

"Have you ever claimed anyone at the club before?"

He let out a long breath. "Once. The last sub I was with, Elena. She belonged to the club before I arrived, and when I joined, I took her."

Ah, another one. How many women had there been? I was beginning to consider where I would fall on his long list of subs.

"What happened to Elena? Is she still there?"

"She's there." He waved his hand about the kitchen, frowning. "She belongs to Gerard Bence, the attorney."

I recalled the slender blonde with the crystal clear blue eyes, and my resolve faltered. I crept closer to him, almost afraid to ask what I was thinking. "Why did you give her up?"

He pushed away from the sink and strutted into the living room. Determined to get an answer, I followed him.

"Answer the question, Garrett," I shouted.

He spun around to me. "Don't ever tell me what to do."

"Cut the bullshit, Garrett. This isn't about Doms and subs, it's about people. Why did you give up that woman? Did you get bored with her? After I humiliate myself in front of those lunatics, is that what is going to happen to me? Are you going to chuck me aside once you've gotten what you want?"

His hands flew to my shoulders, squeezing me. "Don't ever speak to me like that again."

"Are you going to punish me again? Spank me like some silly child? You can't just tell me to do what you want, spank me, boss me around, and think I'll listen to you. It doesn't work that way." I wiggled free of his hands.

"How does it work, Lexie? Because I'm beginning to get the impression that, no matter what I demand of you, there will be no taming you."

"Why in the hell do you have to tame me? Why can't you just accept me as an equal?"

He stepped back from me. "That's not what I do!"

"Well, maybe you should give it a try, because the other way sure isn't working for you. How many women have there been, Garrett? How many times have you made a woman your sub, only to walk away?"

"What are you after, Lexie? More material for your book?" He headed for the front door.

"Are you happy, Garrett? Does all this control you think you have over people make you happy?"

He halted at the door, seemingly swayed by my words. Then his back stiffened and his rigid posture returned, mirroring that uncompromising will of steel beneath his controlled exterior.

I slowly approached, determined to get through to him. He could only run away from the ugliness of his life for so long before it started haunting him. Haunted people always looked the same to me; dead on the inside. If Garrett wasn't careful, he would end up that way. I should know. Until the day he had walked into my life, I had been just as close to death as he was.

"You can chase after all the women in the world, Garrett, make everyone your slave, but I promise you this…until you start taking a good long look at your life, you will never be happy."

"What makes you an expert on happiness, Lexie?"

I reached out to him, gently placing my hand against his back. He pulled away from me. I had hoped we had grown closer, but now I was not so sure. Maybe all I would ever be to him was a submissive mistress. Another woman he could use up and toss aside.

"I'm sorry." I lowered my hand. "I shouldn't have said that."

He slowly faced me. His eyes were as ruthless as the day we had met. Nothing about him had changed. I was the one who had changed.

"There's only one question you need to concern yourself with, Lexie. Do you wish to continue with this? Do you still want to be mine?"

I gazed into his eyes, knowing there could be only one answer. "Yes, Garrett. I do."

As he raised his head, I could see his anger retreating. I had given him what he wanted.

"The ceremony is set for Saturday night," he pronounced, and waited for my reaction.

"How did you know I would consent?"

"I read your book." He cast his eyes to my hardwood floor. "A white robe will be delivered to you Friday. Wear nothing beneath it. A car will collect you and bring you to the club. I cannot have any contact with you until the ceremony. They will be watching."

I thought of his club members spying on my home, and I grew fearful. I did not show him my trepidation. I couldn't. "I understand," I mustered.

He raised his head and his features had warmed a little, offering a glimpse of the man I so desperately wanted to know. "If you change your mind, I can call the whole thing off at any time."

"What would happen to you and your business then?" I shook my head. "Colin made it very clear what he had planned. It would ruin you."

"That's not your concern. I don't want you doing this to save Hayden Parr's business," he admitted. "Eventually, I'm sure I can set things right with him."

Studying Garrett, as he stood before my door, I remembered something Al had said to me. Here was an intelligent, successful man who had never ventured into business on his own. Why?

"You don't need Hayden Parr anymore, Garrett. I think it's time you made a go of it in New Orleans without him."

"Hayden has been good to me," he maintained, scowling.

"It's your contacts here, your sacrifices. I think you would be happier with your own firm." A rush of confidence came over me. "When we have put this ceremony behind us, and you have proven yourself to the club, you should start checking out office space."

He pulled me into his arms. "Now who is giving the orders?"

"Wouldn't you like your own business?"

Garrett touched his forehead to mine. "I always dreamed of having my own place one day. It was just never the right time."

I snuggled against his thick chest. "The right time is now."

Holding me close, he sighed into my hair. "When I take you on that stage Saturday night, I want you to think only of me," he whispered. "No one else. Just me."

I shivered as I envisioned standing naked next to that red velvet chaise.

"I promise I will be as gentle as possible." He kissed my cheek.

I leaned back and admired the perfection of his chiseled features. "I trust you."

Garrett's face lifted into a bewitching smile. "That's the first time you've said those words, and I actually believed it." He dropped his head to me. "Say it again."

"I trust you."

He poised his mouth inches from mine. "Then you're ready." He hesitated, as if debating the need to kiss me or walk away, and then his forehead furrowed. "I need to go," he mumbled. "If I stay.... I'll see you Saturday night."

He turned and opened the door. Without glancing back, Garrett jogged toward the stairs.

Closing the door, I grinned as a glimmer of satisfaction snaked through me. It was the first time I had seen a crack in his well-controlled façade.

"Perhaps there is a way to win with Garrett, after all."

My heart leapt at the thought of breaking through his cast-iron resolve. My elation was soon replaced by dread. Before I could revel in being his, I had to be claimed. That humiliation was something I was not sure I would ever be able to endure.

Day 14

After a sleepless night, staring out my bedroom window, I rose before sunrise in search of coffee. As I stood beside my kitchen counter and waited for the coffee to finish brewing, I spied my laptop. I remembered Garrett asking me once how far I was willing to go for my book. It would seem I now had my answer. I had endured humiliation and pleasure at Garrett's hand. In order to truly understand the inner workings of his world, I would soon pledge myself to a life as his sub. I contemplated if I should be writing fact, instead of fiction, because when I'd set out on this journey I never imagined I would end up here.

The exploits of Ralph and Elise were nothing compared to the real life drama of me and Garrett. How would our story end? Would I eventually bore him and be passed on to another Dom in the club? Or would we find something special, break away from the club, and settle down to a somewhat vanilla life? If I never took the chance with him, I would never have the answers. Shaking off my dreary mood, I filled my mug with coffee. A person could go crazy trying to outthink fate.

Taking my mug to my desk, I turned on my laptop and read the last few sentences I had written. Despite the chaos in my life, Ralph and Elise were building a relationship beneath the rules of their lifestyle. I had Ralph growing as a character because of Elise's devotion, and Elise becoming empowered because of his affection.

Up until this point in the story, I had not mentioned the word love. Ralph was not the kind of character who would profess such an emotion. Was Garrett? The question had always been there, floating in the outskirts of my mind. I kept going back to the picture of him with his nieces, and how different he had seemed. Would he ever be that way with me?

The cell phone on my desk roused me from my mental meanderings. When I checked the caller ID, my stomach did a happy summersault.

"How are you holding up?" Garrett's smooth voice came through the speaker.

"I'm fine." Admiring the trickling of light creeping in through my balcony windows, I inquired, "Why are you up so early?"

"Couldn't sleep. I'm lying in my bed and thinking of you. I gathered you were probably up."

I sipped my coffee. "Hey, I thought you weren't supposed to contact me before the ceremony?"

He chuckled into the phone, warming me up faster than the coffee. "I'm not, but at this point I figured to hell with their rules. I wanted to see if you were all right, and if you had changed your mind about the ceremony."

"You, breaking the rules…that's a first." I could almost see him grinning. "And no, I haven't changed my mind."

He yawned, sounding more relaxed than I'd ever heard him. "You can still back out, Lexie. I don't want you to feel as if you have to do this."

"I'm not going to back out. I want to do it." I got comfortable in my chair, gripping my coffee mug. "I may not be too enthused about Saturday night, but I won't let you down."

"This isn't about me. It's about you."

"It's about both of us, Garrett. If this is what I have to do, then I guess…."

His sigh filled my phone speaker. "Of all the women I have known, you're the first who has truly given yourself to me. I think it is you who has dominated me all along."

"Wow," I mumbled. "I didn't expect that."

"Neither did I." There was a bit of rustling on the other end.

"What are you doing?"

"Getting out of bed," he answered. "I might as well get up."

My imagination went wild with visions of him rising naked from his bed. "Do you sleep in pajamas?" I playfully asked.

"No," was all he said.

I put my coffee down, feeling flushed.

"Are you still in your nightshirt?" His voice became a little deeper.

I glanced down at my shirt. "Yeah, why?"

"Where are you?"

I frowned at my phone. "At my desk."

"I want you to go into your bedroom, and lie down on your bed."

"I'm working…why do I want to do that?" I didn't get up from my chair, and listened to his breath coming over the line.

"Do not question me." The lilt of aggravation in his voice reminded me of whom I was dealing with.

Unsure of what he was after, I rose from my chair and headed to my bedroom. After I spread out on my bed, I gripped my phone.

"Fine, I'm on my bed."

"Close your eyes. I'm going to help you prepare for the ceremony by practicing a run through."

I opened my eyes. "Why do I need to—?"

"No talking," he interrupted.

I rolled my eyes and closed them again.

"Picture us on that stage with no one else in the room. We're all alone. You are in your white robe, and I'm in my tuxedo. All you have to do is listen to my voice as I tell you what to do. I'm going to tell you everything that I'm going to do to you. Do you understand?"

A rush of white heat stirred in my belly. "Yes."

"I slowly ease the white robe from your shoulders. You can feel the soft material slipping away from your body, as it drops to the floor. You are naked before me. I'll admire your creamy skin and fabulous breasts, while I remove my jacket and set it on the chaise behind you. I'll undo the buttons on my shirt while you wait patiently in front of me." He took a breath, and I could feel my body relax while his reassuring voice saturated my mind. "I've opened my shirt now, and I raise your hands to my chest. I want to feel you next to me, so I pull you closer. I caress the curve of your incredible ass, and my hands run up and down along the sides of your hips. Can you feel my hands on you, Lexie?"

"Yes," I mumbled, as the burn between my legs spread up my spine.

"While I'm kissing your neck, my fingers glide down your stomach, very gently. When I reach between your legs and touch you, you moan for me."

The pictures in my head were becoming very clear. As my ache for him grew, I yearned to moan out loud.

"I'm standing next to you, stroking your wetness. I nip at your neck and tell you how much I want you. I want you, Lexie. I want to be inside of you."

My legs rubbed against the bedspread beneath me. My desire was getting the better of me.

"I'm going to take you from behind," his seductive voice continued. "After I turn you around and drape you over that red chaise, I'm going to ease my fingers into you, to get you good and wet for me. I'm going to rub your clit with my thumb. Just when you are so close to coming, I will unzip my pants, spread your legs apart, and thrust so hard and deep into you that I will make you cry out. I'm going to fuck you very hard and very slow. Can you feel me doing that? Can you feel my pushing into you, forcing your flesh apart?"

God, I wanted to feel him doing that. "I can feel you."

"I'm going to make you scream my name out into that room when you come. You're going to be throbbing all over when I'm done with you. Then I'm going to take you home and do it all over, again and again. You will enjoy every minute of it, I promise."

My heart was pounding in my ears, as my insatiable need consumed me.

"Now you want me, don't you?" he teased.

I rolled over to my side, clenching my phone. "Yes, very much."

"You want to come, don't you?"

"Damn you," I sighed, surprised by my bravado.

"Soon, Lexie, I will satisfy your hunger for me. Until then, think only of me, and what I'm going to do to you. Nothing else concerns you. Can you do that for me?"

"I'll try, Garrett."

"'I'll try,' Master," he corrected.

"Master," I repeated.

"I'll see you Saturday night." He hung up the phone.

Letting out a long, frustrated breath, I rose from the bed. Despite Garrett's detailed accounting of what to expect, I knew the ceremony was going to be a lot more difficult to get through. I ached more than ever for him. Shit.

Returning to my computer, I decided to put Elise and Ralph in a torrid love scene, very similar to the one Garrett had just described. I figured if I could not have the real thing, writing about it was going to have to do. When I opened my book, an alert from my e-mail flashed in the lower right hand corner of my screen. The e-mail was from Al.

Attached is contract with Donovan Books. Congrats, Lexie. You've hit the big time!

Opening the attachment, I excitedly read through the five page document. The terms were better than I could have hoped, with proposed contracts for three more books after *Taming Elise* to be part of the *Taming...*series. Sitting back in my chair, a brief flurry of pride came over me. I had always wanted to be with a big publishing house. My previous publisher had been small, yet well-respected. With Donovan Books, I could really reach a wider audience. I had achieved my goal.

Thoughts of Garrett began to cloud my celebration, and I debated if I had actually attained that coveted pinnacle of success. Without Garrett to share it, my victory felt incomplete. In the space of a few days, he had worked his way into my heart. Now every success was going to be meaningless without his approval. What had become of the independent woman I had strived so hard to be? Was I any less of a woman for wanting a man? Was I nothing more than a sub wanting her Dom's approval? Perhaps every one of us needed that pat on the back from the person who held our heart. After all, what was success without the best wishes of the ones who helped you to attain it?

What about Lily?

The unwelcomed question slipped into my mind like liquor at a junior high dance. My mother's approval was something I had never sought. Like any alcoholic substance banned to those under the age of twenty-one, Lily's remarks were sure to be detrimental to my future. I had long ago given up on trying to please my mother. Why re-open wounds that had scarred over?

After gleaning the contract, I sent a reply to Al, telling him I accepted the terms. He could work out the rest of the details. That was what he was getting paid to do.

Business out of the way, I returned to my story, eager to get back to Elise's night of passion with Ralph. As my love scene came to life on the page, I was painfully aware that bringing my two fictional characters together for sex was not placating my need for Garrett. Reaching for my mug of coffee, I took a sip of the lukewarm brew and thought of Garrett's silky voice in my ear.

"Bastard. I'm going to need a cold shower before this day is out," I muttered. "I just hope he does, too."

Day 15

The next morning I was beyond edgy. The ceremony was fast approaching, and I felt doomed to go through with it. I yearned for it to be over, and was sure I would be thankful when it was done. Or would I?

During the night, while tossing in my bed, I had thought ahead to a possible future with Garrett. I knew this wasn't the most ideal way to find a partner. I hoped that after the games had been played, and the intimacies established, we might finally have the chance to just be together. Did I know what I was getting with this man? Then again, did any woman know what she was getting with any man?

Back at my desk I settled down for a day of writing. I had a book contract to fulfill and deadlines to look forward to. I needed to focus on my career and not the man who had re-awakened it.

Deep in thought over which way to go in a scene, I was startled when my front door opened. Luckily I had left the safety chain on the door, keeping the intruder from gaining access. Jumping from my desk, I ran to the door, considering whether or not to grab a knife from the kitchen.

"Who's there?" I yelled.

"Alexandra, open the goddamned door!"

I ripped the chain from the track. "Mom?"

Dressed in a cornflower blue designer pantsuit, her deep brown hair was coiffed to perfection about her oval face. Her makeup was flawless, highlighting the pink in her lips, cheeks, and skin, while the warm gold necklace draped about her glistened in the pale light of my doorway.

"What in the hell are you doing here? How did you get in?"

She held up a gold key ring in her hand. "You gave me your keys. In case you ever got locked out." She peeked into my apartment with her round brown eyes. "Is he here?"

"Is who here?"

She rolled her eyes. "That man of yours…what's his name?"

"His name is Garrett, and no he's not here. It's ten in the morning. He's at work." I looked past her to the staircase, paranoid that she might have been followed. Garrett's warning about being watched still troubled me.

Lily came in the door, dangling a blue leather Chanel purse in her hand. "At least this one works. The last character you were with made loafing something of a profession."

My raging stomach began working on my long-awaited ulcer. "Sid worked. He was a musician."

Lily went to the antique sofa and keenly inspected the fabric. "Sid was an idiot." She waved her hand over the cushion. "When was the last time you cleaned the velvet, Alexandra? I told you to wipe it down and vacuum it dry at least every week."

"It's furniture, Mom, not a puppy."

She dropped her blue purse on my coffee table. "Figures. I buy you something beautiful and you neglect it. Sounds like the story of your life, if you ask me."

I made a mental note to search for Tums. "Why are you here?"

"Because I wanted to see what was going on with that man of yours. Did you sleep with him?" She had a seat on my sofa. "If you haven't, you'd better do it quick. Otherwise, you'll come across as a tease, and he'll dump your ass."

"Gee, Mom. When did you become an expert on men? I don't remember you having a relationship that lasted longer than a weekend at the Holiday Inn."

My mother sat up on the sofa, looking as stiff as a sinner in church on Sunday. "You always were a smart-mouthed kid. It was cute when you were six, Alexandra. Now it just makes you look bitter."

"Bitter?" I shouted, and then I stopped. I was not going to let her get to me. Not today. I had a book to get through, a twisted ceremony to dread, and a future with a dominating man to plan. "Why don't you just tell me why you're here, Mom? I have things to do."

She clasped her hands about her knees. "What things?"

"I have a book to write for starters, and I don't need you to—"

The buzzer at my door rang out.

"Maybe it's him?" Lily said, a little too enthusiastically for me.

I furrowed my brow. "No, it's not him, and I don't like the way you...." I shook my head. "Never mind."

Leaving my mother on the sofa, I went to the speaker at my door and pressed the intercom. "Yes?"

"I have your delivery, Ms. Palmer," a man with a high-pitched voice returned.

I gathered this was the white robe Garrett had told me would be delivered that morning. "Ah...." I glanced back at my mother, cursing his timing. "Can you come upstairs? I'm in 2A."

"Yes, ma'am," he answered.

Moving away from the speaker, I immediately saw my mother's eyes were all over me. "What are you having delivered, waffles to go along with your...," her hand waved over my favorite gray sweat suit, "pajamas?"

"These aren't pajamas, and it's not breakfast. It's clothes."

"I find that hard to believe." My mother rose from the sofa. "The last time you took an interest in clothes was when you were six and tried to talk me into letting you wear your princess costume to school."

"I don't remember that."

She came up to the door. "You were six; no one remembers when they were six." Lily stood next to me, smiling. "It had little roses sewn into the skirt and lace about the hem. My mother made it for you, right before she died. You said you wanted to wear it for her."

"I remember Grandma Bea. She made all of my clothes."

"She used to care for you when I was in nursing school." My mother swept a few hairs that had fallen from my ponytail out of my face. "She always called you her little Lexie."

"I thought you called me that."

"No, Alexandra, I never called you that. It never suited you."

Heavy footfalls came from the landing. Anxious to retrieve the robe, I opened my front door.

An older gray-haired man approached from the stairs. He was not dressed like a delivery man, and wore a black suit with a black tie. In his arms was a long, black garment bag, and as he came to a stop before my door, he held out the bag to me.

"I am to collect you tomorrow night at eight," he said in a girlish-sounding voice.

I took the bag from him, as my mother curiously watched me. "Thank you," I said, not sure if there was anything else he needed to hear.

He nodded to me, then to my mother and turned for the stairs.

Carrying the garment bag to my bedroom, I could hear my mother's high heels tapping on the hardwood floor behind me. Placing the bag on my bed, I glanced back at her.

"Go ahead, ask; it's killing you."

She waved a hand at the bag, making the gold bracelets on her wrist jingle. "Is it from him? Do you have some special date?"

I stood next to my bed trying to come up with an explanation. Sure, I could have lied to her and agreed with her story. It sounded like a good idea and a way to keep her out of my hair. On second thought, she would probably want to see the dress and give me pointers on my makeup. It was time I told my mother the truth about what I was doing. If I was lucky, the shock would kill her.

Placing my hand on my hip, I took a deep breath. "It's not a dress, Mom. It's a ceremonial robe for tomorrow night. I'm going to be inducted into Garrett's club as a submissive. Garrett is a Dom, a man who likes to dominate women and tell us what to do. He is collaring me in a special ceremony at his club. Yes, we will be having sex after that, and no, I haven't slept with him, yet. The reason I'm doing all of this is because I'm writing a book about Garrett. A book, I might add, that just went under contract with a publisher in Atlanta, who is paying me a nice advance and is going to make me a lot of money. I'm even going to make a series out of this, and being with Garrett is research."

She stood in my bedroom doorway staring at me for several minutes. Her brown eyes were dissecting me, determining if what I said was true. Then she adjusted a few bracelets on her forearm, frowning at me. Big surprise there.

"I don't know where you got your imagination from, Alexandra. It must be something on your father's side, because no one in my family would have thought up such a cockamamie story." She motioned to me. "If you're going to have a big date and sleep together, then just say so. I don't need all the dramatics." She spun away from my door and headed into the living room.

"Yes, Mom, we're going to have a big date and sleep together." I quietly chuckled. I should have known the truth sounded too strange to believe.

Gliding across my small living room, she paused at the sofa. "The last bit you told me about the book deal…is it true?"

"Yes. I signed the contract yesterday with Donovan Books. Al is very excited about it."

"Al?"

"My agent. I told you about him."

"Yes, I remember. Well, at least he's earning his ten percent." She picked up her purse. "Tell me one thing, Alexandra. Do you like this man, Garrett?" Her eyes connected with mine. "I mean, really like him."

"You could say I've tried harder with him than most men I've known."

"Even Sid?" Mom tucked her purse under her arm. "I wasn't a fool. You never married Sid because you loved him…you married him to piss me off. Don't throw this one away because you think it will make me unhappy. Worry about your own happiness for a change."

"I didn't marry Sid to make you—"

"Please, Alexandra." She held up her hand. "I'm not going to stand here and pretend that we've got a great relationship. You've always been so different from me, and so hard to understand." Mom's rigid posture relaxed as she studied me with her judgmental eyes. "You want to know why I detested Sid? He wasn't good enough for you, and I didn't want to see you make a mistake with him. Garrett, on the other hand, can be the kind of man you need."

"How would you know what kind of man I need?"

"You need the same kind of man every woman needs: a partner, a friend, a lover, and most of all a supporter. One who will pick you up when you are down, and love your faults, as well as your assets. Lord knows, I've been searching for one of those. Just like your father, they've all come up short." She moved toward the door. "I came here this morning to tell you not to walk away from Garrett to spite me. I can see now that I was wrong. You don't want to walk away from him; you want to be with him…very much."

"I'm going to be with him after tomorrow night," I told her, rubbing my hands together.

"After that collaring ceremony you told me about?" Mother's well-tweezed eyebrows went up.

"I'm going to be his."

Lily shook her head with impatience. "Lord, Alexandra, you're already his, why do you need a ceremony to prove it? Collaring ceremonies, weddings, it's all the same thing. Why do you think I've never married again? You don't need the paperwork, darlin'. You need the emotional commitment. You just have to ask yourself if Garrett feels the same way as you."

"That I don't know," I confessed, in a mumble.

"You'd better find out, fast." She opened the door. "If I was going to go through with one of Mabel Bergeron's tacky ceremonies, I would make damn sure how the guy feels."

I gawked at my mother's back "Wait…you know about the club, about Mabel, and…?" I was too shocked to go on.

She turned on the landing and glanced back at me. "Of course I know. You don't think I've dated some of the city's most connected businessmen and not heard of Mabel's place. This is a small town, Alexandra…everyone knows about her club. I just never figured you to be into such stuff."

"I'm not into it. Garrett is. If I don't do this ceremony with him…it could hurt his business."

Lily dropped her chin. "Did he tell you that?"

I nodded my head.

"So you're doing this for him?"

I leaned against my doorframe. "In the beginning, I thought I was doing this as research for my book.

Somewhere along the way, Garrett became more important than my story. That's never happened to me before. I'm not sure why I'm going through with any of this. All I do know is...I can't let him down."

Lily smirked, coming across as smug. "That's what happens when your heart takes over your thinking from your head. You start making choices you can't explain." She opened her purse and began rummaging through it. "This is good for you. You need to have a relationship like that at least once in your life. It will help your books. The stories you write aren't realistic."

I folded my arms over my chest, smirking back at her. "What would you know about my books? You've never read any."

She pulled her sunglasses from her purse. "Don't be silly, Alexandra. I've read every one of your books. I'm your mother, after all." Waving her sunglasses in the air, she added, "Bring Garrett around for dinner some time."

Lily turned on her expensive heels and went to the landing. In amazement, I watched my mother ease down the steps, appearing every inch the gracious lady. When I was a little girl I had tried to emulate her walk, only to discover it hurt my feet. When I grew older, I tried to do everything the opposite of my mother. My sarcasm started out as a way of getting even with her for being ignored through the years. As I watched her head disappear down the steps, I realized that despite my efforts, I was like her in many ways. Not only did we share a certain drive to be our own woman, we shared the same fragile heart. Hers had suffered through so much more than mine, but we hid our pain in the same way...we shut out those who needed us most.

Shaking my head, I stepped back inside my door. All these years I thought my mother had never bothered with my books. I had misjudged the depth of her emotions. She wasn't the heartless witch I had envisioned, she was simply being …well, Lily. A woman who lived life her way, and the rest of the world bedamned.

Closing my apartment door, I thought back to all the years we had been at odds. Perhaps it was time to cut my mother some slack. She had done the best she could. Maybe I was finally growing up. Reaching a point in my life where I could look back at how I was raised, forgive the faults of my upbringing, and embrace the fallibility of my parent. She was, in the end, only human.

Stepping inside my bedroom, I unzipped the black garment bag on my bed and removed the long white silk robe. The material was not as sheer as I'd thought, saving me at least some embarrassment when I walked into the dark green parlor. As visions filled my head of men and women watching while Garrett and I consummated our union, the robe fell from my hands. What in the hell had I been thinking? I couldn't do this.

I began to hyperventilate and dropped to my knees. I crawled to my desk outside of my bedroom door and grabbed my cell phone. I was in the process of calling Garrett and telling him the entire ordeal was off, when that little voice in the back of my head made itself heard.

You do that, and he's done with you.

My stomach cramped and I covered my mouth, thinking I was going to vomit. The cramp soon passed and I sat on my living room floor feeling thoroughly desolated. The enormity of what I was about to do had finally hit me. Like a bride on the eve of her wedding, fear overwhelmed me. Then again, a bride and groom didn't have to consummate their union in front of the wedding guests. I did. Was that what was really bothering me, or was it the idea of finally being his? I was not sure what was worse: knowing I would be humiliated in public or subjected to his whims in private. What did I really know about this man? Instantly, I heard his delectable voice in my ear from the previous day, describing in detail what he would do to me, and I relaxed.

Wiping my hand over my face, I sighed out loud. "Shit, this is worse than I thought."

Standing from the floor, I headed to the kitchen and retrieved the bottle of scotch from beneath the sink. Wincing as the burn of alcohol went down my throat, my jittery nerves abated. After a few more stiff swallows, I was better. Not calm, just better. Carrying the bottle back to my desk, I wanted to keep my liquid encouragement within reach. I hoped I had enough left in the bottle to get me to tomorrow night.

Day 16

I was standing in my bathroom staring at the white robe hanging on my body and fighting the urge to run screaming out my front door. In my hand was the almost empty bottle of scotch that I had been steadily sipping throughout the evening. I was not drunk, but I was getting there. I wished that I had kept a ready supply of pain medication in my apartment. Mixed with the alcohol, the pills would have made the coming event tolerable.

I had left my hair down—was there a right way to put it?—and had slipped on my tennis shoes, figuring no one would be interested in my feet. With the alcohol in my system, good shoes with rubber soles would be required, in case I needed to make a fast getaway. I had found the courage to put on makeup—nothing more than some blush and lipstick—and as I stared at my reflection, I contemplated why I was doing this. Was it for my book, for Garrett, or for me?

"You can do this, Lexie," I encouraged, psyching myself up. "Get it over with, and then you can have that man you've been hot for since the day you first laid eyes on him. Take a chance, do something wild for once, before you are too old to give a damn." I took another sip from the bottle, draining it. "Who gives a shit if anybody sees my bare ass? At least...." I put the bottle on my vanity. "Fuck it."

Marching into my living room, I collected my purse and glanced over at the clock on my microwave. It was exactly eight.

The buzzer from the speaker rang throughout my apartment. I closed my eyes, saying a silent prayer to whatever patron saint of bondage might happen to be listening above. Did they even have a patron saint of bondage? I was so out of practice being a Catholic. I just hoped the mechanics of Heaven worked like a library; a place where you could pay a late fee and be allowed back into the fold.

Heading to the door, I squared my shoulders and bolstered my courage. It wouldn't be that bad. I had been through worse humiliation married to Sid. I was reminded of the two times I had gone down to central lockup to bail his ass out for fighting in a bar. Both times, I had been treated like the criminal for marrying such a man. I had thought my shame complete, until now.

"Just keep thinking of Garrett," I muttered, opening the door. "He will get me through this."

At the entrance to the house, I was greeted by the gray-haired man I had met the previous day, in the same black suit and tie.

"Are you ready, Ms. Palmer?" he asked in his squeaky voice.

"I'm ready," I proclaimed, and stepped on the porch.

Scrambling ahead of me, the driver then paused beside the black gate at the end of the walkway and motioned to a black Lincoln Town Car waiting at the curb. He held the back passenger door open, gave me a warm smile as I slid onto the black leather seat, and shut the door. From the moment we left my home until we pulled in front of Mabel Bergeron's wrought iron-encrusted mansion, my driver said not a word, making me curious as to what the man was thinking. I itched to ask him how many women he had delivered to Mabel's, dressed in the same white robe, but then thought better of it. I might be more stunned than comforted by his answer.

When I climbed from the rear of the car, he bowed slightly to me and said, "Have a pleasant evening, Ms. Palmer."

I knew then that he had no clue what was about to take place. I didn't say anything, and walked up to the gate at the edge of the property. Ahead, the oak door and huge black cast-iron lanterns taunted me, as if to say, "Enter at your own risk."

When I climbed the steps to the wide front porch, I had to pick up my robe to make sure I didn't trip on it. The hint of a cool breeze blew by me, making me shiver. I wished I could have at least put on a T-shirt or something underneath the robe, to keep me from feeling so naked. After I pressed the brass doorbell, the thick oak door opened.

Much to my surprise, it wasn't Mabel's maid answering her door. It was Mabel. Covered with a red satin dress that amplified her round figure and a few red feathers protruding from her bright red hair, she resembled a dyed Easter chicken on steroids.

"There's the woman of the hour," her annoying voice boomed. "You're right on time."

"Mrs. Bergeron," I said, and then covered my mouth. I had forgotten Garrett's rules about speaking.

"It's all right, honey." Mabel waved me into her yellow-wallpapered foyer. "You can speak freely with me. Your Dom hasn't arrived, yet."

After stepping under the harsh lights of her two-tiered brass chandelier, I felt self-conscious about my skimpy robe and wrapped my arms around me. Remembering my role, I lowered my eyes to the oak hardwood floors.

"Thank you," I mumbled.

Mabel closed the heavy door and came up to me. "You're not like the others I get in here. I could see it that first night. I could also see how swayed he was by you. He didn't want to take you in front of the other men. He respected you." She gazed up and down my figure, adding to my apprehension. "You've got yourself a real find, do you know that?"

"I'm sorry. I don't understand what you mean." My eyes darted about the foyer as my insides twisted tighter.

"Garrett Hughes. Not many get to serve under an elite. I envy you for what you are about to experience."

I stared into her cunning green eyes. "Are you saying that Garrett...I mean my master, is—?"

"An elite master, yes," she cut in. "Why do you think he's with my club? I got word from some other clubs in Dallas that he was in New Orleans, and I sent my son to invite him to join us. It's quite a feather in my cap to have him." She ran her hands over the feathers in her hair. "Excuse the pun." Her raucous chuckle echoed about the foyer.

I recalled the things Garrett had told me about elite masters and how skilled they were reputed to be in the art of domination.

"He never said anything to me about being an elite master."

Mabel's slim lips spread into a concerned frown. "Why should he tell you anything? I've heard from his former sub that Garrett is a skilled manipulator." She flourished her plump white hand down my white robe. "Look at what you're doing for him. He planned this, down to the last detail. Probably why he insisted on the ceremony taking place tonight."

I gaped at her in astonishment. "He insisted on this ceremony?"

"Yes, I wanted to wait to collar you. I thought he'd need more time. Happily, he proved me wrong." Mabel wiggled her finger at me. "I knew you were a Dom the moment I saw you. You have the eyes. He knew it, too. So he set out to tame you, to switch you from Dom to sub. It's the ultimate achievement for any Dom, and he wanted to share his success with our group."

"He said…you were making him do this."

She shook her head. "First rule of bondage, Alexandra; everything is consensual. I don't force anyone to be collared. Garrett knows that." She turned toward the short hall. "Come, I will show you to the waiting area."

As we made our way past the family photos hanging in the hallway, the sting of doubt began to circle my heart. Had he manipulated me to get me here tonight? Was I just a trophy to prove that he was truly an elite master?

Before the last door that led to her parlor, Mabel halted and reached for the crystal doorknob on her left. "You wait in here until Garrett comes to get you." She pushed the door open. "There's champagne already open on the table for you. I suggest you drink before the festivities begin."

I stepped inside the room…closet really. It was only large enough to accommodate a small wooden table and two high-backed red leather chairs. The walls were painted the same shade of dark green as the parlor, and from the center of the high ceiling hung a stained glass chandelier done in alternating shades of light green, yellow, and white.

"Everyone should be here in about fifteen minutes," Mabel spoke out from the doorway.

I spun around to her. "What if I would have said no to all of this? What would you have done to me?"

"To you, nothing; to Garrett…." Mabel sighed, tipping her head to the side. "He would have been shamed for not bringing you to task. Being shamed is tantamount to being shunned in his eyes. I'm sure he would have pursued you until he broke you. That's what elite master's do." With that, she quietly shut the door.

I immediately went to the open bottle of champagne and picked up one of the two flutes sitting on the table next to it. Pouring out the champagne, my hand trembled, almost spilling the bubbly liquid all over the table. My flute was not even half-full when I put the bottle down and chugged the contents of my glass. Deciding not to bother with the effort of refilling my flute, I lifted the bottle to my lips and drank deeply.

"What are you doing?" Garrett demanded, walking in the door.

His tailored tuxedo clung to his strong body, and his hair had been slicked back, adding to the chill in his eyes. Despite my anger and confusion about Mabel's words, my body still melted when I saw him.

He came up to me and pulled the bottle out of my hand. "Are your trying to get drunk?"

I stretched for the bottle. "Drunk? No, I want the bottle so I can crack you over the head with it, you lying, manipulative son of a bitch!"

He held the bottle high in the air so I could not reach it. "What is wrong with you?"

"Me?" I pulled my arm back and punched him hard in the gut.

He bent over, and I took the bottle away.

He coughed once. "Lexie, what is the matter?"

I held up the bottle, ready to clobber him. "Besides the obvious, that I'm standing in a gown, buck naked underneath, waiting for you to take me in a room full of depraved psychopaths and rape me?"

He stood up, fully recovered from my blow—those damned ripped abs—and clasped my arms. "Talk to me. Tell me what is going on."

"Mabel told me you set this up. You did all that stuff to me, the punishing and the pleasure, because you saw me as some kind of prize. Colin wasn't the one who wanted to switch me…you were."

"All right, stop this." He wrenched the bottle out of my hand and put it on the table. "Yes, I went to Mabel and requested to collar you. I had to do it before Colin went to her. I knew if I made the first move, he would have to bow to my wishes."

"You lied to me. She said nothing would have happened if you didn't collar me. Nothing would have happened to either one of us."

"And you believed her?" He pointed to the door. "Lexie, you've seen the people waiting for us in that room. Do you believe they would just let us walk away? You're from this goddamned city…do I have to remind you how corrupt it is? How favors win contracts and how connections have to be nurtured with a lot of money and political pull?"

He was right. Backroom deals and political intrigue were ingrained into the history of my hometown. Maybe it was our sordid past, or maybe it was something in the water. Whatever made New Orleans rife for illegal dealings, it was the way things were.

I glared at him and remembered Mabel's disclosure. "When were you planning on telling me that you were an elite master?"

He rubbed his hand across his chin. "After…I didn't think you needed to know before."

"Why not? I think I deserved to know, Garrett."

"Master," he corrected.

I waved him off and headed toward the door. "I'm done with you and your bullshit games."

Before I could reach the door, he came up behind me and flung his arms around me, pinning me to him. "This is not a game, Lexie, not to me." His lips tickled my ear. I could feel his hot breath against my skin. "You think I've been training you, molding you on a whim?" His hips ground into my backside. "I've been preparing you for me. I want you. But in order to have you, to keep you safe from everyone else in this club, you have to commit to me. I'm doing this to protect you."

I squirmed in his arms. "I don't need your protection, Garrett."

"Yes, you do, Lexie. How long do you think it will be before Colin comes after you, or one of the other men? They won't bother to try to get your consent. You know the kind of men these are. They don't give a damn about women, and they certainly won't give a damn about you."

He loosened his grip on me, and I faced him. "So for you to protect me, I have to be humiliated in that room? Have you...?" I tried to control the panic seizing me. What loomed before me was all too real. I lowered my head to his chest. "Christ, I can't do this. I'm not like those women, Garrett."

"I will be right there. It will be over quickly, I promise. I will not hurt you."

I raised my head to him. "You already have."

The torment that radiated from his dark eyes spread throughout his body. His arms fell from my sides, as if zapped of their immense strength. He took a step back from me and ran his hand over his slicked back hair.

A loud rap on the door shattered the silence in the tiny room.

"You're on," a man's voice called.

Garrett went to the door, avoiding my terrified face. After he opened the door, Colin, dressed in his tuxedo, grinned at him.

"They're waiting." Colin held out a black leather collar to Garrett. "You'll need this."

"We're coming," Garrett barked, and then turned back to me. He grabbed my hand and pulled me toward the door.

I yanked my hand away, and he glowered at me. He faced Colin and muttered, "Give me a moment." Then, he slammed the door.

He was instantly on me, pressing his hands into the sides of my head. "You have to do this, Lexie. You have to go out there with me. If you don't they will rip us both to pieces, and I won't be able to protect you. Do you understand?"

I gasped and wanted to scream. I bit my lower lip, holding back my tears. I had never felt so low. I had struggled for years to be an independent, strong woman. In the matter of a few minutes, it was all going to be taken away from me. How in the hell could I fight back? I was trapped.

Taking my hand, Garrett went to the door. When he opened it, Colin was waiting patiently in the hallway.

Colin smirked at me. "Looking forward to the show."

"Shut up, Colin." Garrett ripped the black collar from his hand and pushed him out of the way. "From now on, keep your eyes off her or I will tear them from their sockets."

Colin was shocked by Garrett's outburst. Instead of challenging him, Colin backed down and stepped to the side. Garrett pulled me into the hall and across to the door that led to the parlor.

Before opening the door, he looked back at me. "Walk three paces behind me, and keep your eyes on my back. Don't look at anyone but me."

My lower lip trembling, I nodded my head.

He opened the door, and the bright lights from the room sifted into the hallway. Mabel's bone-chilling voice was urging the crowd to their seats, ready for the ceremony to begin.

Garrett stood with his back to me. When I saw the collar clenched in his right hand, I truly thought I was either going to throw up or pass out...I wasn't sure which one.

As the din in the room grew quiet, Garrett entered the dark green parlor. Angling my head to see around his wide shoulders, I viewed the chairs arranged in a circle and the stage situated in the middle of the room. Sitting in the chairs were women attired in beautiful long gowns of various styles and colors, with men in tuxedos standing behind them. Observing the blues, greens, reds, and yellows of the different ball gowns made my head spin. While nearing the short stage, the champagne I had quickly downed a few moments before started churning in my stomach. By the time Garrett came to the edge of the stage, I was overcome by a violent shaking. I had never been so terrified in my life.

Garrett stopped right before the stage and held out his hand to me. When my quaking hand took his, his gaze locked with mine. Slowly, he climbed onto the stage and helped me up, supporting my very unsteady body by slipping his arm about my waist. As we arrived before the red velvet chaise, I stared at the offensive piece of furniture, wondering how many women had been spread across it for the sake of the lurid desires of the club.

Mabel stood from her high backed mahogany chair. The feathers in her hair billowed as she tossed her head about, and as I watched those feathers, an unsettling queasiness rose up the back of my throat.

"This is for the rights to this woman and her admittance to our club," Mabel announced. "Alexandra Palmer has freely chosen Garrett Hughes to be her master." She motioned to Garrett. "Garrett Hughes, do you accept this woman?"

Garrett nodded his head. "I do."

Mabel turned her gaze to me, and the burning in the back of my throat was rising higher. I felt lightheaded, and my body became racked by a sudden wave of fire.

"Alexandra Palmer, have you consented to this ceremony?"

I was about to open my mouth to consent when something else came out instead of words. The champagne I had hastily downed made an unexpected reappearance all over the chaise. Garrett was immediately at my side, holding my shuddering shoulders.

The audience around us let out a few surprised gasps and one or two oh my Gods, and then Mabel's voice rose above the rest.

"I guess that answers that question," she chuckled.

"She can't go through with this," Garrett affirmed, his arm about my shoulders. "She's been unwell."

Through watery eyes, I saw a few of the ladies standing from their chairs and covering their mouths. I could feel the wet vomit on my robe, smell the acrid odor about me, and my mouth tasted like…never mind. I clung to Garrett, trying to stay upright.

"She has to go through with it," a man's voice rang out.

I turned my head and saw Colin standing beside his mother, motioning to me and scowling maliciously. Garrett's grip on me slackened, and he took a step closer toward the edge of the stage.

"They have to complete the ceremony. She's not a true member until the ceremony is finished," Colin protested.

All the mutterings in the room grew quiet as eyes veered from the stage to Colin. For a split second, I thought Garrett was going to go after Colin, then he turned back to me. He came around behind me and secured the black leather collar in his hand about my neck.

"Satisfied?" he shouted to Colin. "She's mine and a member of the club."

"You have to consummate the act," Colin ranted. He turned his blue eyes to his mother, pleading, "They have to go on with it."

"Colin, shut up," Mabel bellowed. "No one is going to ask that poor girl to go through with anything after such a display." She glanced back at Garrett. "I'm satisfied the ceremony is complete."

"No, you can't be," Colin yelled. "Since when has a collaring ceremony not been consummated?"

Mabel's enraged eyes tore into her son. "I am the monitor for this club. If I say it is good enough, it is. Second of all, I'm very sure none of the others want to stay in here a moment longer than necessary." She gestured to the entrance. "Let's retreat to the dining room for drinks, and if anyone has the stomach for it, some supper."

The other club members began to hastily exit the room, spurred on, no doubt, by the lingering odor in the air. Garrett helped me off the stage, and as soon as my feet hit the green carpet Colin was barreling toward us. Garrett saw him coming and pushed me behind him.

"You haven't properly claimed her." Colin was right in Garrett's face, sticking out his chest like a proud rooster. "I will take her from you, and you can't stop me."

"Touch her, and I'll kill you," Garrett snarled. "She's mine."

Colin's face was red and his blue eyes were on fire. He was pulling back his right arm to take the first swing when Mabel's throaty voice called to him.

"You'd better think long and hard on that, boy."

Her son stopped, his arm cocked back in mid-air. I could tell by the fury twisting his features that he wanted to rip into Garrett, but he was afraid.

"You raise a hand to another member of this club, Colin, and I will kick you out and never let you back in." Mabel slowly walked up to him. "You have used this club as your personal harem for quite a while now, and I have said nothing. I will not stand by and let you make a mockery of our rules about violence." She pointed her fleshy finger at me. "The girl belongs to Garrett Hughes. The ceremony is done. Now get your ass out of here before I distance you from that trust fund your father left you."

Colin very slowly lowered his arm. He adjusted his tuxedo jacket, gave me one last leer, and bolted for the door.

After he left the room Mabel sighed, sounding more disappointed than frustrated. "He may be my son, but he's also an arrogant little shit." Her green eyes turned to Garrett. "I blame his father. Max Bergeron had a real weakness for pretty women." She folded her hands in front of her. "I suggest you get your new sub out of here before he returns."

"I'll pay to clean the...." He waved back to her red velvet chaise.

"Don't worry about it. We're even now." Mabel smiled as her eyes lingered on me. "I can honestly say I've never seen that before. Probably one of the most memorable ceremonies I've ever witnessed." She paused and then added, "You should be very grateful that you're his. Be careful what you do with that power you have over him."

"What about the others?" Garrett pressed. "Will they side with Colin?"

Mabel shook her head, making her red feathers dance. "They hate Colin. No one will care once they have had a few drinks in them. These are businessmen, Garrett. As long as they know you have control over her, they won't question any ceremony. Nevertheless, I would suggest staying away from the club for a while. It might be best to let things settle down before you bring her back, all right?" She winked at him. "Call me in a few days, and we'll talk again."

We stood by the stage as Mabel sauntered out of the room, swinging her wide hips from side to side. Finally free of the prying eyes of all the other guests, I let out one long, relieved sigh. Despite the condition of my clothes and the horrid taste in my mouth, I wanted to jump for joy. I was free of the ceremony, and my weak stomach was to thank for it. The silence around us was unexpectedly broken by the tinkle of glasses, as the lone bartender cleared away the bar.

"Wait here," Garrett ordered while letting go of my hand.

He left my side and walked across the room, his long stride quickly covering the short distance to the bar. I admired how his tuxedo hugged his wide shoulders and round butt. Touching the collar around my neck, I was comforted by the knowledge that he had put it there. I should have been disgusted or infuriated that I had been made his in such a way. The funny thing was…I didn't care. The man had claimed me. That mattered more than the object he had used to declare his intentions. It was just a symbol after all, like a wedding ring or tattoo. The meaning mattered more than the token.

At the bar, Garrett spoke a few words to the bartender. After being handed a towel and glass of water, he returned to my side.

"I guess that nasty bug you had wasn't quite finished." He poured a bit of the water on to the towel and then handed me the glass. "Drink that."

I took a sip, thankful to wash the awful taste from my mouth. Garrett wiped my face and then, holding back my hair, rubbed the towel along my neck.

"It wasn't the bug," I explained, as he gently wiped my hands. "It was the champagne and the bottle of scotch I had earlier at my place."

"Champagne and scotch don't go well together, Lexie." He wiped his hands on the towel.

"Yeah, I got that. I just needed something to help me get through tonight."

"I'm sorry. I shouldn't have pushed you." He tossed the towel to a nearby chair. "I should have come up with some alternative."

"It doesn't matter now." I took in a deep breath, feeling better. "At least this humiliation I can get over. The other…." I shrugged.

"We need to get you out of here." He put his arm around my shoulders. "Get you out of those smelly clothes."

"Where are we going?" I asked.

Garrett ushered me toward the parlor door. "Home."

* * *

We didn't return to my subdivided mansion on Esplanade Avenue. Instead, Garrett drove me to a converted red-bricked building in the historic Warehouse District of the city. Square, plain, and with cast-iron, tulip-shaped street lanterns in front, it did not stand out from any of the other structures in the neighborhood. The fifteen-story edifice suited Garrett. It reminded me of him: understated, reserved, and yet, formidable.

The first floor had been converted to a garage, and as he typed his code into a keypad at the entrance, I took in the desolate street around us. At any time during the day or night, the French Quarter—only a few blocks away—was bustling with activity. Here among the quiet residences and businesses, all was delightfully peaceful.

After parking his black BMW in his designated spot, we walked, hand in hand, to an elevator with polished silver doors.

"How did you find this place?" I asked, my voice reverberating throughout the garage.

"Actually, Colin told me about it. He used to live in the penthouse, I now rent, before he bought a house in the Garden District."

A tweak of regret made me cringe. "I'm sorry I came between you two."

"You weren't the first, Lexie. When I initially joined the club I had my sights on Heather, but he claimed her before I could speak up. After that first day we met, he told me if I didn't take you he would. I should have known then that he was going to be trouble."

The elevator doors opened, and we stepped inside. "I don't see you with Heather," I confided, as the doors closed before us.

"She would have been a poor choice," he agreed with a slight nod of his head. "Especially after what Colin told me about her."

"What did he tell you?" The elevator rose upward.

He let go of my hand and leaned against the car wall. "She had made the rounds of several clubs, and had a reputation for changing Doms pretty frequently. I've known a few women like that and wanted something else."

"What else?"

His confounding eyes ran up and down my white robe. "Someone I could talk to."

"Really?" I smirked at him. "I thought barking orders at everyone was talking for you."

"You see, that's what I've been missing in a woman." He pointed at me. "Sarcasm."

"One of my specialties."

"So I've noticed."

The elevator doors opened to a shadowy hallway with just a row of brass sconces lighting the way.

He held out his hand to me. "Take my hand. It's a little dark along this hall."

We walked from the elevator and came to a red door near the end of the hallway. Pulling his keys from his jacket pocket, Garrett glanced over at me.

"I think we need to burn that robe."

I played with the material. "Good idea."

Pushing the door open he stepped inside, and a flash of light momentarily blinded me. When my eyes adjusted, a wide-open space came into focus. There was one large room with unfinished red-bricked walls on one side, and a modern kitchen with shiny stainless appliances on the other. Directly ahead, gigantic windows offered a view of the lights along the dark river. Exposed, rough beams in the ceiling harkened back to the days when the building had been a warehouse. Set amid the beams, spotlights illuminated the polished pine floors.

"Wait until you see it in the morning. There's a great view of the river from those windows," he insisted next to me.

I proceeded further into the room, admiring the simple chrome and white leather modern sofa and thick chairs set around a glass and chrome coffee table. "Am I going to be here in the morning?"

I heard the front door shut with a loud thud. "Absolutely."

Wheeling around, I trembled as he strolled up to me with a cocky grin on his face. "Take off that robe."

The slow burn in my loins rose upward while I unzipped the front of the robe and stepped out of it.

"And the shoes," he directed, motioning to my feet.

Complying, I kicked off my tennis shoes and left them next to the robe. I raised my hand to the black leather collar about my neck, ready to take it off when he stayed my hands.

"No, leave that."

He walked ahead and veered to the right before the wall of windows. I scurried to keep up, catching snippets of the room as I padded across the cool hardwood. I was surprised by the lack of pictures on the walls or decorations of any kind. Other than the sofa, chairs, and coffee table in the middle of the room, and some chrome stools set in front of a curved breakfast bar by the kitchen, there was no other furniture.

Garrett ducked into a short hallway. I followed behind him, admiring the old red brick that covered the walls. Running my fingers along the rough surface, I became distracted until the hallway opened into another oversized room.

An enormous low-rise bed edged in oak and covered with a light red bedspread was pushed against the far wall, with another wall of windows to the left. These windows were partially covered with long beige curtains that ran from floor to ceiling, a good eighteen feet. In front of the windows, a red cherry desk had a phone, laptop computer, printer, and a small pile of papers on top of it. Other than a chest of drawers, the room was almost empty.

Light flashed to my right, and I turned to a recessed half-wall. The sound of running water came from behind the wall, and I slowly moved toward it. On the other side, I discovered a master bathroom with a glass shower stall, a Jacuzzi tub, and a double vanity done in white granite.

"You need to wash that smell off you," Garrett suggested, as he stepped back from the round tub.

I approached the small step that led to the tub and gazed into the running water. Garrett scooped me up from behind, making me gasp with surprise. Plunking me down in the bathtub, he then removed my black collar.

The hot water whirled around me as he disappeared from the bathroom, carrying the collar in his hand.

"Where are you going?" I called to him.

"To change."

Sitting back in the bathtub, I played with the water, washing my face and splashing it about my neck and shoulders. To the side, I found a soap dish with a bar of purple soap that smelled of lavender and began rubbing the bar along my arms and neck, hoping to get rid of the rancid smell on my skin. After scrubbing clean with the soap, I scooted back and rested my head against the edge, listening to the rushing water filling the large tub.

"You need to wash your hair, too," Garrett insisted behind me.

I arched my head back, glancing up at him. He had changed into a deep brown robe that added to the depth of his eyes.

"I got most of it."

He swooped down behind me. "No, you still smell." He eased me forward. "Sit up. I'll wash it."

He went to his shower stall and returned with a blue bottle of shampoo in his hand.

"What kind of shampoo is that?"

He placed the bottle on the side of the tub. "Does it matter?"

"Yes, it matters. I don't want to use stinky shampoo in my hair."

After rolling up the sleeves of his robe, he dipped his cupped hands into the tub and poured water over my head. "Trust me, anything smells better than you do right now."

I wiped the water from my face. "You're a real comedian, considering this is all your fault."

His eyebrows went up. "I will take some of the blame, but not all of it, Lexie." He squeezed a dollop of the shampoo into his palm. "You're the one who wanted to do anything for your book." He began working the shampoo into my hair.

I closed my eyes and frowned when the overly heady scent of the shampoo hit my noise. "Okay, yes, I know I went a little overboard with the book. You were the one who belonged to that stupid club in the first place. I really don't get it, Garrett, you—"

"Master," he interrupted.

"Oh, you're kidding. You want me to call you master after the evening I just had?"

"Yes." He pushed my shoulders back. "Rinse your hair."

I dipped my head back into the tub, soaking my hair below the surface of the water. When I popped up, he pulled the stopper, allowing the water to drain. He went to a door on the side of the shower stall and opened it. When he returned, Garrett had a plush white towel in his hands.

"Stand up," he ordered.

I stood from the bathtub, and he rubbed the towel up and down my naked body. The front of his robe opened up, and I let my eyes luxuriate over his muscular chest. Wrapping the towel about my waist, he lifted me from the tub. I grabbed at his thick arms, feeling his rock-hard biceps. A furor of excitement shot up from my groin. When he placed my feet on the white-tiled floor, he began drying my hair.

"I've got a spare robe laid out on my bed. You go put that on while I make us some coffee. I think it's time you and I had a long chat." He handed me the towel.

"A chat?" I almost laughed out loud. "A chat about what?"

He shook his head. "Just meet me in the kitchen," he mumbled, and walked out of the bathroom.

Completely confused, I stood in the bathroom and listened to his footfalls across his bedroom floor. When most men wanted to "chat" it usually signaled the end of a relationship. Garrett and I did not even have a relationship…not a real one anyway. I wanted more, and I had thought he did, too. Perhaps I had read too much into his touch and the way his eyes gazed into mine.

I finished drying my hair and draped the towel about my body. Edging around the half-wall, I stepped into his bedroom. On the bed was a yellow robe that was better suited for a woman than a man. Taking my time as I walked over to the bed, I took in the bare red-bricked walls of the room.

"The guy definitely needs a decorator."

I went to the darkly stained dresser by the door and smelled the bottle of cologne sitting on top. Crossing the room to his desk, I perused a few of the papers piled neatly to the side. There were bills for his business, a few phone messages, and on one piece of paper, a drawing of a house.

The house instantly appealed to me. It was modern in design with a façade of three interconnected squares made of large windows, with a recessed entrance on the lower floor and a jutting balcony on the second floor. It was a home you would see set on a ridge along a forest or on the shoreline of an ocean. It was a house I could live in.

Smiling, I put the drawing down and went to the bed. Slipping on the robe, I questioned why the best piece of furniture in the house was the bed. He didn't even have a nightstand for the white ceramic lamp sitting on the floor next to it. I thought it typical. A woman would worry about furnishing the living room and kitchen to entertain guests; a man would only worry about the bed to entertain himself.

When I emerged in the vast living room, the aroma of brewing coffee called to me. Garrett was behind the curved breakfast bar, filling two black mugs with the steaming liquid. Approaching the kitchen, I marveled at the way he painstakingly poured the coffee, making sure he did not spill a drop onto the white granite countertop. His kitchen was meticulously clean, without a single dirty dish in the sink or a crumb on the countertop. In fact, the entire penthouse was spotless.

"Do you even live in this place?" I asked, taking a chrome stool in front of the bar.

He set a black mug of coffee before me. "What are you talking about? Of course I live here."

I curled my hand around the mug. "No, really live here; like stay here, throw your dirty underwear on the floor, or let the dishes pile up in your sink?" I motioned to the stainless sink behind him. "Either your maid just came today, or you really don't spend a lot of time at home."

"I don't have a maid, and yes, I don't spend a great deal of time here." He drank from his black coffee mug. "Most of the day, I'm at the office or meeting with clients. In the evening, I'm meeting with more clients or contractors or going to job sites and checking on problems. Other than showering and sleeping here, I don't spend a lot of time in this apartment."

"What about your furniture? Do you actually plan on buying more?"

He put his mug down on the bar before me. "I have a house full of furniture in Dallas. I didn't think I should move too much here at first, because I wanted to see how the firm did." He leaned his elbows on the bar. "If things stay busy, I'll have to start hunting for a house in New Orleans and sell my old home in Dallas."

"Why not build?" I rolled my coffee cup in my hands. "I, ah, saw that drawing on your desk of that house. Why not build that?"

He came around the bar and pulled out a stool next to me. "Were you snooping around my desk?"

I nodded, not wanting to lie to him. I figured there was no point. "Yes, I was. I wanted to dig up some dirt on you."

"And what did you learn?" He sat down next to me.

I took a quick sip of coffee and shook my head. "Nothing more than I already knew."

He leaned to the side, resting his left elbow on the bar. His eyes took in my damp hair, yellow robe, and bare feet curled under my stool. "I think it's time you and I talked about boundaries."

I put my coffee down on the bar. "What? Stay out of your desk?"

"No." He reached out for the seat of my stool and pulled me and the stool closer to him. "We need to discuss limits. It's what I do with a sub when I start a new arrangement. You need it for your book."

"Arrangement? Is that what you call it?" I reached for my coffee, needing a distraction from his probing eyes. "Have you ever had a relationship with a woman? Like in the vanilla way?" I stole another gulp of coffee.

He took a moment to think, staring off to the side. "Not completely vanilla, but yes, I've had relationships."

"When exactly was the last time you were in a relationship?"

"I thought the deal was to tell you about the women I have dominated, not the ones I have had relationships with. Isn't that what you want for your book?"

I slapped my mug down on the countertop. "This isn't about the book anymore, Garrett. It's about you and me."

"Master...and it's about research."

I tried to stand from my stool. "Really? I thought fending off Colin and claiming me was about more than research." I fidgeted to get around him.

He grasped my arms. "We never finished the ceremony, Lexie."

I sank down on my stool, feeling his hands on me. "What difference does any of that make now?"

He let me go and stood from his stool. "It makes a great deal of difference to me."

Garrett turned and was about to walk away when I placed my hand on his arm. "There is something I need to know."

He gazed down at my hand. "What is it?"

"Would you have gone through with that ceremony? Would you have taken me in front of all of those people?"

Leaning in closer to me, he whispered, "Despite what you think of me, I am not a monster."

"What I think of you?" I stood from my stool. "What has that got to do with any of this?"

He paused for a moment, as if trying to fathom my thoughts. "You honestly think I would have forced you to submit to me when you were so terrified?" He backed away. "I had no intention of consummating that ceremony. I spoke with Mabel before I came to get you. I told her I planned on putting the collar about your neck, and that was all."

"She went along with that?" I balked. "I find that hard to believe."

"Mabel may seem hard for running that club, but she is also a loving grandmother of four who does not tolerate cruelty in her home. She had every intention of going along with my plan."

"Why didn't you say anything to me?"

"You needed to appear as if you knew nothing. To make it less likely the other members would blame you. I was simply trying to protect you." He headed across the living room, leaving me standing by the bar, my mouth slightly open.

I did not know how to take what he had just told me. I was furious with him for not saying anything and thought of the anguish I could have been spared. I was also grateful he had wanted to protect me. After he slipped into the hallway that led to his bedroom, I took off across the living room to interrogate him further.

"You could have just told me, you know," I blurted out when I walked into his bedroom. "I could have pretended to be afraid on that platform."

He went to his bed and lifted the light red bedspread. "You're not that good an actress, Lexie."

"Like hell I'm not." I came around to his side while he removed a pillow from the bed. "I'm a very good actress." He stuffed the pillow under his arm. "What are you doing?"

He nodded to the bed. "You can have the bed. I'll sleep on the couch."

Now I was really confused. "Wait, don't you want to…?" My stomach danced with butterflies. "I mean, I thought we came here to…."

His intense eyes were analyzing me. "Came here to what?"

"I thought after you put the collar on me, we were supposed to…." I gestured toward the bed. "You know?"

He smiled, shaking his head. "Putting the collar on you was a sign to the rest of the club to stay away from you, particularly Colin. You wanted to find out what it was like to be a sub to me, Lexie." He sat down on the bed. "And so, you have. I told Mabel the truth about you, why you were with me, and that we were just an experiment. That is why she was willing to let you go and not commit to the ceremony. She knew you were just pretending."

I gawked at him. "You mean this was all…you've just been pretending with me? All the groping, kisses, hand-holding, and dinners were just an act?"

He stood from the bed. "You wanted to know how it felt, so that's what I did. You have enough to write your books. Now I can get back to my life."

I stomped my foot on the floor. "Wait a minute! Where do you get off leading me on? Making me think—?"

"Think what, exactly?" He drew closer. "You were the one who set the rules, Lexie. That first day when we met for lunch, you were the one who defined our relationship, not me." He cocked his head to the side. "Are you saying you want to change the rules?"

There comes a point in any relationship when you know you're about to step over the edge. You throw your heart into the abyss, and pray that all the emotions you are feeling are returned. As I stood there, with his deep brown eyes challenging me, I knew Garrett's heart could never be mine. He was not the kind of man who could be swayed by emotion. What beat inside of him was not a human heart, but a heart of stone, impervious to any feeling whatsoever. Despite all of that, and the warnings of my reason, I based my answer to his question on my relentless desire, and decided to hell with the consequences.

"Yes," I finally whispered. "I want to change the rules."

His face never altered and remained as aloof as ever. "How do you want to change the rules?"

"I want to be…your sub, your slave, for just one night." I lowered my eyes to the shiny hardwood floor. "I want to be yours."

He slowly walked around me, studying me, with his hands clasped behind his back. "Why?" he eventually uttered.

"What do you mean 'why'? I thought you would—"

"Why do you want to be mine?" he interrogated beside me. "If you're going to be mine for one night, then I must know why."

"I guess I want to know how we would be together. I haven't been able to think of anything else but you for some time now."

"I'm glad to hear it." His hands went to my shoulders and kneaded my flesh through the fabric of my robe. "You must let me do whatever I desire to you. Do you agree to that?"

I enjoyed the strength in his hands as they massaged my shoulders. "Whatever you desire, yes."

He came around in front of me, his eyes cool and detached. "Remember what I told you I would do to you during the ceremony?"

I untied the belt from my robe. "Is that how you want me?" I let my yellow robe fall to my feet.

As I stood naked before him, he gazed up and down my figure. I thought I should be used to his eyes on me. I wasn't. The way he was drinking in every inch of me made my skin tingle, driving me crazy. Never taking his eyes off me, Garrett reached for the belt on his robe, slowly shrugged off the thick material, and tossed it to the bed.

It was my turn to ogle his strong, lean body, and my pulse quickened at the sight of him. My excitement dimmed when I saw that he was not erect. Recalling how he had become aroused in the shower, excited by controlling me, I turned away. I knew what I had to do to please him. Positioning myself over the bed, I rested my hands on the bedspread and waited, imitating what I had seen Heather do on the stage during her collaring ceremony. I concluded this was how he wanted me. I was his submissive and could only be taken this way and no other.

I felt him coming up behind me, and I closed my eyes, preparing for what was to come. He spun me around to face him.

"What are you doing?"

I pointed to the bed. "Don't you want me this way? Like in the ceremony?"

He held my hands and pulled them to his chest. "No, I don't want you like that. I want you, Lexie. I want the woman you are, not the submissive you've pretended to be."

"You want me, as I am?" I asked, confused. "Since when?"

He nuzzled my cheek. "Since the moment we met."

I tilted my head to the side as his lips glided down my neck. "Why didn't you say anything before?"

He raised his head, and I noticed the coldness I had always seen in his eyes had retreated. "Giving in to you, would mean giving up what I am. I wasn't ready for that," he softly confessed. "I couldn't let you have that kind of control over me."

His words shattered my image of him as the impervious Dom. On the inside he was just as scared, just as fragile as the rest of us.

"Do you still feel that way, Garrett?" I whispered, conforming to his strong chest.

His lips drew closer to mine. "No."

His mouth crashed into mine, and I was caught up in the fervor of his kiss. I explored the muscles in his chest, and the rippled contours of his abdomen. When I reached around to finally get my hands on his round ass, his arms went about me, pulling me close. His hands roamed over the curve of my butt and along my hips. He kissed my neck, and then bit into the tender flesh at the nape. I sucked in an exhilarated breath as his hand traveled down my stomach to that triangle of hair. When his fingers slid into my folds, I moaned for him.

"Do you want me, Lexie?"

"Yes, I want you."

His fingers thrust deep inside of me. "Say my name," he murmured.

"Garrett," I called out as my insides ignited. "I want you, Garrett."

He pushed me back on the bed, reclining next to me on the light red bedspread. As he kneeled between my legs, his erection rubbed against my inner thigh. I was about to reach for his cock, when his fingers drove into me again. Rubbing my clit with his thumb, he began plunging his fingers forcefully in and out.

"I need you good and wet for me, Lexie."

I was writhing on the bed next to him, caught up in the magic of his hands. I could feel my orgasm climbing upward.

"Oh God, yes," I shouted.

I was just about to come when he jerked his fingers away. "Not yet, my Lexie. Not until I'm ready for you to come," he kissed my right breast, "will I let you come."

I dug my nails into his shoulders, arching into him, anxious for him to take me. Swiftly picking me up from the bed, he positioned me on all fours.

"I've been dreaming of taking you from behind."

I clutched the light red bedspread, impatient for him to enter me.

Wrapping one arm around my waist, his hot breath caressed the back of my neck. The stubble of his beard grazed my skin when he kissed me. I could smell the essence of coffee and cologne on him, as the heat from his body enveloped me. He nipped the back of my neck, spread my folds wide apart, and then he rammed into me, making me cry out with surprise. He went so deep, penetrating as far as he could go.

I reveled in the sensation of him inside of me. Then, Garrett slowly pulled out and quickly pounded into me again, harder than before. This time, there was no discomfort, and I instantly wanted more of him. I wanted all of him.

I rocked my hips into his. "Yes," I moaned.

Responding to my need, Garrett began moving in and out, in slow deliberate thrusts. It was the sweetest agony I had ever known. My body throbbed, my toes tingled, and the tension twisting my muscles pleaded for release. Moving faster, he grunted behind me, and even the sound of his exertion turned me on. Just when I thought I could not take anymore, I was seized by the rush of my orgasm. I screamed as the sound of our hips slapping together reverberated around us. He held me while I gave in to the swell of pleasure. I was barely able to stay upright when he made one last deep push, curled into my back, and came inside of me.

Tumbling with him, we collapsed on top of the bed, catching our breath. It had never been like that with anyone. The intensity I felt made me realize I had been missing something in my previous relationships; something sensual, something provocative.

"Now you're mine." His arms tightened around me.

"It would never have been like that at the club," I joked, facing him.

"No." He flipped over on his back. "One of the reasons I wanted to spare you that fiasco."

"Can I ask you a question?" I sat up and ogled his well-defined chest.

He arched a single brow at me. "Is this more research?"

"No." I paused, trying to word my question without sounding too judgmental. "Why does the club appeal to you? I mean, being a master and all, why does it turn you on?"

He sat up on his elbows. "Turn me on? That's an odd way of putting it."

"Let me rephrase that. Why do you like being in charge?"

Lying back on the bed, he put his arm under his head, thinking. "I like...I'm not sure how to put it. I like having my way, is probably the best way to say it. I don't like wasting time letting people think they know what they want to do, talk about how to compromise and then in the end, do what I intended from the beginning. This way I get what I want without wasting time."

I rested my head on his chest. "There's got to be more to it than that."

"Maybe I find most people don't know what they want. When confronted by someone who does, they tend to yield. I just prefer to be in charge." He played with a strand of my dark brown hair. "It's my nature."

"What about compromise? You ever tried it with a sub?"

His brow furrowed and he frowned. "No," he emphatically stated.

"What about with a woman you had a relationship with? Ever compromise then?"

He sighed and his face relaxed. "Frequently, and it usually led to fights, screaming sessions, and eventually a break up." He dropped my hair from his fingers. "This way, I avoid the screaming and the fighting. Better for my sanity."

"Fighting is part of relationships," I insisted. "Goes with the territory."

"No one enjoys fighting, Lexie. Did you enjoy fighting with your ex?"

I thought back to the numerous fights Sid and I had about money and my mother. "No. Sid and I were always fighting. I should have seen that as a sign of things to come. I wanted to leave him many times before I eventually did. I guess I never had the nerve. I went along with our marriage because I felt obligated. I was never happy."

In one effortless motion, Garrett lifted me off his chest. He sat me up next to him in the bed. "That is the same thing you did with the ceremony. You agreed to it, but really didn't want it. You need to tell people what you want, Lexie. If you don't, you'll just be at the mercy of another Sid. Why didn't you stand up to me from day one and tell me to forget about the claiming ceremony?"

I was taken aback by the question. I thought he knew why I had done it, why I had gone through with everything. "I wanted to do it for you. You needed me, and I wanted to please you."

When he let go of my arms, the look of disbelief that seized Garrett's features was disturbing. I did not understand why he would be so shocked. Wasn't that what a good sub was supposed to do? Please her master?

"You would have gone through that for me?" he said, his voice barely above a whisper.

"I wanted to." I shrugged. "Not sure if I could have, though. Talking about it was one thing. Being there on that stage with all those people staring at me...." I shivered.

His hands rubbed up and down my arms to alleviate my shaking. "I'm sorry. I sometimes think I should have kept on walking that first day I saw you at that park. There was just something about you that I couldn't.... I hope one day you can forgive me for all that has happened."

"I have no regrets. If it hadn't happened, we wouldn't be here now." I cuddled into his strong chest. "Didn't you promise after the ceremony to take me home and claim me all over, again and again?"

He curled his arms around me. "Yes, I seem to remember that."

"You also promised I would enjoy every minute of it." I gazed into his eyes.

"Are you asking me or telling me, Lexie?" His lips came closer to mine.

I pressed into him. "I'm begging you."

He grinned. "I like the sound of that."

When his lips kissed me, he felt different. Not the master or the manipulator he had been, but softer and more vulnerable...like me. His mouth became more insistent as his tongue skirted the edges of my lips. I hungrily accepted him, starving for more. This was not the calculated kiss of a man weighing every syllable of my words or testing me. It was the kiss of a man getting lost in his passion. He wanted me. I could feel his arms tighten around me, holding me even closer. He was kissing my cheeks and neck as he positioned me beneath him. His hands skimmed over me, while his thumbs flicked my nipples, and he knelt between my legs. When his fingers dipped into my wetness, I hooked my legs around his waist, yielding to him, needing him.

He arched over me, gripping my hips. "Christ, I want you."

I ran my hands up his arms to his thick shoulders. "Then take me," I breathed.

His penetration was swift and deep, making me arch with delight. He thrust into me with all of his might, and then he stopped.

"Open your eyes, Lexie."

When I did, he was gazing down at me, his brown eyes warmer than I had ever seen them. He kissed me gently and then slowly eased into my flesh, as if savoring every inch of me.

"Keep your eyes on me," he pleaded, as he pushed all the way inside of me.

His eyes stayed on mine as he moved in and out. The tenderness of emotion in his features was mesmerizing. I was completely his in that moment, shielded from the world beyond that bedroom. As his hips moved faster, bringing me closer to climax, a rush of electricity awakened in my body.

"Garrett," I cried.

He bowed his head into my chest, breathing hard as his orgasm began. He slammed into me again, drew in a ragged breath, and squeezed me in his arms.

"Lexie," he groaned as his body shook above me.

I held on to him, resting his head against my chest while our bodies luxuriated in satisfaction. In all the days we had spent together, I had never felt closer to Garrett. I closed my eyes, thankful for that moment. I had seen that part of him he had fought to keep hidden. I had finally caught a glimpse of Garrett Hughes, the man.

Day 17

I awoke to streams of sunlight shining in my face. Opening my eyes was painful, and I quickly covered them with my hand. Eventually, I was able to peek through my fingers to the source of the blinding sunshine. The partially closed long beige curtains to the side of the bed were allowing just enough light through to let me know it was well past morning. Sitting up in the king-sized bed, I looked about the bedroom, orienting myself. Flashes of my night with Garrett came to mind, and the warm ripple of excitement I had felt in his arms quickly returned.

"Was it five or six times?" I giggled, trying to remember the exact number of times Garrett had claimed me.

The funny thing was, each time he took me in his arms the intensity and tenderness from him had deepened. Just when I thought he was done with me, he would roll over, kiss me, caress me, and move me into a new position. Every time his passion had reached a climax, he had called out my name.

A sense of accomplishment made me smile. Sometime during the night, I had changed from his sub to his lover. The man who had made love to me was not an elite master seeking to control me, but a man wanting me…the real Lexie Palmer.

I threw aside the white sheet covering me and noted the rumpled light red spread at the foot of the bed. Soon, the overpowering smell of coffee hit my nose. I searched the floor and spotted my yellow robe where I had left it the night before.

While tying the belt on my robe, I emerged from the hallway and into Garrett's expansive living room. I found him in the kitchen at his cooktop, tending to a pan on the burner. With a spatula at the ready, he flipped some scrambled eggs, and reached for a black mug of coffee on the counter next to him. I observed his movements, treasuring the opportunity to see him doing something as trivial as making breakfast. It made him less intimidating, and sexier than ever to me.

"You're up," he proclaimed when he spotted me across the room. "Good. Come and eat some breakfast before I take you home."

I walked across the hardwood floor to a stool by the curved breakfast bar. Two plates had been set out with some utensils, a butter dish, and glasses of orange juice.

"I thought you said you never cook at home," I remarked, taking my stool.

"No." He turned to me, carrying the pan of scrambled eggs in his hand. "I said I'm never home to cook. I do manage to keep some food in the apartment…hence, breakfast." He scooped some of the scrambled eggs onto the plate in front of me.

I picked up my fork. "Since it's Sunday, maybe we could go do something fun after you take me home. I could change and we—"

"I have work to do at the office," he interrupted. The coldness had returned to his voice, and his eyes were once again impartial. The man I had been with last night had vanished. "I have designs I need to finish up for contractors next week," he added.

I picked at the eggs on my plate. "I should get back to my book."

He took the pan to the sink. "Yes, you have that to finish."

We said nothing for a bit, and the sound of running water seemed to accentuate the silence between us. When Garrett turned from the sink, he picked up the coffeepot from the maker and brought it over to me.

"I would like to read your book when it's finished," he admitted, filling the black mug set next to my plate.

I dropped my fork on my plate with a loud clang and picked up my coffee. "Sure."

His heartless brown eyes were all over me. "You're angry. Is it because I want to read your book? I thought we agreed that—"

"It's got nothing to do with the book," I shouted. "What is the matter with you? Last night we—"

"Last night was last night, Lexie." He calmly returned the coffeepot to the warming plate on the coffeemaker. "Don't read too much into it. We had a good time, but we both agreed to one night, and now we're done."

I banged my coffee mug down on the counter. "It was more than a 'good time', and you know it, Garrett."

"Master," he advised in a raised voice.

"Oh, I see. The asshole is back." I jumped from my stool and was heading to the bedroom when he came up behind me, grabbing my arm.

"This can't go on between us." He wheeled me around to face him.

"Why not? Why do we have to stop after one night?"

His lips angrily pressed together as his arms held me. "I can't have this. I don't want this with you."

"What about what I want, Garrett?" I tried to wiggle free of his grip. "Tell me to call you master one more time and I swear I will—"

He let me go. "I was right about you. You are a Dom, and I could never tame you, never switch you to be my sub."

"Is that what you have been trying to do this whole time? Tame me? Make me give into you?"

"Submit to me, dammit." He turned away, raking his hand through his hair. "You wanted to get research for your book. I tried to show you how it is, being my sub, but it was always there inside of you, that last refuge of unwillingness to comply." His eyes veered back to me. "Last night I thought I had you, had finally made you mine, then…you're not meant for this, Lexie. Can't you see that?"

"Do you ever let it go, Garrett? Do you ever once stop being this paragon of domination, and just let yourself be a regular guy?"

"Not around a sub…and never around you." He marched toward the hallway.

"And last night?" I called behind him. He stopped in the middle of the room, keeping his back to me. "What were you then, Garrett? Because you sure weren't the master you're trying to be now."

His shoulders sagged, pushed down by an invisible weight. "I am a Dom and you must be my sub. Last night was a mistake." His sigh was heart-shattering. "I did something I don't do, and I can never do again. Do you understand?"

"No!" I flung my hands in the air. "Why would you want to throw away a chance with someone? What difference does it make how we come together, as long as we are together? Don't you want me? What in the hell are you so afraid of?"

"For God's sake, will you stop trying to change me?" When he faced me his eyes were as dead as winter. "I'm not going to give up what I am for you!"

His words ricocheted about my head until the shockwaves settled over my heart. I wasn't trying to change him. Couldn't he see that? Or maybe he didn't want to see it. Shades of my marriage flashed before my eyes, and I was again confronted by a man who could not see the real me.

"I'll find something for you to wear, and then I will drive you back to your place." He headed down the hallway toward his bedroom.

Standing in the middle of his Spartan living room, I felt my world come crashing down around me. I thought I had broken through his defenses, but I had only made them even more impenetrable than before. Gutted by the realization that he would never again be the man he was last night in bed, I knew I could not go back to how we had been before. I wanted the gentle Garrett, the tender man who had made love to me. Not the one that ordered me about like an overzealous director on a motion picture set. He was right, I wasn't meant for that. I needed more. Following him to the bedroom, I was eager to get some clothes and return to the life I had known prior to his arrival. I had been safe before, tucked away from the world in my little apartment and writing my stories. I could be that way again. In the end, I was sure I could make myself forget that Garrett Hughes had ever existed.

* * *

We drove in silence from his penthouse. As his stylish black car parked before the converted mansion on Esplanade Avenue, I yearned to run to the sanctuary of my apartment. Before my hand touched the door, he pulled at the rolled up sleeve of the large white dress shirt he had given me to wear. Keeping my eyes on my tennis shoes, I waited to hear what he had to say.

"I should never have brought you into my world, Lexie. This was my mistake." He let go of my sleeve. "I'll tell Mabel you've changed your mind about the club and insist she leave you alone. I'll vouch for you, and she can make sure you're never bothered again."

I turned to him. "What if I do submit to you, agree to let you run my life, and be my master? Would you want to give me up then?"

His hands gripped the steering wheel. "You don't want that, Lexie, you never did."

"Maybe I do now."

"Think about what you would be giving up. It's not you. You're too strong for this."

"That's not true." I reached for the door handle. "Do you even know me, Garrett?"

He didn't answer.

I opened the car door, and without looking back said, "I'll send you a copy of the book when I'm done." Slamming the car door, I rushed up the walkway to the main entrance, not caring who saw me returning home in such attire. I figured at this point, what was a little humiliation among neighbors.

Back in my apartment, I set the deadbolt and immediately went to my bathroom. Flipping on the shower, I wanted to wash the smell of him from me. I needed to remove every last trace of our night together from my life. Throwing his shirt to the floor, I jumped beneath the hot spray of water and began soaping down my body with gusto. The harder I scrubbed, the more empty I became. Finally, as the tears welled up in my eyes, I sank to the bottom of my shower stall and cried.

Day 18

Sitting before my desk, I was staring at my manuscript, unable to type a single word. I was numb from head to toe. The ache in the place where my heart had once been had not let up from the time I had stepped from his car the previous morning. I could not sleep, could not eat, and I hated him for what he had done to me.

What exactly had he done to me? Had he made any type of declaration about his intentions, or had he professed his undying love? No. With Garrett it had never been about words, but actions. It was those actions that had made me believe there was more to us than just a book. There had been moments when I knew I had gotten through to him. For some unfathomable reason, he had pushed me aside. Perhaps I had been wrong about him all along.

Just when I thought my desolation had hit a low point, my cell phone rang. Springing for the phone on my desk, I hoped it would be him. It wasn't. Sighing, I took the call.

"Hello, Mom."

"Where have you been?" Her usually placid voice sounded a bit frazzled— very unlike Lily. "I've been calling your phone since Saturday night. Were you out with Garrett?"

I dug my fingernail into the soft wood on my desk as my exasperation bubbled. "Why were you calling me? Don't you think we've spoken enough for one year?"

"Oh, you're in a great mood. What's wrong? Are you sick?"

My fingernail dug deeper. "What is it, Mother?"

"Okay, Alexandra." Mom gave one of her long sighs, making my eyes roll. "What happened? Is it Garrett? I can hear it in your voice, something is wrong."

I tightened my grip on my cell phone, denying the tears brimming in my eyes. "Garrett and I are done. He...we decided it wouldn't work."

"Uh huh." Then silence.

Worse than my mother's sighs were her bouts of silence. If I was in the room with her, I could just walk away. On the phone—short of hanging up—there was no escape.

I wiped away the shavings of wood I had carved into the desk with my nail. "If you're not going to talk, Lily, I need to get back to work."

"You scared off another one, didn't you?" Her voice was flat and emotionless, another telltale sign of her disappointment in me.

"I didn't scare Garrett off," I argued, my voice teeming with frustration. She always assumed everything was my fault. Ugh!

"Yes, you did. You always scare men away. You're too smart for most men. God knows that was true with Sid. I had hoped not so with Garrett. He's smart, but he's not as brave as you are."

That made me chuckle. "Brave? Since when have you considered me brave?"

"You've always been that way, Alexandra. Ever since you were small, I could see it in you. You never backed down from a challenge and always ventured headfirst into any firestorm. You're just like your father in that way. Elliot was a risk-taker. At least you found a constructive outlet for that trait. Your father didn't."

"That just makes me stupid, Mom, not brave."

"You've never been stupid. I think that's what Garrett likes about you. He's afraid of you, too. You can see it when he looks at you. You scare him, but in the way a man should be afraid of a woman. Afraid of someone who will tame them and make them want to settle down."

"Tame Garrett?" I laughed out loud, almost letting the phone slip from my hands.

"What's so funny?"

I wiped my hand over my eyes. "I think Garrett was the one who wanted to tame me."

"He's already done that, hasn't he? I can hear it in your voice, Alexandra. The man has done what no other could do. He's reached inside that thick armor plating of yours and found the real you."

I shook my head, remembering our fight the previous day. "Garrett never knew the real me."

"Yes, he did. Why do you think he walked away? He knows you need to decide if you want him. You have to be the one to define the relationship. If you don't, you will never believe in it, never trust it." My mother laughed, something she rarely did. I was reminded of our time together feeding the ducks, and how her laugh had always comforted me. "I think this man is just as stubborn and as proud as you, Alexandra. Someone is going to have to give in first. Until that happens, you'll never know what you could have together."

"What if you're wrong? You have a lousy track record with men, Mother."

"I'm never wrong about men. I know them, too well. I've been with a few good ones, a lot of cheaters, some liars, too many rogues, and one swindler. I've never met one like your Garrett, though. I've never been lucky enough to find a loyal one like that. You need to go after him, Alexandra, before you both regret it."

A short lapse of silence filled the line, as I digested her words. Squirming in my chair, I redirected my thoughts. "So why did you call, Mother?"

"That man may be a whiz at figuring you out, but he sucks at fixing garage door openers. I just wanted to tell you that the damn door is stuck again."

Laughter poured out of me. Just when I thought we had made a connection, Lily once again became the acerbic woman I had always known her to be.

"If I see him again, I'll be sure to let him know," I chuckled.

"If...?" Lily snorted. "Just tell him I'll be waiting for him to come and fix it for me."

"I can come over and take a look at it."

"No, baby. You have someone else you want to be with."

After she hung up, her words stuck with me. Even though I hated to admit it, she was right. I did want to be with him. Just being around him made me feel...safe. So how did I tell him that? How did I put into words how he made me feel, and how much I wanted to give us a chance? I was sure of one thing; this wasn't something I could do over the phone. I needed to see him, and give it one last try, before I could walk away for good.

Alexandrea Weis

Day 19

Parking across the street from Garrett's red-bricked office building, I checked my makeup in the rearview mirror while attempting to summon my courage. I had spent the morning debating on either going to his home or office, and had settled on his office. I hoped that being under the scrutiny of his staff would make it easier to get him to listen to me. As I stood from my car, my eyes immediately went to his line of old-fashioned windows on the second floor. It was hard to tell if the lights were on or off in the morning glare. I knew if he was there, he saw me coming.

Heading across the busy street, I stepped beneath the black canopy over the entrance and squared my shoulders, ready for a confrontation. Once inside the beige reception area with its numerous pictures of stylish homes, the blue-eyed receptionist observed me with her silver wire-rimmed glasses and smiled.

"Hello, Ms. Palmer, welcome back." Her friendly demeanor came across as genuine. In spite of that, the pessimist in me assumed that she had been warned I might show up and start trouble.

"Ah, hi. Could I see Mr. Hughes?" I asked, tightly twisting the strap of my leather bag in my hands.

"I'm sorry, Ms. Palmer." The blonde receptionist gave me a wary frown. "He called earlier, and said he would be out for the next few days."

"Out?" This definitely put a kink in my plans. "Do you know out where? Is something wrong?"

"I'm not sure," she admitted. "He just said something came up, and I was to forward all of his calls to his cell phone."

"Thank you." I nodded, thinking of a better idea. "I should go," I said, backing away from her desk.

"If he calls, do you want me to give him a message?" the lovely woman inquired.

I went to the glass door at the entrance. "No, I'll tell him myself," I asserted before heading outside.

Pulling my keys from my purse, I darted across Camp Street to my car. There was one other place left to go before giving up. I only hoped he opened the door when he discovered it was me.

* * *

I was in the dimly lit hallway on the top floor of his building, standing before the red door to his penthouse. My fist was positioned over the door, ready to knock. I hesitated, not sure if this was the right way to handle things. I was also worried as hell about what was going on with him. If he was ill, he would need me, or if he was working, I might only be in his way. Sick of vacillating between the two possible outcomes, I finally banged on the door. After a few loud knocks, I waited. No one answered. I pounded again and listened for movement on the other side of the door, but did not hear any. After a few unsettling minutes, the reality that he wasn't home hit me. I did not know where he was, or when I would have another chance to set things right. Even if he returned in a few days, I wasn't sure if I would still have the courage or motivation to confront him. This had been my golden opportunity, and it had passed me by.

Leaning my head against his door, I reasoned that fate was trying to tell me to get on with my life and leave Garrett Hughes behind. I should heed the message and go home.

Back in the elevator, I went over the time I had spent with Garrett. A photo album of moments with him ran across my mind like a hurried wedding video. We had been good together at times, bad at others. There was something about being with the man that had not only challenged me, it had soothed my soul. He was comfortable. From the moment we met, I had been able to say anything, or do anything, around him and knew I was accepted. I had never had a great deal of experience interacting with people, but I knew enough to understand that kind of contentment was rare.

By the time I slipped behind my steering wheel, I was convinced that Garrett was unique. I had told him once that he was larger than life to me, and he was. My mother had been right. Garrett had cracked the surface, and wormed his way to my very core. How could I rid myself of such a man?

The debate raged in my head during the entire drive to my apartment on Esplanade Avenue. When I pulled in front of the old mansion, my questions abated and my heart plummeted as I spotted the black Lincoln Town Car parked out front.

Garrett had said he would be able to handle Mabel. Perhaps that was not the case. I contemplated staying in my car and driving away, thinking I could avoid the inevitable. Instantly, I thought of Garrett. If she was coming after me, then possibly she had already gone after him.

Imbued with worry for Garrett's safety, I quickly climbed from my car. As soon as I approached the black car, the gray-haired gentleman who had driven me the night of the ceremony stood from the driver's side. He lowered his sunglasses and looked over the top of the car to me.

"Ms. Bergeron requests your presence, Ms. Palmer."

Taking in the busy street, I searched for witnesses. "Requests or demands?"

The driver, dressed in his usual black suit, came around to the passenger side door and opened it. "Respectfully requests," he replied, holding the door open.

Taking one last look at my home, I was flooded with apprehension about ever seeing it again. Returning my gaze to the driver, I nodded my head.

"If Ms. Bergeron requests it…." I slinked into the back seat.

The driver shut my door and the dull thud made me flinch. Quashing my fear, I fought to stay sharp and thought only of Garrett. Whatever was going on, I had to make sure I did everything I could to help him.

* * *

After being promptly delivered to Mabel's lavish pink Garden District home, I stood before her oak doorway, my palms sweating and my stomach tied in knots. Why did I suddenly feel like a fugitive? The smell of blooming gardenias from the gardens next to the grand porch rose up to greet me, making me nauseous. Above, the two black cast-iron lanterns swung back and forth in the stiff late morning breeze.

"Well, there she is," Mabel greeted in an unusual, almost grandmotherly way. "Glad Felix got you here in one piece."

"Felix?" I asked, gazing about the porch.

"My driver." She waved me inside. "Get your butt in here. We need to talk."

I scooted inside the door and was a little put off by Mabel's outfit. Gone were the heavy velvet gowns I had come to associate with her. Wearing a lavender muumuu with silver slippers and carrying a small white Chihuahua in her arms, she was nothing like the imposing monitor of the De Sade Club. Even her face seemed older, and her voice sounded softer than I remembered.

"This is Elvis," she said, lifting the Chihuahua in the air. "Little bugger is blind and almost deaf, so I have to carry him everywhere."

Screaming erupted in the background. It was not the horrific calls of some woman in pain or terror, but the happy squeals of children playing that echoed about the home.

"Ya'll behave back there!" Mabel yelled into the house. She turned to me, shaking her head. "Three of my grandchildren are visiting today. My daughter-in-law dumped them on me, so she could get her hair done."

I stood, a little mystified, wondering how she was going to question me with her grandchildren darting about. "Your grandchildren are here?"

She shrugged, petting Elvis. "The club is only something I do in the evenings when my family is not around...except for Colin, of course." She moved into her grand foyer. "He's the only one of my three boys not married, and the most spoiled."

I followed as she waddled deeper into her home. Expecting to go to the dark green parlor, I was surprised when at the hall she turned left instead of going straight.

We soon entered a bright kitchen with glass cabinets framed in pine, a deep white ceramic sink, black granite countertops, and black appliances. In the corner, a black gourmet stove with six burners and two ovens stood shining beneath the overhead lights. Mabel waved me to a chair at the black iron breakfast table to the side.

After taking my seat, Mabel handed Elvis to me. The little dog didn't seem the least bit bothered by the change and curled up in my lap.

"I thought it was time you and I had a conversation about Garrett," Mabel began, as she traipsed across the kitchen to her built-in refrigerator. "He paid me a visit last night."

I stroked the soft white fur of the dog. "Was his visit respectfully requested like mine?"

She chuckled, a throaty laugh that reminded me more of the woman I had seen in the club. "No. He came to see me. He said he wanted to talk to me about you." She opened the refrigerator door and pulled out a pitcher of iced tea. "He was very adamant that you were pulled from any further involvement with the club. He wanted me to tell the other members that you were no longer interested in participating, and to assure them that he would vouch for your discretion."

I pensively rested my hand on Elvis's back, and the dog raised his head curiously. "What did you say?"

"Say?" She shrugged and carried the pitcher to her counter. "Nothing to say. You want out, that's fine with me."

"Then why am I here?"

Mabel reached into a cabinet filled with a hodgepodge of glasses. "I needed to hear that from you, and not him." She placed two tall iced tea glasses on the black granite countertop. "When he brought you here, I immediately recognized you from your books." She turned to me. "Love your books, by the way. I'm a fan."

I shook my head, more than a little astounded. "Why didn't you say anything before?"

Mabel filled the two glasses with tea. "I was curious if your reasons for being with Garrett were genuine, or merely for a storyline in another book. I got my answer that first night when I watched you with him. For a sub he was training, you were awfully uncomfortable with the entire situation."

"Then why insist I come back for that ceremony?" I waited as she brought the two glasses of tea to the table. "Why not tell Garrett not to bring me back?"

Mabel slid a glass of tea in front of me. "Because I saw the way he looked at you, Lexie. You don't mind if I call you Lexie, do you? Garrett said you preferred it to Alexandra." She put her glass down and took Elvis from my lap. "Come to Momma, baby." Cuddling the dog against her ample bosom, she appeared tender and caring.

"How did you get into this, Mrs. Bergeron?"

"It's Mabel, Lexie. I'm only Mrs. Bergeron to attorneys and bankers. To everyone else, I'm Mabel." She sat back in her chair as Elvis settled in her lap. "My husband, Max, started the club years ago. He called it a gentleman's club. Well, it didn't take me long to discover there was nothing gentlemanly about it. So I insisted on sitting in on a few meetings. Soon I was helping Max run it, setting up rules, and after his death a few years ago, took it over completely." Smiling at me, she lifted her tea. "We're good at games and wearing masks in New Orleans. That's why my club works for a lot of important people. They also like discretion, which I give them."

I ran my fingers along the rim of my tall glass. "I can assure you, Mabel, that there won't be anything about you or your members in my book."

"Garrett already told me that he has read it, and insisted that all identities are safe. He even promised a copy…if he ever returns."

"What do you mean returns?"

"If he returns to New Orleans." She patted Elvis's little white head. "When he came to see me, it was to withdraw from the club. He was heading back to Dallas to talk to his boss about finding his replacement for the firm in the city. He said his job here was done."

I covered my mouth with my hand, hiding my shock. I had never planned on that scenario. I had envisioned anger, resentment, even distancing himself from me for a time. I never imagined him packing up and leaving New Orleans for good.

She leaned forward in her chair, studying my reaction. "He didn't tell you, did he?"

I lowered my hand from my mouth to my glass. "No. I went to his office and apartment today to speak to him, but…." I took a needed gulp from my tea, wishing for something stronger.

"I see." Mabel's green eyes carefully inspected me, as if trying to read my inner workings. She sat quietly petting her dog, as I fidgeted in my chair and drank from my glass. "When you first came to my club, how much did you know of bondage and Doms?" she eventually probed.

"Nothing really." I put my glass down on the smooth surface of the table. "Garrett had told me some."

"You have to understand that the roles we play in my club, Dom and sub, master and slave, are no different from roles we play in real life. We're all into bondage in a way. We're bound to families, jobs, governments, the IRS." She chuckled. "Even love is its own kind of bondage, because we will do anything for those we love. Like you would do anything for Garrett."

My eyes flew to hers, and then I lowered them to the table. "Love? I'm not in love with him, and he certainly—"

A scurrying of running feet and giggling from the hall beyond the kitchen door interrupted me. Mabel stood from her chair and handed Elvis back to me. I placed the little furry white dog in my lap, and he curled back into a ball and went to sleep.

"Stop running in the house, or there will be no cookies later!" Mabel shouted into the hallway.

There were a few more giggles, and the sound of running feet quickly grew fainter. When she came back to the table, Mabel was shaking her head.

"I love the little shits, but sometimes they try my patience." Easing her round figure into her chair, she let out a long sigh. "When you have children, Lexie, make sure they heed you. If not, you will have to resort to blackmail like me."

"I don't think kids are in my future. I was married once, and that ended pretty badly."

"So Garrett told me. Now you have another chance with him." Mabel's eyes returned to me, and the hardness I had always detected in them was gone.

I dropped my gaze to Elvis. "I don't have a chance with Garrett. I don't think I ever did."

Mabel's raucous laugh bounced about the kitchen, making Elvis raise his head and look around. "Oh, honey, you have him, all right. Until he met you, Garrett Hughes was an elite master, who excelled at manipulating others to give in to his demands. He could have taken any woman of his choosing to that claiming ceremony and made her submit, but not you. When he said he wasn't going to take you on that stage, I knew he had fallen in love with you. Love is dangerous for any Dom. It's even more devastating for an elite master like Garrett. He's no longer his own man; he's yours." She leaned forward, grinning. "I told you before to be careful with the power you had over him. Now what are you going to do with it?"

"Do?" I demanded. "What is there to do? He's gone back to Dallas. I think it's pretty clear the life he has chosen, Mabel, and I'm not a part of it."

She stood from her chair. "Life is what we we're given, Lexie. Living is what we make of it. So why don't you go after that man and start living?"

Day 20

The heat of the midday sun was already beating down on the sidewalk, as I stood at the glass entrance to the Renaissance Tower in downtown Dallas. A fifty-six story modern skyscraper, the sleek glass and steel structure shimmered in the bright sunlight.

Reaching for the brass door handle at one of the entrances to the building, my nervous stomach fluttered. This had to be one of the craziest things I had ever done. While making my way across the gray and silver lobby, I questioned what I was doing in Dallas. After meeting with Mabel, I decided that I had nothing to lose. Now I was having second thoughts. Determined to press on, I stepped inside the finely paneled elevator and punched the button to the thirty-third floor; home of Parr and Associates.

As the car made its slow ascent, I picked away specks of lint from my black slacks. I had done a quick retouch of my makeup in the taxi from Dallas Love Field, yet somehow, I felt it wasn't enough. Shouldn't a woman be dazzling when she goes to profess her feelings to a man?

When I exited the elevator on the thirty-third floor, I followed a pale beige hallway until I came to the glass entrance to the Parr and Associates. The two front doors were trimmed in dark wood and covered with a logo of a black rooftop, which covered the name of the firm written in red.

The reception area was done in alternating shades of brown and beige, with a burgundy Oriental rug and overstuffed leather furniture. On the walls were various framed pictures of large mansions I assumed were in the Dallas area.

When I approached a cherry-stained reception desk, a dumpy receptionist wearing a frumpy blue dress glared up at me.

"Can I help you?" she said without a hint of charm in her twangy voice.

It was at moments like this I missed the friendliness of the people in New Orleans. "Yes, I'm here to see Garrett Hughes," I replied, trying to curtail the shaking in my voice.

"Mr. Hughes works at our New Orleans branch."

"Yes, I know that." I put on a tolerant smile. "I'm from New Orleans and was told he was in Dallas."

Her brown eyes scrunched together. "And you came here to see him?"

"Yes, I did." My patience was wearing thin. "Can you find him for me, please?"

"I don't think he's here, Miss," she contended. "I haven't seen him."

Flustered, I caught a glimpse of the name Hayden Parr above one of the framed pictures of a mansion to the side of the reception desk. I turned my eyes back to the infuriating receptionist.

"What about Hayden Parr? Is he in?"

"Ah, yes. His office is on thirty-two. All the administration offices are on thirty-two...but I think he's in a meeting."

I gave the woman a strained smile. "Thank you." I backed away from the desk, and headed toward the glass entrance.

"You need an appointment to see Mr. Parr," the receptionist shouted behind me.

Ignoring her, I walked out of the office and down the beige hallway to the elevators. Once I arrived on the thirty-second floor, I spotted the same glass entrance and logo I had seen on the floor above. Darting toward the entrance, I hurried inside.

This reception area was smaller and paneled in dark wood. The furniture consisted of two leather high backed chairs and one long sofa done in a plush beige material. There were no pictures on the wall in this modestly decorated room, and no reception desk. A pair of double doors stained in the same color as the walls stood at the far end of the room. Speedily crossing the rough stone floor, I grasped the brass handles on the doors and slipped inside.

The long corridor on the other side had thick beige carpeting and there was not a soul in sight. Creeping along, I had no idea what I was going to do. When I spotted a door up ahead, I decided I would peek inside and ask the first person I came to about Garrett.

Not paying attention to what was going on behind me; I was startled when I heard a man's deep voice over my left shoulder.

"Can I help you, Miss?"

I froze and slowly turned around, only to be waylaid by a pair of striking gray eyes. With a wide forehead, sharply carved features, and thick, wavy dark hair, the man in front of me momentarily took my breath away. Remembering my mission, I nervously cleared my throat.

"I'm looking for Garrett Hughes."

The attractive man stared back at me, grinning. He slipped his hands into the trouser pockets of his gray suit and rolled slightly forward on his toes. "Garrett Hughes runs our New Orleans office."

"Yes, I know that," I curtly answered. "The New Orleans office told me he was here."

He raised his dark eyebrows, resembling Garrett in many ways. "They told you he was here? Really? I find that hard to believe."

I bit my lower lip. The hole I was digging with my scheming was getting deeper. "I know he came to Dallas. I figured he was here since he works for Parr and Associates. I'm just trying to find him."

"Why?" he asked, tilting his head to the side.

"Look, can you just tell me where he is, or give him a message from me?" I begged. "I need to speak to him. It's very important."

"Is this about a house?" He sounded more amused than intrigued.

"A house?" I asked confused.

"Was Garrett working on a house for you?"

I tossed a hand up, feeling like I was getting nowhere in my search for Garrett. "No, he wasn't building a house for me. We were working together on another project...a book. I'm, a writer and he—"

"You're Lexie," he interrupted, smiling.

The alluring man's smile, coupled with hearing him speak my name, made me pause. "How did you know my name?"

He held out his hand to me. "I'm Hayden Parr. Garrett told me about you. I didn't think we would be meeting quite so soon." His grey eyes searched me over with a renewed interest.

I took his hand. "Garrett told you about me? When?"

"This morning." Hayden Parr placed his hand beneath my elbow. "We had a long chat about New Orleans and your name came up…several times." He ushered me along the hallway. "Come with me."

"Where are we going?"

"To Garrett's office," he declared, pulling my arm. "That's why you're here, isn't it?"

"Umm, I'm not sure why I'm here," I conceded, having second thoughts. "I'm not sure about anything at this particular moment."

Hayden Parr sported a mischievous grin as we walked along. "Yes, that seems to be catching. I heard Garrett saying almost the exact same thing to me this morning. He was very confused about you, and his role here at Parr and Associates."

"I don't understand. How was he confused about his role in your firm?"

We halted in front of an office door and I noticed the nameplate, Garrett Hughes, Chief Architect.

"I sent him to New Orleans to help expand my business. Today, he comes back and says I picked the wrong man for the job. I don't make mistakes, Lexie." He put his hand on the doorknob. "I must admit I've never seen him quite so befuddled. You must be a hell of a woman, Lexie Palmer, to shake his confidence like that." He pushed the door open. "Wait in his office while I get him for you."

I remembered what Garrett had told me about his boss, and how they shared an interest in the bondage culture. "Tell me, Mr. Parr, are you one of those men who don't like to use the word please, like Garrett?"

Hayden smiled, taunting me. "Please wait in his office, Lexie." He placed his hand in the small of my back, encouraging me forward.

While Hayden closed the door behind me, I wandered into Garrett's office. Done in different shades of brown with cream-colored carpet, the centerpiece of the office was a wide picture window with an unencumbered view of downtown Dallas. Set in front of the window was a long contemporary desk with a laptop computer and papers neatly arranged in small piles on each end. Even the pens had been stacked next to each other to the side of the spotless burgundy blotter. Along the walls on either side of the desk were framed undergraduate and graduate degrees, family photographs, and a few awards and recognitions for achievement. I casually inspected the photographs and was captivated by one large picture of an older couple, dressed in formal attire and holding up champagne glasses to the camera. The woman was petite, a little frail but had a warm smile and deep set brown eyes. The silver-haired man was an older version of Garrett. They shared the same cold eyes, well-defined cheekbones, and jaw, as well as the slightly protruding brow. The other portraits were of his sisters, and a few more of his nieces. I read over the awards he had won for design and recognitions for his outstanding work in architecture. None of the mementos on the wall gave me any more insight into the difficult man.

Counting off the minutes, I began to dread that Garrett wasn't coming. As I peered out the window to the cloudless blue sky, I imagined him upset with his boss for allowing me into the sanctuary of his office.

The blinking red light atop a tall skyscraper, not far off in the distance, distracted me. I thought back to all the things that had happened to me over the past two and half weeks, and I was bowled over by the devious designs of fate. Crafty bitch, fate. Without my knowing she had changed my life, making it damn near impossible for me to return to the existence I had known prior to Garrett. What would happen to my world if he did not want to give us a chance?

"Lexie?"

The smooth voice behind me resonated in every molecule of my being. I knew that voice so well, and had missed it shouting orders at me over the past two days.

"I can see why you came back, Garrett." I did not turn around. I was trying to summon the courage to face him. "Hell of a view."

I heard the office door softly close behind me, and within seconds he was standing in front of me. Decked out in a perfectly pressed beige suit and deep red tie, his dark eyes lingered over my features. The desperation I saw in him enlivened my hope.

"You want to tell me what you're doing here?" He sounded calm. I knew better.

"I came to see you. I think we need to talk."

"How did you get to Dallas?" He went around me and rested his hip on the corner of his desk.

"I flew in about an hour ago. My mother paid for my ticket."

"Did she?" His eyebrows went up. This time I knew it wasn't because he was angry. "I thought you and your mother didn't get along?"

I folded my arms, maintaining my aloofness. "We don't. She has her sights set on you, as her new handyman, and insisted I come to Dallas to find you. I called her after I went to your office and your apartment yesterday, looking for you." I paused, anticipating a heated reaction to my next disclosure. "I even went to Mabel's," I proclaimed.

His eyes shrunk into two fine slits. "Why did you go there?"

"She wanted to see me; requested to see me, actually. Mabel wanted to know if my resigning from the club was what I wanted, or what you wanted for me."

"She had no right to ask you that," he barked.

"I think she was concerned about you…and me. She's the one who told me where to find you."

"Well, you've found me." He went to the front of his desk. "Now I suggest you go home. We have nothing left to say to each other. It's over."

Furious, I stomped up to him. "That's bullshit, Garrett, and you know it."

"Don't curse, Lexie." He wiped his hand over his face. "You never understood me. Believe me, ending this is better. I'm just trying to save you from a lot of disappointment."

I was aghast. How could I be disappointed in him? "After everything I've gone through, everything that you've done to me, do you honestly think I could be disappointed? Pissed off, shocked, outraged, embarrassed, mortified even, but never disappointed, Garrett."

He impatiently ran his fingers over his forehead. "I was talking about the future with me, Lexie, not the past."

The emptiness in his voice surprised me. I had never heard him talk that way. My anger retreated, and I moved closer to him. "So was I. I think we both deserve a chance at a future together."

His eyes nervously darted about the office, and an unbearable silence settled between us. He picked up a few papers to the side of his desk, avoiding my gaze. "I have a meeting in ten minutes, so just tell me why you're here."

"I want to know when you're coming back to New Orleans."

He shuffled the papers in his hands, never glancing up. "I'm not. I came back to tell Hayden to send someone else to New Orleans. I'm done there." He quickly walked to his office door.

"What was it, Garrett? Me?" I called to him. "Or was it what happened that night between us?"

When he spun around, his face was void of all emotion. "Go home, Lexie."

"Not until you tell me why you ran away."

"I didn't run away." He waved the papers in his hand to me. "I just can't give up being what I am. If I stay in New Orleans…. It's better for both of us if we end this now."

I held my head up. "I'm not ready to do that. Whatever you want to be, my master, my partner, or even my mother's handyman, I'm in."

"You're in?" He angled his head downward, his brown eyes hooded over by his wide brow. "What does that mean, exactly?"

I stood before his desk, figuring this was my last chance with him. I either told him exactly how I felt, or walked away. "I'll do whatever you want, be whatever you need. I just want to be with you."

"Be with me?" He went back to his desk and threw the papers on top of it. "As what, Lexie?"

He stood next to me and the smell of his cologne, blended with the steamy allure of his eyes, was spellbinding. "What do you want me to say, Garrett? Do you want me to submit to you? Fine. I submit to you, utterly and completely. I'll be your slave, your sub, whatever you need me to be."

"That's not what I'm talking about." He turned away. "Jesus, do you know what you have done to me? Do you know what you have done to my life?"

I went up to him, and hesitated only briefly before resting my hand on his shoulder. To my amazement, he did not flinch, did not appear to wither under my hand. I rolled my fingers along his shoulder, encouraged by his acceptance of my caress.

"Tell me what I've done," I whispered.

He slowly faced me, and when his eyes met mine, I saw it. The same warm affection I had sensed from him that night when he had made me his. "Fine." He tossed his hand up. "I spend every waking moment thinking about you. I speculate about what you're doing, whether you're eating right, if you're writing, sick, drunk, picking up strange men at parks, or if there is some remote chance that you're…thinking of me."

The rush of emotion that overwhelmed me at that moment made me feel almost giddy. Like characters I had written about in my novels, I felt the same glow of happiness. He was no longer the resolute Dom I could not understand. He was simply Garrett; the man who had captured my heart.

"Say something," he directed.

"What do you want me to say, Garrett? That I'm happy I finally got you to admit that I mean something to you?"

"No." He moved closer to me. "Tell me that you love me, Alexandra Palmer."

Love? I couldn't believe he had used that word. Of all the things I had heard from him, of all the things he had done to me, none had shocked me more than the word he had just uttered.

"What makes you think this is love?" I stoically returned. "Maybe I'm just learning how to be a good sub."

The light trace of a smile shone on his lips. "You would never have been a good sub...too stubborn." Taking my purse from my hands, he dropped it on his desk. "This is love, Lexie. It took me a while to figure it out. After our night together, I knew. That's why I ran away. Oddly enough, you're the one who still needs convincing."

I twisted my hands together. Oh, this was not good. "I've made enough mistakes in the past with men to doubt my judgment. Can you blame me?"

"Mistakes aren't meant to hold us back; they're meant to propel us forward."

"So what do I do? How do I move forward, Garrett?"

He eased up to me. "Well, the first thing you can do is give in to another."

I chuckled, relaxing a little. "I think I've already done that with you."

"Next, you have to let go. Let go of the past and the pain."

I sighed and nodded in agreement. "Then what?"

He shrugged, "If you're lucky, love will find you."

Until that instant, I had not really comprehended the concept of handing oneself over to another. Sometimes being at our most vulnerable gives us the greatest clarity. Only in the arms of someone you trust completely, can you finally open your heart. Sighing, I released all the pent-up pain I had carried around since my childhood. Pushing all my fear aside, I decided to take a chance.

"I guess you're right. I know that I haven't been the easiest person to get to know, and opening up is difficult for me. With time and some patience, I think—"

"Say it again?" he cut in.

I was taken aback by his question. "Which part?"

"The part where you admitted that you love me."

"I never admitted that," I loudly refuted.

His arms went around my waist. "God, I'll never tame you, will I?"

I slid my hands around his neck. "Who says I need to be tamed? I thought you liked me this way."

"No, I never liked you this way." He pulled me to him. "I love you this way, Lexie." He touched his forehead to mine. "But I get to call the shots in this relationship, all right?"

"Since when have you been in charge of our relationship?"

"Never." He grinned. "I'm hoping that will change."

His lips came down on mine. For the first time, I gave myself to him without reservation. There were no more doubts. I trusted him, and realized that I loved him, too. Funny, how it sneaks up on you like that. One day you are just living your life, and then a stranger comes along…and changes everything.

6 Months Later

The early fall sun was pouring in through the wall of windows in Garrett's penthouse apartment when I walked in the front door, my arms laden with grocery bags. Shuffling to the kitchen, I made it to the breakfast counter, where I hoisted the heavy bags up and then caught my breath.

"Damn man would have to live on the top floor," I muttered.

Removing my heavy leather purse from my shoulder, I eased around the breakfast bar and went to the refrigerator.

"Did you get toothpaste?" Garrett asked, walking into the living room from his bedroom.

Wearing only his jeans and nothing else, my frustration with my long trek up in the elevator immediately disappeared, as I took in his wide chest, ripped abs, and thick, muscular arms.

He came up to the countertop and began rummaging through the bags. "I put it on your list."

I watched in fascination as he went through the grocery bags, inspecting every item. When he found the bottle of champagne, he held it up.

"What's this for?"

"I got it to celebrate the release of my new book," I explained, easing around the bar to his side.

"Ah yes, *Taming Elise* hits stores today." He set the bottle on the counter. "Have you finished the other one, yet?"

"You bet. *Taming Candice* just went to my editor, Cary Anderson. She said Donovan Books wants to put it out in time for Valentine's Day." I paused and sheepishly smiled. "You have to finish telling me about June. You know, the race car driver who liked to be chained to the bed?"

He hid his grin behind his hand. "I think we should wait until April to finish that story."

"Why do we have to wait?"

"Because then I can spend our honeymoon showing you exactly what I did to her."

"Very funny." Snuggling against him, I marveled at the feel his body. "How's it going? Are you making any progress?"

"It's coming along." He put his arms around me. "I've just got a few more details to add. The contractor will have what he needs to start construction next week. I was also thinking of making variations of this design to show some new clients we picked up. I think word is getting out about Parr and Hughes Architecture. I've gotten a ton of referrals."

"I like the sound of that…Parr and Hughes Architecture."

"Me, too." He kissed my forehead. "I can't believe Hayden made me a partner in the New Orleans firm."

"You deserved it. After all, you're the business."

"Perhaps...at least I'm earning enough to build our house."

"Did you make any more changes to the plans?"

He nodded and pulled away. "A few. I'll show you." He took my hand and led me toward the bedroom.

At his red cherry desk, my eyes went to the plans laid out before me. The design for the contemporary home I had first seen as a simple drawing on his desk many months ago, with its three interlocking squares on the façade, was now a livable house complete with a den, four bedrooms, four bathrooms, a gourmet kitchen, and even a fish pond in the back garden.

Inspecting the plans, I was amazed at how a simple drawing of his dream home had turned into such a complicated project.

"I added another closet downstairs, like you wanted, and made your office a little bigger." He pointed to the first floor of the plans, and I followed his finger to the office he had put in for me, against the rear of the home, that was meant to overlook the fish pond.

"How long do you think it will take to build?"

"Nine months, give or take," he answered, studying the plans. "Any idea how Lily will feel having us right down the street from her?"

"Oh, she'll love having you close by to fix everything." I motioned to the plans. "You really think it will take that long to finish?"

"Who knows? Contractors have their own schedules and can't be rushed."

"Why don't you bark orders at them like you used to do with me? Might get them to move faster."

He held my face in his hands. "That was who I used to be. I'm not that way anymore, you know that."

"Maybe you should make an exception for our contractor," I offered. "Use your Dom ways on him."

"My former Dom ways, you mean." He chuckled. "I doubt he'd listen to me. Ralph Lawrence only listens to Mrs. Ralph Lawrence. He's not the easiest contractor I've ever worked with, but he's the best."

"I just hope I don't have to juggle any book tours while moving into our new home."

He tossed his arms around me. "You can do it. You can conquer anything you set your mind to."

I poked his firm chest. "I haven't conquered you."

"Oh, yes you have. From the moment we met, I was conquered by you."

I giggled as he nuzzled my neck. "Does that mean I get to be the master now?"

"No," he angled his head back, "but I'm willing to negotiate."

"Negotiate? You?" I smirked into his soulful eyes. "Oh yeah, this should be good."

The End

Alexandrea Weis is an advanced practice registered nurse who was born and raised in New Orleans. Having been brought up in the motion picture industry, she learned to tell stories from a different perspective and began writing at the age of eight. Infusing the rich tapestry of her hometown into her award-winning novels, she believes that creating vivid characters makes a story moving and memorable. A permitted/certified wildlife rehabber with the Louisiana Wildlife and Fisheries, Weis rescues orphaned and injured wildlife. She lives with her husband and pets in New Orleans.

To read more about Alexandrea Weis or her books, you can go to the following sites:
Website: http://www.alexandreaweis.com/
Amazon page: http://amzn.to/1orDPLT
Facebook: http://www.facebook.com/authoralexandreaweis
Twitter: https://twitter.com/alexandreaweis
Goodreads: http://www.goodreads.com/author/show/1211671.Alexandrea_Weis
TSU: https://www.tsu.co/alexandreaweis

Made in the USA
Middletown, DE
18 November 2015